Joonie

Dedicated to 'little cheetah'
Mezaan Manzoni-Jacobs

Love your animals, love God, and be the best that you can be.

Joonie

Rayda Jacobs

First published by Jacana Media (Pty) Ltd in 2011

10 Orange Street
Sunnyside
Auckland Park 2092
South Africa
+2711 628 3200
www.jacana.co.za

© 2011 Rayda Jacobs

All rights reserved.

ISBN 978-1-4314-0099-7

Set in Sabon 10.5/14pt
Printed and bound by Ultra Litho (Pty) Limited, Johannesburg
Job No. 001432

See a complete list of Jacana titles at www.jacana.co.za

My father, who had always wanted a boy, named me Junaid when I was born. He had a friend, Junaid, he played cricket with, and liked the name especially when he learned it meant warrior. If he wasn't going to have a child with male genitals, he was at least going to have a child with a boy's name starting with the letter J, same as his. My mother, Merle, who secretly relished the attention showered on me, thought the name Junaid too masculine for a girl and called me Joonie, a kind of compromise between Junaid and June, the month in which I was born. Fifty years later, I still like the name. Joonie has a nice ring to it. I also like the name Junaid as it is unusual sounding.

Masquerading as a boy drew me closer to my father, although he sometimes forgot I was really a girl and kicked the ball too hard when we played football on the field across the road from where we lived on one of the avenues. He took me everywhere with him: to the airport to watch the planes arrive and depart, and I would dream of flying off to a foreign country when I was big; to his clients on building sites where he provided quotes and told the bricklayers and plumbers what to do; to the hardware shops where he bought bags of cement and CreteStone. Later, in the storeroom in the yard of the house in Grassy Park where we lived in the servants' quarters, he would show me the fittings and pipes and explain how things worked. I liked sitting in amongst the pipes and porcelain toilet bowls on an overturned crate watching my father fix a tap or do some drawings of things he liked to build.

He would have a brown packet of pink stars or gumballs hidden behind some of the tools on a shelf and would give me some, and say things like, "What you going to do one day when you're big, Joonie?"

And I would tell him things I thought he might be proud of. "I'm going to be a runner, Dad. And I'm going to fix things."

"Fix things?" he would laugh. "You're going to be a fixer?"

"Yes, Dad."

"But why a runner?"

"Because I'm fast, Dad, and I know I can beat Stephanie who always comes first. She brags a lot when she wins."

He laughed. I always amused him. Once I stood behind the bedroom door listening to his whispered conversation with my mother and heard her say, "You spoil that child, Joe. Just because she's pretty doesn't mean she's an angel. She can be bladdy naughty."

"She's really my child, Merle?" he teased. "Look at me. My hair's hardened from cement. I'm dark. There's nothing coloured about this child."

They both laughed; why, I could not understand.

Still my childhood wasn't all peaches and cream. Having a tomboy haircut and wearing boys' clothes didn't spare me from bullies and rogues.

One morning it was raining heavily when I had to go to school. My routine was to walk to Auntie Olive's house a few streets up the road where my cousins Beryl and Charmaine would be waiting for me. On this particular morning there was no one outside their house and I waited for a few minutes. After a while my navy-blue raincoat was dripping with water. My walkers were soaked. I took them off. I couldn't wait anymore and dragged my feet through the rushing water in the sluits and walked to school with my shoes under my arm. I heard a car approach from behind me. It was Uncle Lionel in his beige Peugeot driving Beryl and Charmaine to school. He stopped the car and told me to get in. I could smell the liquor on his breath, but was only too glad to get into the car where Beryl handed me the dog's towel and told me to dry my feet and wring out my socks and put them back on. It was one of those miserably dull winter school days where you sat in a cold classroom with damp hair and wet shoes wishing for the day to end.

A few mornings later, Joonie, in a freshly pressed navy-blue gym, a white shirt, and black school shoes, was chatting to a classmate waiting for the bell to ring when she noticed her uncle's Peugeot come up the road and stop near the school gate. She was puzzled. He hadn't driven Beryl and Charmaine to school. They had walked with her and had already gone off to their classroom.

"Maybe something happened at home," Lorraine said.

"Maybe." But she felt uneasy. She had always felt uncomfortable in her uncle's company and about his insistence on kissing her on the lips when she greeted him.

"I'll go and see." She walked to the gate. Her uncle got out of the car. He was dressed in a suit and wore a brown hat on his head. He was smiling. It couldn't be bad news, she thought.

"Uncle Lionel ..."

"Don't you greet?" he asked, grinning.

She leaned forward and gave him a peck on the cheek.

"The bell is going to ring. Are you looking for Beryl and Charmaine?"

"No. Can you get into the car for a few minutes? I want to talk to you."

She looked back at Lorraine who was watching her. "I'm not allowed to leave the school grounds."

"I'm your uncle. Just for a minute."

He opened the door. She got in hesitantly and sat on the edge of the seat. She waited for him to speak, but he kept smiling at her, a smile that made her feel most uneasy.

"How old are you, Joonie?"

"Seven. Uncle Lionel, I have to go."

He put his hand into his suit pocket and brought out a chocolate with a red wrapper. "I bought this for you."

She liked chocolate and wanted to take it, but something inside her said no. He was still smiling when he put the chocolate bar down in the wide space on the seat between them and took her hand into his. She pulled away from him.

"You mustn't be afraid of me. I'm your friend – more than an uncle. I can give you things."

He opened his fly and took out the thing between his legs. She gasped. She had never seen a man's private parts before.

"Do you want to touch it?"

She was horrified by the suggestion and wanted to get out.

"Don't you like my little rocket? Come on, you're not like the others. You're a naughty one."

She wrenched the door open and ran from the car. Lorraine noticed and came running up just as the bell rang, summonsing them inside.

"What happened?"

Her breath came in short, sharp gasps; she couldn't speak.

"Did something happen?"

"No."

Lorraine walked with her to the classroom. Miss Jansen, an oldish teacher in a grey skirt and red jersey, asked them why they were late.

"Her uncle came to the gate," Lorraine said. "I think something happened, Miss."

Miss Jansen told the class to take out their reading books and asked one of the pupils to read.

Joonie sat at her desk, not following any of the words. Her head felt thick and fuzzy. She couldn't think of what to do or who to tell. She wouldn't know how to explain what her uncle had done in the car, but she knew it was wrong. She got up and ran from the classroom.

Miss Jansen followed. She found Joonie trembling behind the outside toilets.

"What is wrong, Joonie? Is it your parents?"

"No, Miss."

"Why are you shaking?"

She didn't answer.

"Is it your uncle?"

Joonie looked up at her.

Miss Jansen looked at her kindly. "Do you want to tell me?"

She looked down at her hands; without meaning to, she started picking at her nails.

"Joonie?" Miss Jansen paused for a moment. "I think I should call your father to come and pick you up. You don't look right to me."

Miss Jansen walked with her to the principal's office where she made a telephone call. Her father, tall and striking, took one look at her and she could see he knew that something had happened.

"Please excuse us," he said to Miss Jansen, and with his hand on her back he steered Joonie out of the principal's office.

"What's wrong?" he asked, squatting down beside her in the passage.

"Uncle Lionel came to the school."

"Uncle Lionel?" he asked in surprise. "What did he want?"

Joonie didn't know how to tell him. It wasn't an everyday complaint. She was sure that telling her father the truth would get her uncle in trouble. Her father might also think that she had done something wrong.

"Is it Uncle Lionel?"

She looked up at him. "He asked me to get into his car. He wanted me to touch him."

He stared at her, his left eye twitching. "What?"

She became tearful. "I didn't do anything wrong, Dad."

"Where did he want you to touch him?"

"I can't say it ... I opened the car door and ran off."

The twitching in her father's eye became worse. He took her hand and walked her out to the van. He didn't say a word. She sat nervously in the front seat next to him. He put his arm around her.

"You did nothing wrong, Joonie." He started the van and went screeching down the road.

Joonie sat trembling. She knew where they were headed. She also knew that her father didn't much care for Uncle Lionel because of his drinking and cheating. Her mother was going to be angry – she would have nothing to defend her brother-in-law with anymore – and would look at her as a mischief maker. Worse, Uncle Lionel's wife, Auntie Olive, would have it in for her now. Auntie Olive had never liked her and had once called her a little white bitch and put chillies in her mouth while her mother was in hospital having her appendix out. When Ma, her grandmother, found out about the chillies, she told her father, Joe, who told her mother, who told Auntie Olive to keep her hands to herself and to put chillies in the mouths of her own children.

Joonie knew the day was going to end badly and prayed that her cousins were not going to find out. How could she possibly tell them what their father had done? They wouldn't believe her. And if they did, they would be terribly ashamed.

The van stopped at the green-roofed house with the broken gate. The road was so narrow another car could hardly pass. Joonie saw Auntie Olive, dressed in sloppy tracksuit pants and a jersey, sitting on the stoep. The Peugeot was parked in front of the gate.

"You stay in the car, Joonie." Her father got out. Joonie could see her aunt was surprised to see him as he had not been to her house since the chillies incident. Auntie Olive looked towards the van and saw Joonie looking at her. Auntie Olive's frown grew deeper.

"Where's Lionel?" her father asked.

"Lionel just came in from the shop. He's inside."

"He wasn't at the shop."

"What do you mean?"

Her father walked past Auntie Olive into the house. Joonie opened the door of the van and quietly ran after him, past her aunt, into the kitchen where the previous night's dirty dishes were still in the sink and Uncle Lionel was seated at the kitchen table smoking a cigarette and studying the racing form. He saw her father too late and the next thing he knew a crackling punch to the right side of his face knocked him clear off his chair.

Joonie covered her eyes with her hands, trembling with fright.

"What are you doing?" Auntie Olive screamed. "Are you mad?"

"Ask him what he did!"

"What did he do?"

"He got Joonie into his car and took out his cock and asked her to touch it!"

"Sies!" Auntie Olive screamed. "How can you come here and accuse my husband of such a shocking thing?!"

"Ask him if I'm lying. Ask him!"

Auntie Olive turned to her husband. "Lionel …?"

"The girl's lying," Lionel said, struggling to get up from the floor.

Her father punched him again. Joonie couldn't bear to watch. Uncle Lionel lay twisted and bleeding on the floor, Auntie Olive screaming at the top of her lungs, swearing she would never speak to her one and only brother ever again.

Joonie turned and quietly snuck back into the car. She was trembling, and felt nauseous at the thought of what she had seen between her uncle's legs. He had tried to do adult things with her. What had she, just a seven-year-old, done for him to single her out and act in such a lewd way? He was her uncle, a family member who came to the house and ate at their table. What made it worse was that he had called her a liar when he was the liar and she was telling the truth. She had told lies sometimes, yes, but she wouldn't dream of making up a story like that. No one spoke about such things in any case. It was too shameful. All that happened was to go to the house of the man who'd tried to do something like this and beat him half dead with a cricket bat – like her father more or less did.

The weekend after the incident with Uncle Lionel, her father thought it a good idea that she spend some weekends with his mother at her cottage in Chapel Street. He also thought it would keep her out of harm's way if she had something meaningful to do in her spare time and bought her a pretty little pink-and-white diary to write in while she was away. She was thrilled. She liked the tiny metal clasp with the lock that no one but she would be able to open, and she liked the idea of spending weekends in District Six. Ma, with her own knack for adventure, was her favourite grandmother. She didn't like her mother's mother, Ouma Ball, in the same way.

The first few pages in her diary were taken up with little events that happened at school and her stay with her grandmother on weekends. She loved staying with Ma. Lying cuddled up with her in her bed, watching the rain beat at the window, Ma told her that she had done the right thing to tell. "If you keep silent about something like this, Joonie, the man gets away with his crime, and some other girl might suffer – who may not be as lucky as you."

She was surprised by how openly Ma had spoken to her. She was a young girl. Children were spoken to as children. Ma had spoken to her from the heart, as if she was an adult. It was a bad thing her uncle had done. She had to know the things men were capable of. It was no use sparing her ears and leaving her vulnerable, Ma said. She believed that children were not always safe in the care of men, and she said so.

She always felt better after she had spent a weekend with her grandmother. After their private little conversation about men, Ma let her be a girl again and gave her a warm bowl of custard. She discovered that Ma had her own secrets. One of her biggest secrets was Saturday afternoons when Ma would soap and wash her hard hair and put on lipstick and a pretty dress. At six, on the dot, there would be a light knock at the door, and a tall man carrying a heart-shaped box of chocolates would step into the house. Ma would tell her to play nicely with her colouring book in the lounge and go into the bedroom with him. At first the door was left open and Ma would sit on a chair in the middle of the room and he on a chair a short distance away. After a few weeks, as she got used to his presence, the door was closed. The man would have a cup of tea afterwards, and then take his leave. She and Ma would eat the chocolates when he was gone. Usually, there would be three or four chocolates left the next day and Ma would tell her to take them home with her and not eat them all at once. Ma would be a little quiet the rest of the Saturday, and on Sunday morning be her old self again.

Joonie wrote a lot in her diary, especially in the early morning when she liked to sit at the window to catch the first light of day and hear the milkman delivering bottles of milk to the neighbours. No one had to tell her what was too risky or dangerous to put in the diary, and that there should be no mention of her grandmother's escapades. She just knew instinctively what wasn't fit to be recorded in her book of secrets, despite the tiny lock that was supposed to keep its contents safe.

But there was so much activity where her grandmother stayed, she feared she would fill up the pages before her eighth birthday, when she would ask her father to buy her another diary. Ma knew all the neighbours. Even in those days, in Ma's early fifties, people came to sit with her on her stoep with the overhanging creepers and tell her their deepest, darkest secrets. Joonie loved listening to the stories. Ma let her sit in, but she had to sit on the step. "Jy kan voor die kind praat," she would say. Around the corner on Hanover Street it was bustling with traffic and noise; behind the creepers on the stoep all secrets were safe.

Mostly the problems were health complaints and stories about men who told lies and had girlfriends on the side. One day, however, there was a story Ma hadn't heard before. A young girl who had heard of Ma's success at solving women's problems appeared on the stoep with a bloody nose and two teeth knocked out of her mouth. She was newly married, had a three-month-old baby and didn't want to report her husband to the police as he was the breadwinner and they would all starve.

"Is this the first time he's beaten you?" Ma asked. The

woman said no. "Why don't you just take your baby and go back home?"

"I'm ashamed," the girl said. "My parents had warned me about him. If I go back it would mean that I've failed."

"Forget about failing. We all make mistakes. Go back home to your parents. A man who hits you once will hit you again. He has no control over his rage. If you go back to him, you will pay a dearer price in the end. You are sixteen now? Seventeen? You have your whole life ahead of you. Your parents' house is the best place to be."

"I am pregnant again," the girl confessed.

Ma looked at her, momentarily stumped, then sent Joonie to the kitchen to put two strawberry ice blocks in a glass and mash it up with a teaspoon of condensed milk – her standard treat for someone who came to discuss their troubles on the stoep. Joonie didn't know what advice her grandmother gave, but a year later the girl appeared with the baby, a toddler now, and a fruit vendor carrying a pocket of oranges and said she had found a job as a shampoo girl at a hairdresser on Hanover Street and was back home with her parents, earning enough to provide for her children's needs. She thanked Ma for the advice Ma had given her all those months back and gave her the oranges.

At the end of the year, having passed Sub B, Joonie spent Christmas and New Year with Ma. It was exciting in District Six at that time; the streets were decorated with colourful overhead streamers and everybody was in a festive mood. Ma told her the two of them would go out into the streets the next day. Joonie wanted to look extra pretty and asked Ma to buy a few dinkies for her pin-straight hair. She wanted to see what she would look like in curls and put over a dozen dinkies in her hair. When she took them out the next morning, she was horrified to see that her hair had shrunk by several centimetres and looked like a steelwool cap clinging to her head. Ma stuck her head under the tap and washed it all out with soap. An hour later, she and Ma were on Hanover Street watching the coons stream down the slope of the hill in their yellow and red and blue satin outfits. She loved the music – the saxophones and guitars and the sticks they tapped on the road as they bounced by. On their New Year's Eve stroll, she and Ma became part of the wave of people that washed through the streets of District Six and up Wale Street. Bouncing next to Ma, the two of them followed the Atcha Americans with their big feather headdresses and axes all the way from the Bo-Kaap back down Wale Street into town. Her grandmother even blew on one of the men's whistles and smeared some black Nugget shoe polish on her face.

If her mother and father taught her how to be a God-fearing Christian, her grandmother taught her not to feel ashamed of a little fun.

That was Ma for you. Joonie didn't have the kind of relationship with her own mother that she had with her father's mother. Merle, her mother, was lovable and protective, but over-cautious and a stickler for rules. Ma was a chancer. "You are your own best adviser, Joonie," she would say. "Don't do anything you know is wrong, but don't be put off by other people's fear." Ma didn't have an education beyond Standard Seven but she was an avid reader of monthly magazines with crossword puzzles and had wisdom and guts. In time, her mother Merle became the one who mostly said no, and Ma the one who said go for it.

It was a nice set-up. When both women disagreed with her schemes, Joonie would run to her father, who could never deny her anything. Also, staying with Ma, she need never fear running into Uncle Lionel. He wasn't a favourite of Ma's and Ma had spoken many times to Auntie Olive about the kind of man he was. Ma had also spoken to her and told her not to hold what had happened with Uncle Lionel against her cousins. Beryl and Charmaine were innocent and family; Uncle Lionel was a rotter. "Never get into any man's car except your father's," Ma cautioned.

Her lovely life was rudely interrupted when she turned nine and her grandmother was forced to give up the house she loved to make way for the whites. Ma didn't want to move from her cottage with the high ceilings and polished red stoep. She had grown up in District Six and knew every little shop, alleyway and trestle table where fresh fish was sold. She said she would miss staying at the foot of the mountain and long for the intoxicating smells and sounds of District Six. Ma lingered on with the last of the neighbours until the bulldozers came. She gave the best of her prized possessions to her children: the oak sideboard with its original glass doors to Joe; her antique mantelpiece and wing-backed chair to Auntie Olive, and to Auntie Laverne she sent a thousand rand. Not that Auntie Laverne deserved a cent, Ma said, for running off to the United States.

Along with the antique mantelpiece and wing chair Ma also gave Auntie Olive a real dressing down when she came to pick up the furniture a few days later. She wasn't allowed to sit in on this conversation as it was Ma's daughter, but Joonie heard enough, listening on the other side of the kitchen window. Ma told Auntie Olive not to take what had happened to me lightly and that a man who would expose himself to a girl, especially one who was his niece, had a tendency "om met kinders te foeter" and was a sick shit. "He'll always be driven by that thing between his legs and you'll cry long tears, my girl."

Joonie cringed where she sat eavesdropping under the kitchen window. She had never heard her grandmother use such language. In any event, after Ma's children had removed the furniture and Ma had packed everything that was left, she moved into the servants' quarters with them in Grassy Park and tried to make the best of her cramped situation. It wasn't easy for anyone.

Joonie didn't see Uncle Lionel again until she went to OK Bazaars with her mother just before Christmas. Her mother had promised to buy her a diary if she got a good school report, and wanted her to choose one she liked. While her mother was paying for the bright gold-and-green diary with the castle in the forest on the front cover, she saw him standing at the sweets counter. She pulled on her mother's sleeve and pointed in his direction with her head. Her mother turned her back on Uncle Lionel, nudged Joonie in behind a tall shelf with colouring books and crayons, and as soon as she had received her change they left the shop through the back entrance.

That night Joonie made her first entry in her new diary. She wrote only three words, and left the rest of the first page blank: *I hate him.* She knew that her mother didn't like her to use the word hate – "it's a very strong word, Joonie" – but Joonie couldn't think of a word equally vile to describe what she felt. She hated her uncle.

In January she went to a new school in the quiet suburb of Claremont. Her father dropped her off in front of the school on his way to work each morning. She felt special being driven to school. Her father said the school was in a good area, and she could see the houses were bigger than in Grassy Park and all had gardens with tall trees, and sometimes even a swimming pool.

My new school was different in many ways from the school I'd attended in Grassy Park. In the Grassy Park school, some children came to school without socks, or without shoes, and you didn't pay for anything except your books. In the new school, in a posh area with nice houses and green lawns, my father paid school fees, which came to a lot, my mother said, but they were paying so I could have a good education and achieve what they never could. There was a netball court and also a swimming pool. There were many rules. You couldn't run up and down the stairs; you had to walk. And you had to greet the teachers and stand still on the step if one of them wanted to pass. You had to say good morning and good afternoon, and you were not to wear your uniform out in public after school. The biggest thing about the new school was that the teachers and more than ninety per cent of the pupils were white; the rest were like me, coloured or Indian.

It took me a few days to settle in, but soon I knew how things worked and got to know girls and boys I would never have met otherwise. There existed a whole other world on the school grounds than in the classroom. You learned how to make friends and you learned the value of good marks and good looks. If you were at the top of the class, everyone wanted to be your friend. If you were pretty also, you were almost sure to make the shortlist for Spring Queen by the time you reached Standard Five.

The principal, a stern-looking man with thick spectacles, was in charge of this pageant and at the end of the first term of third year in primary school summoned me to his office. A summons to the principal's office usually meant a caning. I couldn't think of any wrong I had done, but went to the small room at the end of the passage. I knocked respectfully and waited to be asked to come in. The principal opened the door and smiled. He said he had talked to the other teachers and my good marks and good behaviour were a fine example to others and that they had all voted for me to be Spring Queen. I was thrilled. I had seen pictures of the Spring Queens of the previous years and had imagined myself in a long dress and a tiara up on the stage with my princesses.

Then his voice changed, and I became aware of his breathing. I froze. It was the same breathing I had heard in Uncle Lionel's car.

"Would you like to be Spring Queen?" he asked. "There's something about you, a sparkle."

His voice sounded different from the one he used to scold us. I kept my eyes averted. I had heard the stories floating around the school grounds about him quietly standing behind the Standard Five pupils while they wrote in their exercise books, pretending to straighten their collars but trying to sneak his hand down the front of their shirts.

"Do you *want* to be Spring Queen?" he asked.

I moved away from him.

He brought his face close to mine. "Do you?"

"No," I said and looked straight at him. He frowned, not having expected a negative response. I was as shocked as he was by my reply. The conversation ended with me staring at him, waiting for him to dismiss me. Walking home later, I wondered what had possessed me to pass up such a chance.

I said nothing to my parents about the principal asking

me to be Spring Queen, although I was dying to tell them. I went to bed that night dreaming about how I might've looked up on that stage in a long white dress with a train. For at least a week or two, I felt enormously bolstered by the fact that I had been considered smart and pretty enough to be asked to be the Spring Queen.

The next year a new teacher, Miss Bosman, started at the school. The principal was away on sick leave, and the pageant duties fell to this bubbly young woman with curly dark hair. Miss Kennedy, the acting principal, decided that the Spring Queen shouldn't only be selected on good looks, but also good marks, effort and discipline. I didn't have a clean reputation when it came to discipline and once was given extra homework to do for arguing with a teacher. Without saying anything to my friends, I eased off on my pranks in the classroom and worked hard on getting top marks in arithmetic. My plan worked. At the end of Standard Four I stood on a stage with eight princesses and spoke some forgettable words into a crackly microphone.

The Spring Queen event was a good popularity boost. In my last year of primary school, everyone wanted to be my friend and I basked for a while in the glory it gave me. I was made privy to secrets. I got an apple or a guava that had come from someone's tree. I was asked for my opinion on personal matters. I was invited to birthday parties and given a special place at the table. Some girls even copied my pert little pony tail and tied their navy-blue ribbons in the same cheeky way and carried their books under their arms like me, instead of in a satchel. Primary school had been more than a learning experience; it had been fun.

After the Christmas holidays my father enrolled me in high school. His reasoning for putting me back into a coloured school was simple: "So you don't forget who you are."

JOONIE

In Standard Nine a girl called Hilary, a rough-and-tumble kind of girl with a thick black plait down her back moved into our neighbourhood and enrolled in our school. I liked Hilary. She would come to school in the morning all neat in her blazer and gym and by the afternoon her plait had come undone and her socks were drooping at her ankles. She was the epitome of a tomboy and was far more physically active than I. She was also smart, with an odd kind of humour and a strange horsy laugh. We got along well as we weren't soppy kind of girls and liked rabble rousing with the boys. She was the only friend I brought to the servants' quarters in the yard to play Scrabble with me in between our study breaks.

At the end of the second term, Hilary said we should have a party to celebrate our good marks. We drew up a list and invited all the snobbish girls in our class who spoke English with a "better-than-you" accent to see what kind of boyfriends they had. I was so disappointed. The girls looked great in their spaghetti-strap dresses and patent leather stilettos, but the boys were lanky and awkward-looking and could tell you what year Cecil John Rhodes was born, but they had the grace of a giraffe on the dance floor. I have to admit that it made me feel good. I was from a scrappy little home in Grassy Park, but I had been to a fancy primary school and had a good-looking hunk on my arm for the dance. A few days later he called for another date and I said no. I was a fickle fairy in those days and at the beginning of my chop-and-change spree with boys. I didn't see the same boy twice in a row. I didn't allow myself to get close and never took anything from a boy that he would have to come back for, or that would obligate me to him. In fact, I wasn't at all serious about boys; getting top marks at the time was my primary goal.

When the school year neared its end, my father asked

me whether I had decided what I wanted to do. I wanted to say "an actress", but knew that that would take me nowhere. So I said I wanted to be a lawyer. Not the one who defends criminals, but the one who puts them in jail. "That's a prosecutor, Joonie," my father said. He added that he had twenty thousand rand saved up and could do one of two things: pay for my university education, or buy a house. Considering all the years we had stayed cramped up in a granny flat, it took me only moments to answer.

"Definitely the house, Dad," I said. "I can apply for a bursary."

"Well, all right then. Study hard and get that bursary."

Two things happened in my matric year that changed everything.

It was past five in the afternoon when Joonie got off the bus at the cemetery on Voortrekker Road in Maitland and walked down a side road to a modest cottage with a small stoep. It wasn't a pretty neighbourhood. Across the road was a derelict manufacturing building, next to it a spray-painting place, and next to that an ugly box of a house with white occupants. Seventh Avenue was a far cry from the vibrant community her grandmother had come from at the foot of the mountain in District Six, but a step up from Grassy Park. The house in the bleak area close to the cemetery, where the cottages were crammed together like fish sticks and nothing exciting happened except for the growling of the dogs rummaging through the street bins in the middle of the night, was the only one her father Joe could afford.

Still, it was a house with three bedrooms, a big kitchen, a small lounge, an inside toilet and she had her own room for the first time in sixteen years. She no longer had to share a room with Ma who groaned in her sleep and polluted the air with her silent farts.

"I need some eggs from the shop," her mother said when she reached home.

"I have homework, Mom, and Hilary's coming soon. We're going to concentrate on our English prescribed book today. We've started studying for final matric exams. Do you have a list of what you want?"

She handed Joonie a slip with only three items on it.

"Can't the eggs wait until later?" she asked. "We have

two eggs in the fridge, and there's still some milk left in the bottle."

"Just go and get me the eggs. I need to make a cake for your father. It's his birthday tomorrow, have you forgotten?"

"And a packet of Cavalla for me," Ma added from her spot near the coal stove. Ma was in her sixties now and always looked for the warm spots in the house to ease the pain in her legs.

"They don't make Cavallas anymore, Ma. I told you."

"Bring me a packet of Stuyvesant's then."

Still in her school uniform and white ankle socks, Joonie walked down to the corner café. She didn't like the area very much as it had all the same telltale signs of hardship and poverty but none of the whorish glamour of District Six. As she approached the shop, she saw several boys her own age – three coloured and one white – hanging about at the door. She didn't have to look at them to know that they were sizing her up. One of them whistled.

As she passed them to enter the dark store she tried not to look at the guy in the tight black jeans and white T-shirt with a sultry Dennis Hopper look eyeing her from where he leaned against the pole.

"You new in the neighbourhood?" one of the other boys asked. "My name's Keith, and that one over there with the kwaai hair is Blair."

She didn't answer, but allowed herself a glance at Blair. In seconds she had taken in everything. He had that same nervous edge as Hopper and looked like someone right out of the movies, and she liked movies. Her favourite all-time bad boy was Jack Nicholson in *One Flew Over the Cuckoo's Nest*. She paid for the eggs and the cigarettes, and turned to leave. They blocked her at the door.

"Can I pass, please?"

"Leave her alone, guys," Blair said, smiling. "Can't you see she's wearing a gym?"

They laughed. She walked past them, her heart fluttering like a bird in her chest. She walked on, not daring to turn around. As she turned to go through the gate she stole a last look and saw Blair, still standing on the same spot a hundred or so metres away, watching her.

"You look flushed, Joonie," her mother said when she entered the kitchen. "Did something happen?"

"Nothing happened. I've got the eggs and the cigarettes. Mr Ali didn't have the magazine you wanted. You know you have to buy that at CNA. He sells comic books, not magazines from England."

Her mother grunted. "Can't you just say that nicely, without pouting? When I look at your face these days I always think something's wrong. You know I like my magazine. They always have something about the royal family in there, and this year is a big year for them. It's the Queen's Silver Jubilee. She's been on the throne for twenty-five years. Also, Princess Anne gave birth to Peter Phillips in August. They're celebrating all year. There'll be lots of pictures."

Joonie smiled. Her mother was a follower of royal events and even wore her hair in the same style as the Queen. She knew every published detail of life at Buckingham Palace; from the divorced American Simpson woman who'd snatched the king from his throne in 1936, to the photographer who'd captured Princess Margaret's heart. She had Queen stories, Princess Margaret stories, and had told the story numerous times of how as a young girl she had stood with Ma in the street waiting for the Queen Mother and the young princesses to pass them in her carriage when the royal family visited Cape Town in 1947, and how the Queen Mother had looked at her and smiled.

"I saw you at the corner talking to some boys," her grandmother said.

"You got eyes in your back, Ma?"

Her mother looked up. "You talked to boys you don't know? And you don't even know the neighbourhood."

"I'm seventeen, Ma. I can talk to boys."

Her mother looked at Ma. "Hear that, Ma?"

"That's kids for you today. They have all the answers. When they're small, they're such little angels, and then they grow up."

"You meet any neighbours today, Ma?" Joonie asked to steer the conversation in another direction.

"I met the old lady across the road. She lives by herself. She has a grown son and daughter living a few roads from here, but not a soul visits her, she says. She was standing on the stoep waiting for someone to come along so she could ask them to go to the shop and buy her a half loaf of bread and a can of pilchards."

"Did someone come?"

"No. I went."

Joonie's brows shot up in surprise. "You went with your bad leg, Ma?"

"Yes."

"You must invite her to come and sit with you on the stoep after lunch. The sun is on that side of the house in the afternoon. Tell her some of your stories – the one about the time the Starlights were planning a fight with the Golden Globes and went around to all your neighbours telling them to stay indoors to avoid getting hurt."

The wrinkles around Ma's cheeks crinkled into fine little pleats as she smiled. "The woman's seventy-nine; she'll die of fright."

"You're heading for the big six five, Ma."

"Don't advertise my age. I don't look it."

Joonie made herself a peanut-butter sandwich, picked up her books from the table and went to her room with the bright burgundy-and-cream bed covers with her old dolls and teddy bears propped up against the pillows. She changed into jeans and a T-shirt and shook out her silky brown hair.

There was a knock at the front door. She thought it was Hilary and went to let her in. She blushed when she saw Blair standing there.

"Hi," he said, smiling. "I thought I would come and make your acquaintance. My name's Blair. I live on the next street."

"Oh."

"Well, not really. My mother lives there. I live with my father in Johannesburg. I'm here on holiday for a few weeks, to recuperate. I was in a motorbike accident last November. I was supposed to write my matric exams and then go into the army, but I couldn't do either. I wrote the exams at the beginning of this year, along with the pupils who had to rewrite some subjects. I'm still waiting to get into the army, but they have the stringiest tests. You have to be super fit and healthy. Do you have a name?" he asked, almost out of breath.

"Joonie."

"Joonie? That's a nice name. Does it mean anything?"

"Little June, I think, but spelled with a double 'o'."

He tried to sort that out in his head and for a moment didn't speak. "I've never done this before, you know," he said.

"What?"

"Knock on someone's door I don't know."

"Why *did* you knock on the door?"

"I wanted to meet you."

"I'm not white."

The words were out of her mouth before she could stop them.

"What's white?"

"Oh." After a short pause, she added, "A question with a complex answer."

He laughed.

"How were you injured, or is it too personal to tell?"

"No, not at all. I don't have a weak heart or anything like that. I had severe whiplash as a result of the accident. I wore a neck brace for a few weeks. And I have a back injury. I have therapy twice a week."

"Are you okay?"

"Yeah – especially now that I've met you. My father knows people in the army, so he's arranging for me to be tested again at the beginning of next year."

"Do you *want* to be in the army?"

"I was drafted, like everyone else." He stopped abruptly when he realised what he had said. "Well, like all the white boys. And it is to protect our country. It's not a bad thing if you look at it in the right way. The army protects the country and its citizens."

She felt stupid for having asked such a question. "I'm sorry. I didn't mean that in a bad way. Of course it's an honourable thing to do. It's just that I don't know anyone who's in the army."

Ma came limping into the passage and saw them. Blair greeted. Ma smiled and nodded her head and then disappeared into her room.

"Can I call you?" he askedShe felt the blood rush to her face. "Why?"

"You know why."

"Do you want the telephone number of every girl you meet for the first time?"

He smiled shyly. "No. Just yours."

She gave a mischievous smile. "Okay. You get a silver star."

He laughed.

She was suddenly aware of his closeness and how she might appear to him. She knew from Hilary and from others at her school that she was considered to be attractive. She didn't think so, and would always find something wrong with her appearance. But the truth was that she did have beautiful hair, and smouldering eyes, and an athletic body, and was once likened to the young Jane Fonda.

She gave him the number and said, "It is easy to remember. It has three sevens in it."

Hilary appeared at the gate. "Who is this?" she asked, walking up to them.

"This is Blair. We've just met ten minutes ago. Blair, this is my friend, Hilary."

"Donner!" Hilary said, looking him up and down. "And hallo. Pleased to meet you."

Blair smiled at both of them and turned to go. "I'll call you tonight."

"Okay."

As soon as he was out of earshot, Hilary turned to her. "He's gorgeous, Joonie. Is he white?"

"Yes."

"And he wants to see you? That's great. Why can't I get someone like that?"

"Someone who's white?"

"No. Someone who's so delectable and has such a great bum; like two ostrich eggs. You're a lucky sod."

"Don't make anything of it. I haven't said ten words to him. I don't even know if he has a brain."

"Who cares about his brain? As long as you have the brain."

Joonie laughed. "You're right. Very delicious indeed."

They went to her room, but instead of studying they talked about Blair. Around six, she heard her father come home and soon after her mother called them. Supper was being served in the kitchen. Hilary often ate supper at their house.

"That boy was at the shop?" Ma asked.

"Yes. I am allowed to have friends, not so?"

Her mother intervened. "Of course you can have friends; the right friends. We don't want you to get hurt."

"Why would I get hurt?"

"You know what I mean. White boys like coloured girls, but they don't marry them."

"Mom! You're making too much of this."

"Maybe I should go," Hilary said.

"No, don't go, please," her father said. He turned to Joonie. "What your mother is trying to say is that you should stick to your own kind."

"What's my own kind, Dad? I don't think like that. Ma married a man who was so bleached out everyone believed he was white. Who stopped Ma from being friends with him?"

"Don't bring me into it," Ma said.

"And in those days it wasn't like it is now," her mother added.

"Whatever. I don't know why we're even talking about this. This guy is just a friend. In fact, he isn't even a friend yet."

"Keep it that way," her mother said.

She turned to her father. "You put me in a white school, Dad. Isn't that a bit hypocritical?"

"I did that so you could have the benefit of both worlds and trust you to use judgment. Look how you speak to me now. You would never have lectured me about your rights if I'd not given you that opportunity."

She put her arm around him and hugged him. "I love you, Dad."

The phone rang. She reached for the receiver behind her on the kitchen dresser. She blushed when she recognised his voice.

"Can you speak?" Blair asked.

Joonie looked at the four pairs of eyes around the table staring at her. "Not right now."

"I'll come and see you tomorrow."

"Okay." She replaced the receiver.

"That doesn't sound to me like an ordinary friend," Ma said. "Sounds to me like *Love Boat*."

Even before the short September school holidays Joonie was seeing Blair every day. He would wait for her at the bus stop in Voortrekker Road and carry her satchel, and have a sandwich and tea with her in the kitchen. She had brought him to her house to test him, but he was as at ease with her family as he was with her, and her parents liked him despite their earlier concerns. He was respectful, funny, and laughed easily. Her mother, she knew, had a thing about colour and hair, and while she grumbled here and there, was secretly proud of her daughter's fair looks and her friendship with Blair. Once, he even went with them to church for the experience, and to see the new reverend ordained. They did many things together and sometimes her mother played dominoes or cards with them, and her father would return home from work to find them all having a good time. After supper, she would wash the dishes and Blair would dry them, and they would sit with her science project or he would help her memorise dates of historical events for the upcoming final exams. She was aiming for top of her class. Blair wanted to start work as a game ranger, but there were two reasons he couldn't, at least not immediately; one, he had no choice about being drafted and had to go into the army if he was found fit enough, and, two, his father *wanted* him to pass the physical examination as he believed the army would give him purpose in life. His father was calling every other day to find out how the physiotherapy at Tygerberg Hospital was going and when he was returning to Johannesburg.

Joonie's affections for Blair deepened. She had never had a real relationship with a boy and the experience left her light-headed and reckless. She had gone beyond two and three and ten dates and felt genuine adoration. Blair spoke proper Afrikaans – not the mixed Afrikaans from the Cape Flats, which she was good at, but an Afrikaans that made her body tingle when he called her his "bokkie".

He started every telephone conversation with: "Bokkie, waar's jy? Ek mis jou." When the family was at home, she and Blair would hang around in the living room and snatch kisses. When no one was around, they would go a little further, but no exploration up her thighs. Hilary, who sometimes went with them to a movie at the cinema, marvelled at the growing affection between them. "You're a lucky duck," Hilary would say. "I wish I had someone like that. Are you two going steady?"

"I guess so."

"Do you think you can marry someone like him?"

"Of course."

"And have you …?"

"Have I what?" But she knew what Hilary was referring to. They were both straight-to-the-point girls.

"You know? Got under the sheets?"

She blushed a little despite herself.

"No."

Hilary looked at her, a faint smile on her face. "Truth?"
"Scout's honour."

She'd hardly defended her honour when Ma had a gallbladder attack and was taken to hospital and Joonie and Blair were alone in the house for six hours. God in all His Might couldn't stop what happened next. They had hardly seen the ambulance off and made it into the kitchen when Joonie lost her virginity up against the fridge with a scream that could be heard all the way at the corner café where they had first met. It was both blissful and tearful and Blair held her in his arms.

"Joonie, jy's my bokkie, vir altyd," he whispered in her hair. "Ek is lief vir jou. Moenie bang wees nie."

The experience was everything she wished it would be and the next afternoon they walked hand in hand to his house. Keith and the others whistled as they walked by. Blair responded with a crooked smile. On approaching his house, he dropped her hand; a thin blond woman was standing on the stoep.

"That's my mother, Ronelle," he said.

They walked up to the stoep. "Hey, Ma, dis my vriendin, Joonie."

His mother didn't look at her. Joonie felt slighted.

"Your father called twice today. He wants to know when you're coming back. There's a letter from the army."

"I've decided to stay in Cape Town."

"Nonsense. You have to take your physical test in a few weeks. Your father wants to talk to you. Call him."

Blair took Joonie's hand. "Come inside with me for a minute."

His mother stepped aside, a fed-up look on her face. Joonie gingerly followed him into the stuffy house with its old cabinets and spindly-legged coffee table and cheap white couch. She tried not to listen to his conversation with his father, but his voice was argumentative, and soon he put down the phone.

"Don't worry, Bokkie. I'm not going."

She said nothing, but she was worried for the first time.

The next afternoon when she got off at the bus stop in Voortrekker Road, he wasn't at his usual spot leaning against the bus shelter waiting for her. She walked home and waited for his call, trying not to think herself into a panic.

At four o'clock there was still no call. Close to suppertime she braced herself and walked over to Blair's mother's house. She knocked on the door. His mother appeared in the doorway.

"Can I speak to Blair, please?"

"Blair's left," his mother said in a flat voice.

She felt confused. How could he have left so suddenly, she wondered? He hadn't mentioned anything to her the previous day, hadn't phoned her. Nothing. And he wasn't the kind of person to just leave without a word. "I don't understand. He didn't tell me."

"Look, he's not a friend for you. Please don't come here again."

Joonie watched the door being closed in her face. She stood rooted to the ground. The thing she had silently dreaded had happened. He had vanished. She looked at the closed door. Old feelings of shame washed over her. She had got carried away thinking they were a match, forgotten that she was a coloured girl from the Flats. His poor-white status still made him better than her. What had she expected? That they would waltz off into the sunset and live happily ever after? Even storybooks had more realistic endings.

She returned home and called Hilary when her mother wasn't in the kitchen to listen in. "Don't worry," Hilary said. "Blair doesn't look like the kind of guy who would just take off. He had called you his bokkie, hadn't he? Give it a few days," Hilary tried to reassure her. She got under the blankets. The uncertainty of her situation left her weak. One moment she felt she had been manipulated; the next moment she believed that there was a good explanation. Perhaps he had tried to reach her. Perhaps he had been forced onto a plane and gone straight into the army. She couldn't believe that he had deliberately strung her along and had no feelings for her. He would call. He would explain.

But the call she waited for never came; no message, no letter, no word from his friends. She stayed in her room for two weeks and missed the first day of the final exams.

Hilary called her after school. "Where were you, Joonie? You missed the English exam!"

"I'm not feeling well."

"Is this about Blair?"

She didn't answer and told Hilary she would phone her some other time.

The next morning her mother appeared in her room. "Get out of this bed."

"I'm not going to school," she said.

"What about that bursary you promised your father? He believes in you."

"I can get a job."

Her mother was outraged. "What's the matter with you? Are you going to ruin your life over a boy and end up in a factory? You always get excellent marks. Almost all A's. You talked about studying law. Is this what Blair's done to you? It's your final exams. Get up or I'll get you up with a stick!"

She had never heard her mother speak to her like that. Reluctantly, she stirred under the blankets and got up.

"I didn't study for today's exam."

"You're clever with your mouth. Put that cleverness down on the page. Just get up and go. Ma's making your sandwich in the kitchen. And bring Hilary with you so the two of you can study for tomorrow's exam. I don't know why you've stopped seeing her. She's a good friend."

Joonie knew she was right, and studying with Hilary in the afternoons and talking about Blair was comforting. She had been neglectful of her friend since her involvement with him.

She wrote her exams. She didn't know where the answers to most of the questions came from, but wrote as if she had set the exam paper herself and knew all the answers. Her mother and father went to the school and pleaded with the teacher for her to be allowed to belatedly write the exam she had missed. The teacher said it was impossible as a new exam would have to be specially prepared for her. In the end there was a compromise, and while she was not allowed to write the English exam, which she was best at, it was decided that if her other marks were good enough, she could pass; they would take her September results into consideration.

However, it didn't really matter one way or the other. She had become quiet. She'd lost her zest for life and for long hours sat at her bedroom window looking out. She missed Blair terribly. She didn't see Hilary or any of her other school friends. She didn't care whether she got matriculation exemption and whether the University of the Western Cape would admit her to do a BA LLB; Stellenbosch and UCT only took white students. The week before Christmas her father said she looked pale and asked if something was wrong. She said no, she was just feeling a little down.

"Why haven't we seen Blair?" he asked. "It is more than three weeks since you've finished writing your exams. The last time he was here was a day or two before you started writing."

She didn't know what to say, just mumbled that they'd had a misunderstanding.

Her malaise continued. Ma plied her with bowls of custard, but nothing helped. Christmas came and went in a haze of unhappiness. The following morning at the breakfast table, the smell of coffee in the kitchen made her feel nauseous and she rushed to the toilet.

Ma watched with a worried look on her face. She came into Joonie's room and sat on the side of the bed. "What's going on, Joonie? You've changed so much. Look how thin you are. And you hardly smile. Where's the girl I know?"

Joonie didn't respond.

"Is there something you want to tell me?"

"I can't tell you this, Ma."

"You can. I've always looked after you."

Joonie lowered her head into her hands. "My breasts are sore, and I feel nauseous in the mornings when I smell the coffee on the stove. I think I might have ... something ..."

"Are you pregnant?"

Hearing the words spoken was too much. She started crying into her hands. "I think I am. I don't know what to do. Mom and Dad are going to be so disappointed in me."

"Of course they're going to be disappointed. I'm disappointed, too. I didn't expect it of you. You're a smart girl. We trusted this boy coming to the house."

"It only happened once."

"It shouldn't have happened at all. Did you tell Blair?"

"Blair's disappeared."

"What do you mean he's disappeared? Disappeared like gone forever? The other day you said he'd gone up to Johannesburg to see his father."

Ma's tone made her lift her head and look at her. "His

mother told me that he's not a friend for me. She closed the door in my face."

Her grandmother's eyes became hard and her voice was sharper than usual, "You see there? That's the true nature of these railway-line whites. She's a rude bitch. I saw her at the café in her cheap floral dress. But a white identity card makes her better than you. Not in my book."

Seated on the bed next to her, Ma put her hands squarely on Joonie's shoulders. "Now listen to me, Joonie. You pull yourself together and forget about Blair. This is your problem now. *You* have to make the decision. And the decision you make now is the one you must live with. Do you want to have the baby?"

Joonie lowered her head, unable to give an answer.

"You must be sure. I can help you if you don't want it, but you have to be sure it's the right thing for you."

"I don't want Mom and Dad to know."

"So you want to get rid of it?"

"I don't know."

"I tell you what. Think about it for the next few days. You have time still. When you know what you want, I'll take you to this woman in Retreat. She helps girls in your situation."

Joonie felt better for having told her grandmother. The secret was too much to bear on her own. Six days passed. Her grandmother reminded her that every day that passed complicated the situation further. "You have to decide," she urged.

"I can't bear to tell Mom and Dad. I'll do what you say."

"I'm not saying anything. It's your decision, Joonie, a decision only you can make."

She went to lie on her bed until her mother and father had gone out for the afternoon. It was the second of

January – Tweede Nuwe Jaar. How different to the fun time she and her grandmother had had in District Six, she thought. If only she could erase the day her grandmother had been taken to hospital and she and Blair had lost control and given in to their desires. She got up and went to call Hilary on the telephone in the kitchen. "Happy New Year, Hilary. I know we haven't spoken in a while, but if you only know what's happened to me. I wasn't ready to tell you until now."

Hilary came to the house. Joonie made hot chocolate and grilled cheese sandwiches and told her everything. Hilary listened quietly. If she was shocked, she didn't show it. Joonie was so thankful she felt like throwing her arms around her friend, but she, too, kept her emotions under control. They talked for a long time. Hilary helped her come to some kind of decision.

On a windy Monday a week later, Joonie went with her grandmother in her grandmother's friend Iris's brown jalopy to a small council house in Retreat. Iris, the same age as her grandmother, had straggly hair and was puffing on filter cigarettes, even as she drove. She kept her eyes on the road and didn't say a word.

The house looked scrappy with its sand patch in front. Iris said she would stay in the car. Ma struggled out of the front seat and walked with her to the front door. No one answered the bell. They went around the back and found a goat lying in the doorway, out of the way of the southeaster, tied with a rope to the leg of the kitchen table. The goat, reposed like a lion, regal and far-seeing, wouldn't get up and she had to help her grandmother over the animal, careful of its horns.

One of the women waiting in the kitchen got up and gave Ma her seat. Joonie asked her where the toilet was. "I believe it is in the yard," the woman said. Joonie

JOONIE

stepped over the goat a second time and went back outside. She saw the small outbuilding and got a whiff of the stench before she entered the toilet, pinching her nose. There was damp newspaper on the cement floor, yellow drops on the seat and brown spatter in the bowl. She stood still for one second and then went back out into the wind and squatted behind the toilet, letting out a hissing stream. Her foot slipped in the sand and she peed on part of her foot. She had one crumpled tissue in her pocket to wipe herself with.

Feeling windblown and soiled she went back inside, wondering what she was doing there. Was it the right thing to do? Would she regret it? Would God punish her? As she stood there waiting her turn, she thought that God might understand and forgive her mistake, but that her parents wouldn't, and that she had to see it through.

Finally, it was her turn and a young girl, in a skimpy, threadbare dress appeared and asked her to come through to the front room.

"You go," Ma said. "I'm here if you need me."

Joonie followed the girl down a short dark passage to a bedroom with two single beds with pink candlewick bedspreads and a picture of Jesus Christ on the cross pasted on the wall with tape.

"Die's Ouma," the girl said. "Praat Afrikaans."

She looked at the old woman with the rheumy eyes and gnarled hands sitting on the bed and wondered how on earth this woman could help her. Before she could open her mouth to speak, however, the old woman moved her face in her direction and spoke in a crackly voice. "Ek het gedroom jy kom."

She looked at the woman in amazement. Was she referring to her? How could she have dreamed that she would be coming? They didn't know one another.

"Jy's swanger. Jy wil die kleintjie hou, maar jy's bang."

She was silenced by the old woman's ability to look into her heart. How had she known that she wanted to keep the baby but was scared? The woman was ancient, blind, and the difficulty with which she searched for the right words gave Joonie the confidence to speak.

"I *am* afraid – and ashamed."

"Don't be afraid ... you must keep the child. She will be a blessing to you in your old age."

"She?"

"Yes. You are going to have a girl."

She didn't need more to convince her. The old woman's words made it real and for the first time she pictured herself with a little girl; she, Joonie, a mother of a little baby. She held onto the old woman's words. She had to believe that the old lady was right. She had known her predicament before she had opened her mouth. She couldn't wave it off as though it was nothing. And how could she dismiss the advice? The old woman had saved her.

On the way home in Iris's rickety car, she sat quietly on the back seat listening to the wind whipping at the windows and Iris grinding the gears. She believed in her heart that she had been stopped by God from making a big mistake.

That evening at supper, which consisted of sweet yellow rice, peas, roasted potatoes and mince frikkadels, she picked at the food on her plate and glanced at her grandmother for her cue.

"Dad?"

Her father looked up from his plate. "Are you feeling better today? You look better."

"I am, Dad, but I have something to tell you and Mom."

"What?"

"It's not easy for me to say it – you've given me so much."

Her parents gave each other a perplexed look, and then turned to her.

"I'm pregnant."

Her mother's fork dropped from her hand. "What?"

"I'm going to have a baby."

"You're joking, right?"

She didn't answer.

"Do we need to ask whose baby this is?" her father asked, his voice hardly audible.

"It's Blair's."

His face clouded over. He looked thoughtful, sad.

"How could you," her mother said in a brittle voice. "After all we've taught you, after all we've warned you about." She put her face in her hands.

"It just happened once. We didn't plan it."

"I don't care how many times it happened. It happened."

"Where's Blair now?" her father asked.

"I think he's in Johannesburg."

"You think? You don't know? Does he know you're pregnant?"

"No."

"Joonie's not good enough for her son," Ma chimed in. "The woman shut the door in her face."

Her father scraped back his chair and left the kitchen.

"Now what?" her mother said, looking at Ma and at her. "I don't know what to say. You'll have to get rid of it. You're too young to have a baby. There's your education to think about – and the sooner we do something, the better."

"I can't."

"What do you mean you can't? You want to be an unwed mother and throw your life away?"

"I'm not throwing anything away, Mom. I'll continue my education. I thought you said it was wrong in God's eyes to destroy a life when your friend at the church, Mrs Pietersen's daughter got pregnant and did away with it."

Her mother reached across the table and smacked her. "Don't get smart with me. You know very well what I meant. What's wrong in God's eyes is what you did; having sex with a boy you're not married to. If you don't want to have an abortion, you'll go and stay with your godmother Alice in Swellendam for a few months, have the baby, and then give it up for adoption. No one need ever know you were pregnant."

"I'm not hiding out."

"Then have the abortion and get on with your life." Her mother's despondence was fast turning into irritation. "You've made a mistake. It is not a life yet until God provides it with a soul. Do it as soon as possible."

"I'm sorry, Mom. I can't do this to please you."

Her mother's eyes narrowed with anger. Her grandmother, fearing an altercation, quickly intervened. "Don't upset yourself, Merle. Let her make her decision."

"I'm calling the reverend."

"What for? We've just met him the one time. We don't know him. He'll tell you it's wrong, anyway. The deed's done. There's nothing you can do."

Her mother turned on her grandmother. "I don't want to be rude, Ma – I've never been rude to you; you're my mother-in-law – but if you don't mind me saying so, you've encouraged Joonie in a lot of ways."

Ma looked at her, surprised by her guts. "Well, I'm glad you're finally saying so, Merle, and you're not wrong. Joonie's close to my heart, yes. She's the grandchild who has time for me. Laverne doesn't have children who I can spoil and she's not here anyway – and Olive's children don't have time for me. Don't think I encourage Joonie to do wrong. Oh no. I know her tricks. But let's not make this about us, Merle. We've always understood one another very nicely. Let her make this decision. She's the caretaker of what's in her body."

Her mother turned red. She knew she had been spoken to, albeit in a sweet voice, and was no match for her husband's mother. Joonie's mother retreated a little. "I'm calling Reverend Martinus to ask him where the church stands on abortion, and to speak to you."

Her grandmother looked concerned. "There's been talk about him, Merle. And we don't even know him. He's new at the church. And it seems like some of the things people are saying about him might be true."

"Joe!" her mother called out to her father in the bedroom.

Her father came back into the kitchen. He had his windbreaker on. Joonie watched him. She could tell that he felt deeply disappointed, almost as if he had been betrayed.

"Where are you going, Joe?" her mother asked. "Don't leave this to me to sort out. Talk to your daughter. We should call Reverend Martinus and ask his advice."

"I don't want the man in my house."

Her mother swallowed. "He doesn't have to come here. We can go to the church."

"I want nothing to do with him. You know he's been accused of molesting a young girl in Bible class. True or not, I'm not taking advice from someone like him."

"It's not been proven, Joe. The Lord tells us not to judge."

"The Lord doesn't have my problem. I don't want to hear about the Lord right now. I don't like the man. He's your reverend, not mine. Besides, I don't need someone to tell me how to handle my own household."

Joonie couldn't take her father's disappointment in her any longer. "You're not going to talk to me, Dad?"

"What is there to say?"

"Dad ...?"

"Not now, Joonie." He walked past her, looking straight ahead. A few minutes later they heard the front door open and shut and the car rev off into the night.

She couldn't sleep. She feared that her father would go out drinking with his friend Alan and come home in the early hours of the morning whacked out of his mind. She kept listening for his car, and peering out the window. Somewhere around one in the morning she came out of a fitful sleep and heard him stumble around in the house. She listened until she heard the toilet flush and the bedroom door close. Only then did she relax. Her father wasn't a drinker and didn't keep liquor in the house, but had turned to it once or twice during a crisis. She had shattered his dream. He needed time to digest what had happened and to accept that she was fallible and might still make many more mistakes. It was Ma's intervention that had saved her. Her grandmother knew that by taking her to see the old woman that she would come to the decision to have the baby on her own. She had never before thought about it, but an abortion seemed like a quick fix to her and she would never forgive herself if she had it done.

For the first time in weeks, Joonie fell into a deep sleep and didn't wake up until nine the next morning. When she smelled the aroma of the coffee drifting in from the kitchen, she knew that she would again throw up, but now she felt different about her condition. The vomiting episodes were cries of communication, she told herself. Her baby was growing inside her. The thought of being a mother was taking shape in her mind.

She entered the kitchen to find her mother turning eggs in the pan and her grandmother buttering rolls.

"Good, you're up," her mother said. "We have an appointment with Reverend Martinus at eleven."

"He can't change my mind, Mom."

"We'll see."

She glanced at her grandmother. Ma gave a little nod to indicate that she should humour her mother. She excused herself, went into the bathroom to wash, and got dressed. After a boiled egg and a cup of lemon tea, she accompanied her mother by bus from Maitland into town and followed a few steps behind her up the steep slope at Zonnebloem to meet Reverend Martinus. A tall, middle-aged man in a dark suit with a cheap shine from having been ironed too many times opened the door of the back room of his home-made church.

The reverend shook hands with them. He listened respectfully as her mother asked whether an abortion was a sin if it was done in the early stages. He sat stiff-lipped and straight as a board in his red-velvet padded chair as he contemplated the question. He was obviously used to pondering parishioners' concerns and put on a lofty show by leaning back in his plush chair, squinting his eyes in thought.

Her mother, made nervous by the long silence, talked about the white boy Joonie had met who had got her in trouble and went on about her near-ruined future. It could be salvaged if she just wasn't pregnant, she said, looking at him pleadingly.

"There *is* a way," the reverend began. His syrupy smooth voice could lure even the most hardened sinner back to God, Joonie thought, but to her it didn't sound genuine. "A way," he continued, casting a brief look at her, "which can help her get back on the right path.

Joonie needs to involve herself more with the church and meet new friends and put her old ways behind her. She should spend some time helping with rummage sales and fundraising affairs, and spend one or two weekends with me and my wife, Katleen. People will know what a charitable girl she is, that she has time for the Lord and the people around her. And when the baby's born, she can give it up for adoption. There are many good homes out there and many women who can't have children. It will be better to do this than killing the unborn baby in the womb."

Her mother seemed surprised by the advice, and about spending weekends at his home. A frown appeared between her brows. "I'll think about your advice, Reverend," she said. "Is there a toilet I could use?" Reverend Martinus pointed down the corridor.

When her mother was gone, the reverend's stiff lips curled into a smile. "You've been a naughty girl, Joonie," he said, looking deep into her eyes.

She stared at him, amazed by his boldness. Was he making a pass at her? The words in themselves were not out of line, but accompanied by the lust in his eyes, the tone of his voice and his grin, he was coming on to her. There was no mistaking what he was trying to do. She folded her arms defiantly. What had made him think that she was open to this kind of talk? Did he think her a girl with loose morals?

"I think you're the one who's being naughty, Reverend."

His brows shot up with delight; he leaned forward to say something, but her mother returned and he was back to his creepy smile.

"You must come to church on Sunday, Joonie, and you must come to the house."

Her father, who knew nothing about the visit to the

reverend, didn't ask questions when he saw his wife dressed in her best Sunday outfit a few days later. Joonie didn't want to go to church, but her mother reminded her of her condition and made her feel guilty. In the end, she went with her mother but sat with a hardened heart in the third pew amongst the modest congregation, listening to the reverend talk about the Day of Atonement. A plan took shape in her mind.

The following Saturday she let her mother steer her with minimal fuss to the Reverend Martinus's house to spend the weekend in the holy man's abode.

The house was quiet. The children were at their school bazaar with an aunt, the reverend explained, and his wife Katleen was asleep upstairs. Joonie remembered the rumour that his bloated wife suffered from a mysterious illness, which no one knew how to treat except with a glass of Johnny Walker, which they said would make her just strong enough to reach for the next glass.

After her mother had left and the reverend had excused himself, Joonie passed the time by writing in her diary, and then lay down on the old springy couch in the lounge to read what she had written the past few days. She felt nauseous from the dusty smells of the house and didn't want to use the toilet with the broken seat and the grimy blue woollen mat on the floor. There was no food cooking on the stove. She had met no parishioners or fundraisers. She didn't know how she was going to survive in the dark stuffy house with the dusty curtains until the next day. Perhaps she had read too much into his behaviour and her imagination was working overtime. After a few pages she fell asleep and drifted off, the diary open on her chest.

She was awoken by the sound of a creaking floorboard. She didn't open her eyes, just listened, fully alert. It was the reverend coming down the stairs into the lounge. She knew it was him by the heavy tread and the smell of his cheap cologne. She didn't move. He tiptoed to where she lay with closed eyes on the couch; she could feel him approach. After a moment she felt his hand on her breast. She made a soft moaning sound. Emboldened by her response, he put his hand on her thigh and stroked it. She opened her eyes and sat straight up.

"What're you doing, Reverend?"

"You're a smart girl, Joonie. You know what."

"I want to go home." She knew now that she had been right to be suspicious, and that her father was right not wanting to have anything to do with the man. She had no pity or shame for what might happen now.

"Why? We're having such a nice time. No one can hear us."

"You're taking advantage of me."

"You like it, don't you?" He reached for her other breast. "Come here ..."

She pulled away from him and got up. She reached into her pocket and brought out her small battery-operated tape recorder. He stared at her and then at the recording device in her hand, his mouth slightly open. She pressed a button. There were some scratchy sounds as the tape rewound, but the words he spoke, when she played them back, were crystal clear.

She put on her jacket and held up the recorder. "Evidence, Reverend."

He sat down on a chair, totally shaken. "You tricked me."

"You trick the people in your church, Reverend. You're an imposter. You were right. I *am* a smart girl. Five thousand rand can buy this from me. Or everyone in your congregation gets a free copy."

He had regained his composure and his right brow

arched in indignation. "You think anyone will listen to you – a pregnant schoolgirl?"

"Why don't you call my bluff and find out?" She picked up her pen and book.

He grabbed at her. She kicked him on the shin. He let out a small yelp and backed off. "Do you want me to scream and wake up your wife?" she asked.

He sat down again, hanging his head.

"What's it going to be, Reverend?"

"I don't have money in the house."

She felt a rush of excitement at the prospect of actually getting away with it. "I can wait until tomorrow. Make it ten thousand."

"What?"

"I'll meet you in front of Mr Ali's café on 7th Avenue in Maitland at three o'clock. If you don't come with the money, the news will be out by suppertime."

He looked at her with knotted brows, his fists clenched at his sides. "You vile piece of shit! You deserve to get fucked!"

"Who's your naughty girl now?"

"Oh, Lord, you *are* a sinner."

"Oh, Reverend, you *are* using the Lord's name in vain."

She left the house and started to walk down the hill to catch a bus. She had a bounce in her step. She glanced over her shoulder. There was no sign of the reverend. She grimaced. He was scared; it was a good sign and looked like she might pull it off.

Not once that evening did she think that the Reverend Martinus wouldn't show up with the money the following day, but all night she tossed in her bed, wondering what her grandmother and parents would say if they knew what she was doing. She did not even want to contemplate God's judgment of her actions; it was sure to be wrong and extremely so.

The next afternoon she waited next to the pole in front of the very café where she had first met Blair. She was glad that Keith and his friends weren't around. She didn't want them to see her with the reverend. But there was no sign of the reverend and she wondered whether he was going to call her bluff after all and not pitch. Had she underestimated him? Maybe he was still coming, she thought, but with the police.

Suddenly nervous, she asked herself what had propelled her to even think of blackmailing him, never mind actually doing it. It was stupid and dangerous and all just to prove a point.

At three-thirty, a full half-hour late, she saw a blue Toyota with a missing hub cap turn the corner and come to a stop within metres of where she was waiting. The reverend got out. He didn't greet her.

"Where's the tape?" he demanded.

"In my pocket."

"How do I know you haven't made copies of it?"

"You don't."

He stood watching her, thinking what to do. Finally, he took a folded brown manilla envelope from his pocket. "How about two thousand?"

"No bargaining, Reverend."

"Five thousand, for God's sake. It's the church's money. I have a bond to pay."

She lost her bravado for a minute. How could she take money that belonged to the church? Her hesitation lasted only seconds. She lifted her chin in defiance. She was in it and couldn't pull out now; he was deceitful in any case. "You know the price."

"Please consider what you are asking of me."

"Ten thousand or I go to the police."

He threw the envelope at her. It hit the side of her head.

"I would never have thought that someone your age could do something as wicked as this."

"Sticks and stones, Reverend. Save it."

She tossed the tape at him and stuffed the envelope down the front of her jeans and sauntered home as if she had just been to the café to buy her grandmother some cigarettes. It had been that easy, she thought, and so disgusting. She had never had more than two hundred rand to her name, and that had come from Christmas presents. Why had she done it? She had threatened him with the ease of a common gangster. She had set him up. She was wilier and more wicked than he was. There was a right way to deal with people like him. Her actions were akin to helping a blind person cross the road and then abandoning him in the way of oncoming traffic. It wasn't a packet of fish and chips she had stolen; she'd robbed her mother's church of ten thousand rand.

Her thoughts swirled about in her head as she debated whether she should return to the reverend's house and give back the money and tell him she'd only scared him. When she reached their front gate, she still hadn't decided. She went inside and hid the envelope with the money under her mattress and went to look for her mother.

Her mother and grandmother were both in their rooms having a nap; her father was dozing off on the couch in the lounge. She knew he would be up to listen to the cricket broadcast, his favourite programme on the radio. She returned to her room and threw herself on the bed, her thoughts in turmoil.

At supper that evening, she watched her mother watch her father pick at the food on his plate. He had not brought up the subject of her pregnancy once, at least not as far as she could gather.

"You don't like the food today, Joe?"

"You know I don't like peas, Merle. You haven't made lamb curry in a long time. A person gets tired of chicken and peas. Ever since you've been to England, I'm getting peas. If you want to put peas in a mince curry, that's okay, but all these peas rolling around on your plate a person can't stick a fork into; that's for the birds."

Joonie watched with detached amusement. It was unusual for her father to complain about the food. She was sure her pregnancy was weighing heavily on his mind.

"You agitated today, Joe?"

"No. You got something you want to say, Merle? The cricket match between the Springboks and the Aussies is starting in a few minutes. I want to listen to the radio. There were no local matches this afternoon," her father said testily.

"I've got plenty to say. I want to hear *you* say something – anything."

"I've got nothing to say."

"Just like that you're going to remove yourself from the situation?"

"Does anyone listen to me? If it's not Ma speaking up for Joonie, it's you. I'm only the guy who changes the light bulbs around here."

Joonie listened. She wished there was something she could do to restore his faith in her.

"Don't make this about you, Joe. You know very well what we're talking about. I spoke to someone yesterday at Social Services who gave me the name of a woman at an adoption agency. I phoned her. She told me that Joonie didn't have to worry about anyone finding out, and that it was all very private and confidential. They will find a good home for the baby once it is born. She gave us an appointment for next week to come and speak to her."

"Are you for real, Mom? You keep on."

"And you have a big mouth for someone in your situation."

"Don't go off the point, Merle," her father said.

"See there? No wonder she's like this. She has no idea what it takes to raise a child. She's a child herself, for God's sake. You want a child raising a child?"

"I'm not giving her up," Joonie said.

"Her? You know it's a girl?"

"Yes, I know, Mom. I want to have her and keep her. It wasn't rape. I had feelings for Blair."

"Blair took advantage of you and ran off. This isn't a doll you can set aside when you're tired of playing mommy. You have to be there every minute. You won't be able to go out, you'll be up at all hours changing and feeding."

"If she keeps the baby, she must take the responsibility that goes with it," her father said.

"Thank you, Dad."

"Don't thank me so quickly, girl. You won't like the rest of what I'm going to say."

"Before you say it, Dad, I want to tell you my plan. Ma thinks it's a good idea."

Her mother glanced at Ma sitting poker-faced at the table. "Ma backs all your schemes. What is it?"

"I want to go to New Jersey …"

"Where?"

"Auntie Laverne's alone over there. I can stay with her until I have the baby and then come home."

"Out of the question!" her mother said. "You don't know Aunty Laverne. You were in nappies when she left. She's not the same every day. Ask your father; it's his sister. She hasn't been in touch with the family for years. We don't even know if she's in the same place, married or living alone. Plus, you're not leaving South Africa. You're seventeen, for heaven's sake. You can't just sneak into another country. You need papers, a visa. If you want to leave the country, there are all these rules – and, besides, you're too young to go on your own. Laverne's cuckoo. She'll say yes, you can come, and when you get there, ask who you are. Speak to her, Joe."

Her father took his time formulating his thoughts. He picked up his fork as if he was going to start eating again, and then put it down.

"Your mother's not wrong, Joonie. Your auntie *is* a little strange sometimes, but she has a good heart. I'm not worried about Auntie Laverne. I'm concerned about you. America's a faraway place. It's a different breed of people over there. Here, black or white, despite everything, you can knock on anyone's door and ask for a piece of bread. You know the way a South African thinks. There, you don't know, you know no one. Not even Auntie Laverne!"

He rested his hand on her arm. "They have a different kind of racism going on over there. Believe me. And you're a young girl, with no worldly experience, and expecting a baby on top of it. Don't you think it's extreme, travelling thousands of kilometres to solve your predicament? I'm less concerned than your mother about your age. I'm trying to fathom your reason for wanting to leave. It feels like you're bolting. I don't want you to bolt. You bolt once, Joonie, and you'll bolt the rest of your life."

She didn't fully understand what he meant, but knew she should take heed of his words. *Was* she running away?

"Can I say something?" Ma intervened.

"You've said enough, Ma. Let's hear from Joonie."

Ma continued as if he hadn't spoken. "Going to the States might be the very thing she needs to grow up. Laverne's impulsive and irrational at times, but not as daft as everyone thinks. It will be good for Joonie to be away at this time and good for Laverne to have a member of the family with her. Who knows? Maybe Laverne'll come back. One of my children or grandchildren must make me proud."

"You must be plenty proud now, Ma," her mother scoffed.

"That's enough, Merle," her father cut in. He turned to her. "What is it, Joonie? You don't want to face your friends – you're embarrassed? Is that why you want to leave?"

"The pregnancy did something to me, Dad. It's a whole lot of things. I can't explain it. I just feel the need to be in charge of my life. Right now, I don't want to be in this neighbourhood, expecting a baby, being reminded of Blair."

"America's a cold place, you know?" he continued. "They say the hairs freeze in your nose during winter and it can go down to minus twenty degrees. That's cold. You'll miss the good weather we have here and you'll miss the family. Going to America is a big move. All young people want to go there, but it can be lonely also for those whose plans don't work out. Those people become casualties of what they call the American Dream – starting small and ending big – and end up on the pavements of New York."

"You're frightening me, Dad."

He laughed for the first time in weeks. "That's good. It will keep you on your toes and –"

"I don't know where you're going with this conversation, Joe," her mother interrupted. "She's not going anywhere. Besides, there's no money for plane tickets when we've just bought this house. Don't give her ideas."

"I'll pay my own fare."

"How? You don't have money."

"I do."

The tone in her voice stilled them.

"Under the mattress."

Her father laughed. Her mother also; only her grandmother was silent.

"A trip to the United States doesn't cost two hundred rand, girl."

"I know, Dad. It's 1978. It's probably three or four thousand."

She got up and disappeared into her bedroom. Moments later she returned with the sealed envelope the reverend had given her and put it on the table.

"What is that?" her father asked. "Are you saying there's four thousand rand in there?"

She didn't answer.

"Where did you get it? You've just written matric; you don't have that kind of money."

"It doesn't matter, Dad."

"Oh yes, it matters very much."

"I got it from the reverend."

They frowned at her, not understanding. "Why would the reverend give you four thousand rand?"

The kitchen became quiet. Even Ma leaned forward on the table to hear.

"I tried a little experiment while I was at his house."

"An experiment? What kind of experiment?" The expression on her mother's face was almost fearful.

"I wanted to test him. Mom thinks he's a saint, but I have proof that he's not. The day I was at his house, his children were out at a fair and his wife was asleep upstairs. I wrote in my diary and fell asleep on the couch. I heard a floorboard creak and woke up. It was him, coming down the stairs in his gown. He stroked my leg. I told him to stop. He told me I knew what he wanted. I pressed the button on my tape recorder in my pocket and recorded him."

"He touched your leg?"

"Yes, Dad. And he put his hand on my breast and said we could have a nice time."

Her father pushed his chair back with a scraping sound and stood up. "Bastard! I told you about him, Merle. I'm going to that rinky-dink little church right now and punch that fucker out."

Joonie became frightened. She had caused real trouble now. "Wait, wait till you hear the rest, Dad. It gets worse." She waited for him to sit down first before she slowly said, "I took out the recorder and showed him. I told him that I would give copies of the tape to the church and his wife if he didn't pay me five thousand rand."

"You what?" Her father was out of his chair again.

Her grandmother broke out in a hacking laugh. "You blackmailed the reverend?"

"Yes."

"What is the matter with you?" her father exploded. "Blackmailing someone is a crime. You could go to jail for this."

She knew he was right and was disgusted that she had been able to carry such a thing out. "I wanted to expose him, Dad. He's an imposter."

"You extorted money from him."

"He touched me, he wanted to have sex. He thought because I was pregnant I would do things with him. The words just came out of my mouth when I saw how I had frightened him."

"You took advantage of the situation."

"I know."

"Why?"

"I told you."

"That's not the whole truth."

"I wanted to hurt him."

"How much did he give you?"

"Ten thousand."

"*Ten* thousand rand? I thought you said five."

"I got reckless – and increased the amount."

Her father turned his back on her and slammed his fist into the wall. "No! I don't believe it! I just don't fucking believe it! Did you have something to do with this, Ma?"

Ma sat like an innocent. She'd had nothing to do with it, but was nevertheless enjoying the details of Joonie's revenge.

"I had bugger-all to do with it." Ma rose from the table and took the iron poker and vigorously stirred the logs in the grate of the coal stove. With her back to them she said, "That creep deserves it, preaching the Word of the Lord, and preying on girls. The church is where he meets his victims. What a nice set-up. Well, we all know now that he's a fraud. This had a bad smell from the start."

Her mother sat back in her chair with her hands to her face. "You've shocked me, Joonie. Truly, I didn't know you were capable of something like this. It takes a willful and mean nature to record someone without them knowing and then threaten to use the information against them."

"I did it because it irritated the hell out of me that you couldn't see what kind of man he was. That day you took me with you to church he made a move on me when you went to the toilet. I wanted to tell you, but you wouldn't have believed me. So I set a trap."

"You set a trap? What the devil were you thinking?"

"I wanted to see for myself if I was right. So I took my little recorder along. I regret it now, but that's what I did. I can give back the money if you want."

"Don't be glib. It's no use giving back the money if you don't believe that what you've done is wrong."

"I know it was wrong, but I wanted him to know that I saw through him, and I wanted to hurt him for thinking I was someone he could take advantage of." She said it with such vehemence that they all turned to look at her.

"Now what?" her father asked. "What do we do with the money?"

"Don't give it back," Ma said. "And don't go over there, Joe. You don't want to be locked up for beating a preacher; he isn't worth it. And you don't want Joonie going to jail."

Joonie listened to the voices around her. It was hard to believe that she had caused all the upset in the house.

"We can give the money to charity," she suggested.

"That doesn't absolve you. It doesn't make things right. You've cancelled out the man's crime by your own actions."

"It's done now, Joe, nothing to be done about it," her grandmother said. "You give a good portion of that money to the poor, Joonie. Buy groceries and blankets and take it around to the neighbours. Give as much as you can. Tell them you're going to America. You want their good wishes."

She looked at her father, waiting for him to say something. "Dad …?"

Her father looked like a wounded animal. "Maybe it *is* better if you go away for a while."

When I think back to that day – my naivety, my stubbornness and lack of regard for authority, my blind determination to have my baby in a foreign country – I can't believe how reckless I was for a seventeen-year-old. The trip to America was a chance to make good and to return home within a year with some kind of achievement. That's what I told myself. In reality, however, I was camouflaging my shame and running away.

Filled with a sudden zest for a new beginning and adventure, feeling normal for the first time in months, it was decided that I should speak to my aunt in America. The question was, who was going to make the call to Auntie Laverne. Ma didn't want to do it. She was still upset with her daughter for running off to New York when she hadn't even finished school and not keeping in touch with them. She just joined a family from Athlone who were emigrating there, saying she was going to look after their children.

In the end it was my father who called his sister. Auntie Laverne was home and they spoke for a long time.

She must have asked about me, for I heard my father say, "She's tall. She has brown shoulder-length hair and pouty lips. Very pretty. Too pretty for her own good, and full of tricks. She wants to ask you something."

He handed the receiver to me.

"Hi, Auntie Laverne. How are you?" I said, the hand next to my ear a little shaky.

There was no answer except for some strange sobbing

sounds. I looked at my father, confused, mouthing over the receiver that my aunt was crying.

"Just go on talking," he said.

"Auntie Laverne, is everything all right?"

"Everything's all right, my girl. I'm here. It's really you, Joonie?"

"Yes. I don't know what time it is over there or if we're calling at the right time, but it was my idea to call you to ask if I could come and live with you in New Jersey for a while."

There was a gasp at the other end of the line. "You want to come and live with me?"

"Yes. Just for a year. I'll buy a one-year return ticket."

"Oh, Joonie, you can come for twenty years if you want. I can't believe that you called me. Just pack your bags and get on the plane."

"I'm going to have a baby, Auntie Laverne. I must be honest and tell you."

"A baby?"

"Yes. I'm three months pregnant. I'll come home after the birth."

"I would love to have a baby in the house and you can stay as long as you want. Oh, I don't believe this call. When will you come?"

My aunt sounded really excited. "Soon," I said. "Maybe in three, four weeks' time, at the end of February. Dad said I must tell you that he doesn't want me to come there if it's going to put you out."

"Put me out? I will never be put out having you here. My brother's a worrier. You just book your ticket and let me know when to meet you at JFK airport."

A few days after the discussion around the kitchen table that made her father miss a cricket broadcast for the first time ever, Joonie took a thousand rand from the sealed envelope and went shopping with Ma. She filled the back seat of her friend Iris's car with loaves of bread, cans of pilchards, beans, bottles of fish oil and bags of rice, as well as packets of pink stars, lucky packets with fake rings and gumballs for the children. She was not giving the groceries to the people in Maitland and asked Auntie Iris if she would drive to where they used to live in Grassy Park. She had been in Grassy Park for most of her life, and wanted to give to those people who really needed it.

Their old neighbours were taken aback when she knocked on their doors. They came out of their houses to say hello to her grandmother, who was too comfortable in the passenger seat of the car to get out. Even though they hadn't seen Joonie for years, they received their parcels with smiles and laughter and wished her well on her trip. One neighbour insisted she have a cup of tea; another said it was the first time someone had given her something for nothing and wished Father Christmas would come down her chimney in January every year. A visitor with two small children, seated at the table, said her son had stolen her food money out of her purse, and asked if she could have a parcel also.

Joonie was thrilled that the food parcels were causing so much joy and handed fifty rand each to two other women with babies. She knew that the money she had obtained by wrong means and was being charitable with didn't belong to her, but it nevertheless helped her to feel better about what she had done. She felt ready to plan her trip in all earnest.

There were lots of preparations for the trip; packing, saying goodbye to friends, shopping for the cold winter months she'd been warned about and, most of all, trying to obtain a visa to visit the United States for a year. She didn't know where to start. She knew it would not be as easy for her as for someone who was white. In the end, Hilary suggested that she obtain the services of a travel agent to book her flight and get her a visa. It probably cost a bit more, but she was happy to put the reverend's money to such a good use.

A few days before her departure, she found herself walking to the house on the next street where Blair's mother lived. She didn't know why she was going there – maybe for a last glimpse or for a sense of his presence. She stopped on the opposite pavement and looked at the cottage with the broken hinge on the gate and the green door. She and her family lived in an identical cottage, but her father had slapped on a fresh coat of white paint and had replaced the old rusted metal window frames with new ones, and the many flowerpots on the polished red stoep made it a pretty place and inviting to look at. She stood for several moments. She remembered the last time she had stood there with Blair. So many dreams she had had, so much to look forward to. Walking home sniffling into her sleeve, she knew she was on her own.

On a hot, windy February day, Joonie emerged from their house in a black pants suit trimmed with gold braiding. Ten or more of their old neighbours were standing on the stoep and in the street. They had come by bus and train to say goodbye. She was passed around for hugs from neighbour to neighbour, accepting the small packages of dried fruit and sweets and chocolates pressed into her hand, receiving kisses and well-wishes she never expected.

At the airport, more presents of nightgowns and thick woollen socks and caps were heaped on her for the cold American winter. Hilary also gave her a book to read on the plane, and a diary to write things in. "Record everything of importance," she said. "I want to know every detail when I see you again." People wanted to know why she was going away. Her mother replied that she was part of an exchange-student programme. Her mother knew nothing about exchange students, but the pamphlets and literature on social programmes Joonie had received from the travel agent had given her an inkling.

Loaded with cellophane packets of toffees and chocolates, even a box of mince pies, Joonie had to rearrange the things in her suitcase before checking it in. Her cousins Beryl and Charmaine and their brother, Stephen, had come to the airport with their mother, Auntie Olive, and seemed both sad and surprised that she was going away. They had been together a lot as children, but had not seen much of each other after she went to high school. There wasn't much time to talk except to thank them for coming to the airport to see her off and to take the round cake tin with a fruit cake in it Auntie Olive wanted her to give to her sister, Laverne. Joonie saved her goodbyes for her mother and father for last. She wiped her mother's tears with the back of her hand and reminded her that her ticket was a one-year return ticket. "When I come back, Mom, I want to see you with a different hairstyle. It's a pity I'm not going to London so I can see the Queen."

"Ag you," her mother laughed. "Leave my hairstyle alone."

She turned to her father who stood on one side, trying to look happy. "It's time for me to go, Dad. I'll miss Ma. Tell her every day that I love her."

"You know why she didn't want to come to the airport, don't you?"

"I do."

"She's going to miss you. Saying goodbye to you here would have been too hard for her."

He hugged her tight and stuck an envelope into her pocket. "Take care of yourself, Joonie. Write every week, and come back. I'll look forward to reading your letters on Sundays."

"I promise, Dad – a letter a week."

"Call me when you get there."

"I will."

The boarding call sounded. She picked up her overnight bag and followed the stream of passengers ahead of her, not daring to look back. It hit her at that moment, crossing the tarmac to the plane, that she was leaving her parents and grandmother for a whole year. A year was a long time to be away. As she ascended the steps, the breeze lifted her hair and she took a last deep breath of the smells of the Cape so she would remember it in the concrete jungles of America.

She stepped onto the plane showing her boarding stub to the stewardess. As she turned right into the first aisle, she felt a sudden flutter in her belly, so swift it was over before she realised what it was; it was her unborn child reminding her she was there.

Hers was the aisle seat in the second row behind the emergency exit. She had never flown before and copied what the passengers around her did, fastening her seat belt, settling down. As the engines revved up and the plane gunned down the runway, she felt her heart in her throat, and when the nose of the plane lifted and the land dropped away, a wave of heat rose up to her face and she thought she was going to faint. She looked at her hands knotted together in her lap so she wouldn't feel dizzy. For five or six frantic minutes she listened to the roar of the engines and expected that the plane would capsize and plunge into the sea. After a while she couldn't even tell it was moving. She looked around to see if anyone else felt as she did, but people were reading or looking out the window, relaxing. By the time the seat belt signs were turned off, the meal served and the trays collected, she felt stupid for having felt so afraid.

She stepped into the aisle and took out Hilary's diary, which she had placed on top of her things in the overhead locker. She smiled as she leafed through the blank book. Hilary might not care what she looked like and talk tough like a boy at times, but she was a good friend; her only true friend from school, she thought; she would miss her. Writing in the diary every day would keep them connected. Staring at the cloudless sky outside the small window to her right, she decided she would go back in time and start at the beginning of her life, or what she imagined was the start. Maybe it would even turn out to be a book.

Out of the blue the face of her cousin Stephen, Auntie Olive's son, popped into her memory. Stephen as he looked at her at the campsite at Harmony Park during the Christmas holidays when she was eleven years old. She didn't like Harmony Park very much. It was a tatty beach with bushes and trees along the tar road leading past the sea, where coloured people were allowed to swim hidden from view. Where the shore sloped down and dipped into the sea, it was deep almost as soon as you stepped in. She couldn't swim. She and Stephen were splashing each other in the waves that crashed onto the shore, the water up to their waists. The next moment, he was standing close to her, looking at her in a peculiar way, and while she was still trying to fathom his expression, he reached out and touched her between her thighs. She smacked him. Hard. But she lost her footing and was swallowed up by the sea, flailing her arms, trying to keep her head above the waves. She glimpsed her cousins Beryl and Charmaine sitting on the blanket on the shore, but they seemed kilometres away and couldn't possibly see her as the swirling waters pulled her back. Stephen swam quickly towards her and turned her on her back. She felt suddenly afraid of him, considered pushing him away when he reached her, but she was terrified that they would both drown and allowed him to put his left arm under her head and shoulders and paddle back to shore with her floating on her back. As soon as her feet were on firm sand she ran to her parents. They were drinking tea from plastic cups and her mother pointed to the flask next to her on the blanket, but Joonie told them she wanted to go home.

She sat back in her seat and wondered what had prompted the memory. Stephen was four years older than her, and married now to a girl he'd made pregnant. He seemed still happily in love. They had last seen each other at a family funeral the previous year. They had talked. There was no sourness between them. It had been a "childhood thing", stupid and spontaneous; there was no need to carry a grudge. And he had saved her from drowning.

They were almost halfway to Johannesburg, and passing over Kimberley, before she leaned forward and wrote something on the first page: *black swimming suit – eleven – blood*. She circled the words, and turned the page. She didn't write anything on the second page.

After hours of a long, uncomfortable and dreamless sleep with hazy faces with bad breath all about her, the pilot finally announced that they were an hour and a half from JFK and would soon start to descend. It occurred to her only then that she had one telephone number, and that if her aunt wasn't waiting for her at the airport and wasn't home when she called, she would have nowhere to go.

But her fears were groundless. Auntie Laverne hadn't forgotten. She seemed almost overexcited and was constantly touching her neck and running her fingers through her long, bright orange tresses. To Joonie she looked like a rock-'n-roll singer from the sixties in her purple top and sleeveless sheepskin jacket and swinging beads and neatly tweezed eyebrows. She remembered a photograph of her aunt as a plump girl in her teens, but Auntie Laverne in real life had slimmed down. She was younger looking and prettier than Joonie had imagined, and was accompanied by a fit-looking man, quite a bit older than her.

Auntie Laverne gave her a clumsy hug, as if she didn't know whether to give her a peck on the cheek, as Joonie noticed that people around them were doing, or kiss her on the mouth. Then she stood back and took a long look at her, smiling and shaking her head.

"I can't believe my eyes. Here, honey, put this on. It's freezing. This isn't Cape Town weather, girl," she said and handed her a brown fur-lined jacket.

Joonie was shivering from the icy blasts wafting in through the sliding doors of the airport and was only too glad to snuggle into something warm.

"This is Billie Bob. Billie's my best friend."

Billie Bob smiled at her. "This is your first time in America?"

"It's my first time anywhere."

"You will like it here, except for this cold weather maybe. We've had a rough winter; two more months, we're almost at the end of it."

They collected her luggage. Auntie Laverne talked non-stop about all the things she had lined up and the friends Joonie was going to meet. Joonie noticed words like honey, girl, honey-girl, and washroom, for the toilet. Her aunt was hip, and easy to talk to.

"How far to New Jersey, Auntie Laverne?" she asked when they were ready to go.

"Oh, just twenty minutes to Cliffside Park. New Jersey is on the other side of the river. You can see the New York skyline from where we live. I actually had a part-time job in Manhattan once and took the bus to work every day; a twenty-minute ride."

Joonie listened to her aunt ramble on and thought that there wasn't a thing wrong with Auntie Laverne except for her taste in hair colour. She even had a man at her side that no one at home knew about. She took a good look at him in his jeans and windbreaker as they left the baggage hall. He looked a little old for her aunt, but still had a strong body and seemed caring of her.

Outside, on the third floor of the parkade, she felt the cold bite into her ears.

"The forecast is snow for the weekend," Billie Bob said. "You'll get used to the cold. It really is a lovely time here, all year round, when you get used to the seasons."

The first snow fell before Christmas. We've had some big storms, people unable to pull out of their driveways – but it's starting to ease off now. It's February; in April the weather will get markedly milder."

"Now listen to me, Joonie," her aunt said. "I don't want you to call me Auntie Laverne. I'm only thirty-three, for heaven's sake. Call me Verne, or Vernie, whichever you prefer."

She was surprised. Her aunt was indeed different from her sister Olive back home. Joonie wondered, with a smile, what her mother and father would say to hear her address her aunt as Verne or Vernie. But she liked the idea. She knew they would get along well together. Her aunt made her feel welcome.

"All right, Verne – if you want me to."

"I really want you to. I'm too young to be anyone's aunt. I was an afterthought, you know, a laatlammetjie, born when your father was fifteen. Ma had me quite late."

Joonie wished her aunt had said how she should address Billie Bob. She was amused by his name, but she couldn't just call him Billie Bob. Was she to address him as uncle?

They got into a long brown Ford LTD station wagon with wooden strips on the side, snaked down to the ground floor, and drove off.

"Now you have to tell me everything, Joonie. The whole scoop. How's my brother? Auntie Olive? Ma?"

"They're all fine. Dad's working hard as usual, still listens to his cricket on the radio, builds the odd cabinet or cupboard in his spare time. He recently built a dinghy, a small wooden boat, from instructions in a woodworking book. The boat's in the garage now and the car is parked outside. It was broken into the first night, but still stands out in the street. Dad's in his woodworking phase now."

"And your mom?"

"Mom still has that goofy QE hairstyle. Her Queen Elizabeth with the kiss-me curls."

Her aunt laughed merrily. "Oh, I miss home. You don't hear these kinds of stories in New Jersey. And Ma?"

"Full of beans. Ma's still the boss. Dad says Ma just loves him for his wallet. He's joking of course, but every so often Dad has to dig into it and give her a few rand. Ma has this friend Iris from when they lived in District Six. Aunt Iris is half the size of Ma and smokes like a chimney. The two of them get dressed up and go in Aunt Iris's old brown jalopy to this place on a Saturday afternoon where they have a brandy and place bets. Ma knows about horses. Dad pretends he doesn't know, and gives her the money. When her horse comes first, Ma buys Dad a carton of cigarettes. There haven't been any cartons of late."

Auntie Laverne's eyes sparkled with delight.

"Ma and I have had some real escapades together," Joonie continued, smiling. "She hasn't lost her sense of adventure. She doesn't want to *hear* about it, she wants to be *in* it."

"That's Ma all right. She should've been a poker player. She knows everything. She knows what you're going to do before you've even thought of it. And Auntie Olive?"

The question caught Joonie by surprise. She hadn't thought what she would say about Auntie Olive and her husband if she was asked. Since that episode when she was seven, Auntie Olive had dropped from her top-ten list of favourite people. "She joined the Apostolic church," Joonie said, pleased to have thought of something neutral.

"She's a born-again now?"

"I think so. I heard Ma mention this to Auntie Iris."

"Olive's a stickler for the church. She thinks the church can fix everything."

"Ma doesn't think so."

"How do you know?"

"I know."

"Really. And Uncle Lionel? Is he still tipping the bottle?"

She felt her jaw tightening. "I don't know anything about him."

Auntie Laverne didn't ask any further questions. They drove in silence for a long while. Joonie was tired from the long trip and sat snuggled up in the warm jacket on the back seat, staring at the old buildings along the road from JFK to New Jersey. They stopped at the toll where Billie Bob handed the guard a few coins. Joonie couldn't believe that one had to pay money to be able to drive through the huge gates. It reminded her of the first *Godfather* movie she saw some time ago, and how James Caan, playing Sonny in the film, was shot dead by gangsters while stopping at a toll booth. She wanted to pinch herself: here she actually was in the great United States of America, driving through one of those very same toll gates.

Billie Bob looked at her in the rear-view mirror. "Do you play any winter sports, Joonie?"

"I played field hockey at school, but not anymore. We're big on rugby and cricket, which are played throughout the year. Soccer also. Winter and summer is all the same to us. The weather's not extreme. What do you do, Uncle Billie?"

"I own a Seven Eleven on the corner of the street where your aunt lives. We sell milk, bread, popcorn, cool drinks, ice cream, all kinds of food items – things people run out of but don't want to drive all the way to the supermarket for. Your aunt said you've just finished high school?"

"Yes. I'm hoping to get a part-time job here if I can, before the baby comes – take a night course. Don't know what though. And I don't know if anyone will hire me, having no papers to work here."

"There're lots of people in this country without visas working as cooks, dishwashers, waiters and the like, being paid under the table. Depends what you're prepared to do."

"Anything that I'm able to do. It will only be for a few months. I promised to return by the end of February next year. I have a return ticket that is valid for a year."

"Are you good at maths?"

"I can add, multiply, divide and subtract fairly well. Not good at algebra and the other stuff, though. What am I going to do with algebra? I'm not planning to become an astronaut. English was my best subject."

He laughed. "That's good enough. One of my guys in the shop, Stavros, is going to Athens to visit family for a few weeks. If you're interested you maybe can take his place while he is away. You can start right away because I need more help in any event. We'll talk about it at home."

The Ford LTD swooped down the highway and she looked out at the sky scrapers and office towers zooming by. They exited the highway, turned into an avenue with huge trees, green lawns, landscaped gardens surrounding double-storey houses with white marble columns. The houses looked like they could have been built a hundred years ago.

"Gee whiz ... this is where you live?"

"Oh no," Auntie Laverne laughed. "I live on a deurmekaar street close to Billie's shop. The houses are older than these, but close to everything."

"You still know your Afrikaans! First, 'laatlammetjie' and now 'deurmekaar'."

"Oh yes. I like speaking the taal."

It was Joonie's turn to laugh, remembering her mother's

return from England a few years ago and her mother trying some choice English expressions on them.

They turned into a bustling street. Joonie counted a grocery store, a delicatessen, a radio-repair shop, a bakery, a tattoo parlour, a pharmacy, a newsstand, a record shop, a hairdressing salon, and The Pussy Willow Jazz Club.

Billie Bob brought the station wagon to a stop in front of a solid brown brick double storey. It had a big wooden porch crammed with chairs, pots of dead, frozen plants, a round card table with two boxes of damp-looking cards, and a birdcage with a blanket thrown over it. Joonie was amazed that all these things could be left out on the porch. In Cape Town, anything left outside like this would've vanished into thin air. There was no gate, just an open piece of lawn and steps leading from the pavement up to the porch. The houses were all in the same style, built closely together, with deep porches and narrow driveways between them.

On the porch she put her hand luggage down to look around. A group of young boys were playing hockey in the street. She looked closer; it was the first time she saw children of so many different races playing together. She looked at Auntie Laverne, but her aunt was rummaging in her handbag, looking for the front-door key. The sounds of traffic, children's voices and drifting soul music stirred something inside her, making her feel she could live in such a colourful place.

Auntie Laverne lifted the blanket on the cage. "I used to have a parrot called Georgy. I taught him some Afrikaans expressions, like 'jou moer'." She sniggered. "He was with me for more than ten years. Last year, Billie Bob and I went away for the Labour Day weekend. When we came back, there had been a freak storm and he'd died in the cold."

JOONIE

How could she have forgotten to bring the parrot indoors, Joonie wondered? It wasn't a crazy thing to do, but a pet was one of the first things one would consider when going away for a weekend. She studied her aunt as she talked to the empty cage and remembered her mother telling her that her aunt had been a nurse in a psychiatric ward and that working around crazy people all day had affected her.

"Do you like my house?" Auntie Laverne asked, opening the door.

"I love it," she said, following her aunt inside. "It seems like a really friendly home. Warm, comfortable. I love the wide wooden-plank floors and the high ceilings."

"The bathroom's old and the plumbing's a little decrepit, but everything works. I like these old houses. We're a real mixed neighbourhood: Hungarian, Portuguese, Italian, West Indian, Hispanic. People from the same country live in small pockets here; it helps with homesickness to speak a little of your own language now and then. Of course, you know how our people are. Suddenly, they can't speak Afrikaans anymore. It's as if by disowning the language, you can disown the place you come from."

Joonie laughed. She had noticed that her aunt's own English was quite a step up from the rest of the family at home. Her mother still said things like: "I'm going to buy me something" instead of "buy myself something", and everyone who got their education from teachers who couldn't speak English properly themselves were guilty of misusing the words borrow and lend, and would say, "I borrowed him money", and used "much" when they should say "many", and "many" when they should say "much". Even Hilary said things like "he gave me too much apples".

Auntie Laverne showed her into the living room, with a

small dining room on the side. She couldn't help but smile at the way her aunt had decorated the place with wooden giraffes and rhinos and lions and other African knick-knacks, all sitting on the sideboard. There were white lace doilies on the low coffee table and on the back of a brown velvety couch, and a framed picture of Table Mountain on the wall, as well as two springbok hides on the floor. She had never seen such a mishmash of things.

They sat down on the couch while Billie Bob brought in her luggage and took it upstairs, where she assumed her room was.

"You miss Cape Town, don't you, Auntie Verne?" she said looking around the door.

"Verne."

"Okay, sorry. Verne."

"Of course I miss Cape Town. You never forget the place you come from. Many South Africans have a lonely time of it here. They love the star quality of America but smart at its flamboyance. They go on about opportunity and freedom, but their struggle is on a different level. Displacement is the immigrant's plight; the constant struggle between the attraction of material wealth in the new country and a longing for the familiar sounds and smells of the mother country – and for South Africans, it means another identity crisis. You feel displaced wherever you go. Of course, there're also those who come here, fall in love with this old whore of a city across the river, and never look back. Make no mistake; New York really is the bastard mother bitch of them all."

Joonie laughed at the way her aunt put it. She liked her humour, her choice of words. Her aunt wasn't like the aunts at home. The family, she thought, had no idea how witty and Americanised Auntie Laverne really was.

"It's strange that you don't live on the other side of

the river. That part's called Manhattan, isn't it?" She had almost said "auntie" again, but had caught herself in time.

"Yes. I lived there when I first came, but it got too much. I like Cliffside Park. You're close enough to spit on the steps of the Empire State Building, but you're out of the hoer en rumoer. The writer E B White once wrote that there're roughly three New Yorks: the New York of the person who has been born there and who takes the city for granted; the New York of the commuter who comes into the city every morning to work and leaves again at the end of the day, and the New York of the person who was born somewhere else and has come to the city in search of something. Of these three New Yorks, he says, the last – the city of final destination – is the greatest. It is this third city that accounts for New York's highly strung disposition and poetical deportment."

Joonie was fascinated by her aunt's knowledge of the place she had adopted as her home. "You should be a writer, Verne."

"Those aren't my words, honey, it's White's. But yes, I would have lots to write about. And now, I must let you go. I don't know why I went on like this; you must be tired."

And just like that Auntie Laverne was up and gone, leaving a faint flowery scent in her wake.

Joonie went upstairs and found her bedroom in the loft. She was glad to be finally alone after such a long time flying, and loved the privacy of the spacious room tucked in the roof of the house. It was warm and carpeted, a radiator against the wall making a soft whirring sound as it generated heat. On the other side of the room stood a small bookcase containing several novels, a cupboard and a chest of drawers. There was a lamp on a small round bedside table. Nearby a fluffy red tabby lay curled up between two cushions on the white lacy bedspread. The cat meowed lazily to let her know she wasn't moving from her spot.

Joonie sat down next to the cat, picked it up and cradled it in her arms, and fell asleep with her clothes on. In the middle of the night she woke up with the cat licking her ear. She listened to the sounds in the house – the soft groan of the radiator against the wall, the traffic on the main road. She put on her night clothes and crawled into bed, thinking of home: Ma's baked-custard bowls with chunks of syrupy stewed fruit on top, her mother's killer chicken roasts with brown potatoes, her father sitting in the sun at the kitchen table, doing his crossword puzzles. Already they seemed like a distant memory, even though she had left them barely twenty hours ago. Aeroplanes are magic, she thought.

In the morning she struggled to get into her jeans. It was as if the life inside her had lain dormant until she stepped off the plane and had puffed up overnight to remind her it was still there. It was a fitting reminder. She was in New Jersey now. She was pregnant. The year would pass swiftly. Her aunt and Billie Bob could help with only so much; the rest was going to be up to her. Was the United States going to be kind to her? Or was it going to spit her out like she'd been warned?

She unfastened the jeans and put on a pair of loose-fitting pants Ma had made for her on her old Singer sewing machine, and took out her writing pad and her diary. She wrote to her parents that she had arrived safely and was having a wonderful time. She ended the letter with: "Auntie Laverne is great, and a lot of fun. She doesn't want me to call her auntie, simply Verne. I can't get used to it, but I'm trying."

After almost an hour, she put the letter and her

diary aside and headed for the kitchen. She noticed two nightgowns thrown over a chair on her way down and smiled. She was happy for her aunt. Billie Bob seemed like a nice guy.

The small old-fashioned kitchen, which she entered for the first time, had cream walls and a freshly-varnished oak floor. The oak dresser facing the door was laden with mugs and dishes and sported a dozen or so glass jars containing canned peaches, figs and watermelon on the top shelf. Some photographs were pinned on a board on the wall behind the table. On one she recognised Auntie Olive and Ma, but the other people with them on the faded picture she didn't know. She was delighted to spot a small picture of her walking hand in hand with her father down Adderley Street, clutching a football under her other arm. She was wearing chequered shorts and a T-shirt and looked about five years old. Her dad must have sent the photo to Auntie Laverne. It was one of those snapshots with frilly edges taken by a street photographer; she had never seen it before.

The table was set with blueberry muffins, orange juice, toast, ginger jam and grapefruit. Only then she noticed Auntie Laverne standing in her panties and bra at the gas stove, cracking eggs into a pan. Joonie found this a little disconcerting, but pretended that she had not noticed anything out of the ordinary. She was getting to know her aunt.

"How many eggs for you, honey?" her aunt asked over her shoulder.

"Two's fine, thanks, Auntie Laverne."

"Verne. Not Auntie Laverne."

"Okay. Verne. Sorry."

"Did you have a good sleep?"

"Yes. The cat slept with me. What's her name?"

"Skollie."

Joonie laughed. The cat was a lay-about all right. "Skollie slept with me all night. She kept me nice and warm."

"I noticed. She didn't come to our room. Billie's just having a shower and getting dressed. He wants to talk to you about doing some part-time work as a cashier once you're over your jet lag."

"Fantastic. Thanks."

"You'll be working eight-hour shifts. He'll pay you the minimum wage, but you'll score as you won't have to pay tax. He's going to pay you under the table, as they say here. How does that sound?"

"It's just what I want until the baby comes. And the shop's right across the road. It can't be more convenient."

"Next week we'll go to an obstetrician, to check you out, make sure everything is all right." She paused. "You know I haven't got children."

"I know."

"It's not because I couldn't have them. There was this Moslem boy I met in Standard Eight, Enver. My mother didn't want me to see him, and his parents also didn't want us to be friends. You know how it is with the Moslems; they want you to turn. I wouldn't have minded, he was a nice boy and I knew a lot about their beliefs. Anyway, Enver and I continued seeing one another on the sly. Then after some weeks I realised that I had not had a period. I thought it was a fluke. I missed another one. A friend told me to sit on a pot of steaming onions so the fumes could cause a haemorrhage. Nothing happened."

Joonie couldn't believe what she was hearing. It seemed that there were a lot of similar experiences in the family.

"I knew then that I had to tell Ma. She was angry and told me there were no Abdols and Mogamats moving into her house. I was Christian and that was how it was going to stay. My father was still alive at that time. Ma said nothing to him about the whole thing. Without asking me, she took me to a doctor on the Foreshore who recommended a scrape the next day. The word scrape sounded ominous, and naturally I felt scared. I didn't sleep much that night and kept wondering what they were going to do to me. In those days it was even harder to talk to your children about certain things. The strange thing was that when I woke up after the procedure, I couldn't stop crying. I should've been happy that my problem was over, but I wasn't. I was sobbing, lying with my head buried under the pillow and the nurse wanting to call in someone to come and talk to me. Even now I can't tell you why I was crying, but I felt sad and weepy, and kept thinking that I had killed my baby and I hated my mother for not giving me a choice."

"You hated Ma?"

"Yes. She tried to spare me from shame, but I hated her for not even asking me if I wanted to keep the baby. That wasn't her decision, was it? That's one of the reasons I ran off."

"Are you still angry with Ma?"

"No, but sometimes it's hard for me to be around people with babies. Here it is good to have family. Someone once said that an immigrant lives in a borrowed environment. He lends his skills and borrows from the Americans. I've lived here almost twenty years now and have never applied for citizenship. Don't get me wrong. I love the flamboyant nature of America, its aggressive belief that it's number one in the world, but I'm still a girl from the Cape and fiercely South African. With you here now, I have a chance to have a family. I admire you for keeping your baby."

She was touched by her aunt's story. "It wasn't easy. I had to be strong against Mom and Dad, especially Mom – but Ma helped me."

"Ma? You are lucky. I was never able to conceive again. I don't know if they damaged my womb with that scrape, or if something was left up there, but I'm barren as the Mojave Desert. I hope, Joonie, that you will let me be your baby's godmother."

"Of course ... Verne. I'm so very glad I've come." She thought back to the wise words of the old woman who'd told her to keep her baby and take her away. If it hadn't been for her grandmother taking her to see that old lady, she, too, would've lost a baby. It was strange to her that Ma had acted so differently when Auntie Verne was in the same predicament.

"What about the father of your unborn child, Joonie? You haven't mentioned him once."

She took her time answering. "He's a white boy, Verne. He made me feel good about myself. He told me he loved me. I believed him. Then he disappeared."

A frown appeared on Auntie Verne's brow. "Maybe he still loves you. Sometimes people love each other, but they just can't be together; the laws back home prohibit many things. They screw up lives. They certainly screwed up mine. Does he know he will be a father?"

"No. His mother lives around the corner from where we live. He lives with his father in Johannesburg. I met him while he was recovering from a motorbike accident in Cape Town. I think he has joined the army. His father wanted him to."

Her aunt got up and scratched around in a drawer. "Have you seen my pills, Joonie? They were somewhere around here; a little brown bottle."

"I've just come downstairs, I haven't been in the kitchen

until now." She thought it odd that her aunt should look in the drawer where they kept the knives and forks.

"Maybe Billie knows where they are. What do you think of him?"

Joonie was surprised by the question. "I like him. And I think he likes you."

Her aunt turned a little red. "Do you think so? He's a good man, you know. Still married to his wife, but there's no problem there. She knows and they live apart. He's just waiting for his younger son to finish college before he files for divorce."

"Do you think you'll marry him?"

"Hmm. Maybe. You're here now. You're going to have a baby. We can be a family."

The words were innocent enough, but there was just a hint of something in the tone that disturbed Joonie.

She started work as a cashier five days later. Billie Bob showed her how to handle the cash and operate the till and in no time she was packing fresh loaves of bread on the shelves and serving customers on her own. At the beginning she could not follow what some of them were saying. She first had to get used to the various accents, and to the different names for some familiar items. Sweets were called "candy", a cooldrink was "pop" or "soda pop", takkies were "sneakers".

The shop was busy, especially after three in the afternoon when high-school kids her age started drifting in to buy cigarettes or chips or something to drink. Nearing the end of her shift on her third day, a handsome guy entered the shop. She noticed him because of his tight jeans and cowboy boots and guessed he was in his twenties. He had longish dark hair, a prominent nose that gave his face character, and a reddish-brown complexion. He looked Greek to her, and waited in front of the magazine stand for her to finish serving the customer in front of her before he came over.

He held out his hand. "I'm Stavros," he introduced himself. "I work the four-to-eleven-o'clock shift. You're Joonie?"

She felt a little nervous shaking his hand and noticed it to be warm despite him having walked in from snowy weather without gloves. "Yes. I'm to cash up and take the money and the slips to the house once you arrive, Billie Bob said."

"That's right. He asked me to come a few minutes early today to see that you're okay."

"I've already cashed up. I have the receipts ready."

"Good. How do you like being in America?"

She pulled in her stomach slightly. "I haven't really been out yet, except for a walk around the block yesterday with my aunt. I'm still trying to get used to the cold."

"You never get used to it – even though you grow up with it."

"Were you born here?"

"Yes. My parents emigrated here from Athens in the fifties. I'm a journalism student at the university. I work in the shop for extra cash. My parents are divorced. I'm sort of in charge of my mother who doesn't need babysitting but is making a meal out of her suffering."

She gave a little embarrassed laugh, taken aback that he would so easily talk about his family to a complete stranger. But she liked it. He, too, laughed; the ice had been broken. "I have your typical Greek mother."

"What's a Greek mother?"

"A mother who can't let go of her son. No girl is good enough."

How strange that he should've said that, she thought.

"I'll watch you from here," he said. "I can see the house. Be careful. It's slippery out there."

She picked up her bag. "Thanks. It was nice meeting you."

As she walked towards the door, she could feel his eyes on her back. What was he thinking? Teenage slut?

For a week Stavros arrived half an hour early every day. He seemed to enjoy chatting to her before she finished her shift. At the same time, he would stock the shelves and pack the milk into the fridge so that she didn't have to lift anything heavy. He told her bits and pieces about himself, but mostly wanted to know about her and the country she came from.

By the time he left to spend two weeks with his paternal grandparents in Athens, another routine had developed: by now Stavros arrived only five, ten minutes before she left. But he always made a point of walking straight to her and having a chat, and on the day he left for his Easter holidays, he dropped by the shop on his way to the airport. The conversation took a new turn.

"Are there really lions wandering around in the streets of Cape Town?" he asked.

She laughed. "You're the third person asking me that. I think people hear the word Africa and imagine all kinds of things. We have lions, yes, and elephants and giraffes and all kinds of wild animals, but they're protected and only found in game reserves. The general population is quite safe."

"Really? How come I thought otherwise?"

"Maybe the tourism industry is to blame. I don't know why people think of Cape Town as wildest Africa."

"But you do have apartheid there? People do live segregated, don't they?"

She loathed talking about the politics of her country. "Yes. And even if the laws change one day, people aren't just going to wake up the following day and be different in their thinking. It's hard to change attitudes. The whole country – black and white – will have to do their part."

"Do you think that is possible?"

"I don't know. Time will tell."

"Are you white?"

"See what I mean? You're thinking in terms of colour. I'm of mixed race. Some people don't mind being called coloured. I do. I'm a South African. That's my identity."

"I didn't mean to offend you."

"I'm not offended. And I'm sorry for barking at you."
"You're angry."
She smiled. "Maybe. Sorry about that."
He smiled back at her, and handed her a gift wrapped in tissue paper. "I won't be here for Easter. It's just something small."
She was surprised by the gesture. They hardly knew one another. "Thank you. I didn't expect this. I don't have anything for you. Maybe when you come back?"
Stavros put his cheek to hers briefly. "Enjoy your first American Easter. I'll see you in two weeks' time."
She watched him leave. Somewhere in the back of her mind she searched for that saying about Greeks bearing gifts. Quickly, however, she dispelled any frivolous thoughts. A handsome young guy like him wouldn't be interested in a pregnant girl.
She waited until she was in her room before she undid the tissue paper. Inside was a fluffy white baby blanket with a satiny silver ribbon woven through it. She stared at it, holding it to her chest. It was her first baby gift – and the first gift given to her as a mother-to-be.
The Wednesday before the Easter weekend, a van arrived at the house. Her aunt told her to put her hands over her eyes and not peep while the delivery men carried in a big box.
"You can open your eyes now," she said when they had gone.
 She gasped when she saw a wooden rocking cradle, padded out with cushions and soft blankets. "Oh, Auntie Verne!"
"It's your Easter present, honey. It's my present to me also. I'm enjoying all this. On Sunday we're having lunch with some South Africans in Manhattan. You'll meet the gang: Millie, Veronica and Reggie – all South

Africans, except for Reggie's wife, Ursula, who's English. Don't know how long that's going to last, though. Reggie went through that whole white-woman-trophy-on-the-arm syndrome. Eventually, though, you revert to your own kind."

After a few seconds she reminded Joonie, "No calling me 'auntie', least of all on Sunday."

"Okay, Verne."

That night she lay on her bed staring at the cradle. The cradle symbolised so much: motherhood, a baby, a new environment, a new life. She took out her diary and recorded the events of the day, then wrote her father a letter.

> *Dear Dad*
> *I am so sorry that I'm only replying to your letter now. I have been thinking a lot about you and Mom and Ma though and hope you are okay. Happy Easter! Here all the shops are overflowing with Easter eggs and bunnies and Auntie Verne says that a part of New York will be blocked off tomorrow for the traditional Easter Parade. There will be no floats, but apparently masses of people walk down Fifth Avenue each year, showing off their Easter "bonnets" and outfits. I hope we'll catch a glimpse of the parade because we are going to have lunch with some of her South African friends in Manhattan.*
>   *I'm very okay, but so tired by the time I get home from the store in the afternoon that I just want to drop into bed and sleep. Can you believe it that I've been working for almost two months now? My first pay cheque was $1,200! And no tax deducted. I'm buying something every week for the baby. I don't know how long I'll be able to work, my feet*

already ache from standing behind the counter for half a day. But I'm earning money, Dad. I'm paying my own way. And I'm having a great time. Auntie Verne's the greatest. I don't know why you guys were so worried about her. She just bought the baby the most beautiful cradle – a rocking cradle made of wood. We're having her name carved on it – Bobby Jo. These are the kinds of names you hear here. I like it. Her nickname will be Bokkie. She'll be an American baby, Dad. She'll have all the privileges just having been born in this country. But she must know her South African roots also. And so she'll be my little springbokkie. I can hear Ma saying that I'm talking a lot of nonsense now, so I'll shut up, but I'm just so excited, Dad. Not to mention Auntie Verne – she's so pleased you'd swear it was her baby.

I promise I'll write more regularly, but now I have to go to bed.
Lots of love
Joonie

On Easter Sunday, she was awoken by loud voices. At first she thought it was coming from outside, then realised it was her aunt shrieking at Billie Bob. She tried not to listen, but it was impossible to ignore her aunt's raving. From what she could make out her aunt was upset over Billie Bob wanting to spend the day with his sons. "You men are all the fucking same! Go to your family and don't come back!"

Joonie couldn't believe her own ears. She had never heard her aunt say a harsh word to the man who shared her bed. She felt quite bewildered. The stairs creaked; someone was coming up to the loft. She heard a soft knock at the door.

"Come in," she said, feeling a sudden cramp in her belly. She had become more uncomfortable of late, prone to cramps.

Billie Bob came into the room. "I'm sorry you had to wake up to such a racket, Joonie, and sorry to disturb you."

"It's all right, Uncle Billie."

"Your aunt's acting a little strange. It happens when she doesn't take her pills, and from what I can make out she's lost the container and hasn't taken them for almost a week. She can't afford to be off them. She's addicted to them and becomes symptomatic if she doesn't take them every day at the same time. I need your help while I sort her out."

"I'm happy to help. Tell me what to do. Auntie Laverne asked me about her pills before, but I didn't think it was that serious.

He handed her a card. "She's always misplacing her pills. Call the all-hours pharmacist and tell him that we need an urgent refill. I'll pick up the pills in twenty minutes."

There was a sound at the door. It was Aunt Verne, still in her nightgown, holding a huge Easter egg. Joonie stared at her aunt who now seemed rational and calm, as if nothing had happened. But there was a dull look in her eyes.

"Give me a cigarette, Billie."You don't smoke, Verne. You gave up ten years ago. Remember?" he said quietly.

"I didn't. Ask Joonie. Joonie knows I smoke. Hand me my smokes, Joonie. It should be in the top drawer over there."

"This isn't your room, Laverne," Billie Bob said. "You don't have cigarettes in here."

Auntie Laverne walked over to the small chest of

drawers against the wall, plonked down the Easter egg and opened the top drawer, which was filled with Joonie's underwear and personal items. She lifted up panties and bras and scratched around, mumbling to herself. "Did you take my cigarettes, Joonie?"

"I don't smoke, Auntie Laverne."

The "auntie" slipped out before she could stop it, but her aunt didn't notice. Turning to Billie Bob she said, "She's lying."

Joonie stared at her. With a single accusation her aunt's behaviour told her that something was very wrong and she felt suddenly afraid. How could anyone change just like that? She was reminded of her grandmother's friend Maggie in District Six who used to sit with her on the stoep and talk about her mean daughter-in-law, and then when she ran out of pills would walk right past Ma without a word, pretending not to know her.

"Go make the call, Joonie," Billie Bob urged, making a sign to her to remain calm.

"I asked for a cigarette, Billie," Auntie Laverne repeated.

Billie Bob handed her one. She put it in her mouth but didn't light it.

Joonie went briskly down the stairs to the kitchen to call the pharmacist. The man on the other side of the line accepted her explanation without hesitation and promised that the pills would be ready to be picked up. After Billie Bob left to fetch the pills, Joonie helped her aunt to her bedroom and coaxed her back into bed. She thought it safer to have her aunt off her feet than wandering about.

As soon as he arrived back, Billie Bob gave Auntie Laverne a pill and a glass of water; he made her swallow a mild tranquiliser as well. She almost immediately fell into a deep sleep.

"I have to see my two boys today, Joonie," Billie Bob

said where the two of them stood at the side of her aunt's bed. "Would you mind keeping an eye on things while I'm gone? I know you're a little shocked. Your aunt had a nervous breakdown eight years ago. I don't know if you know that she used to be a nurse in a psychiatric ward? When she had the breakdown she ended up in the same ward where she'd been working. I was a porter at the hospital at the time. I remembered her from the time when she was a nurse. So I visited her and took care of her when she was released three months later. I know the real Laverne – the Laverne before the breakdown. This other person only appears when she forgets to take her pills."

"You mean she has a split personality?"

"It's an alter ego, I think. You've been here almost two months now. You know what your aunt is like. She's caring and generous. This other Laverne is suspicious and mean."

"Do you know why she had the breakdown?"

"I think it had something to do with the baby she lost – an abortion she had to have when she was very young; she was still living in South Africa at the time. She had no choice, it had stopped growing inside her, she said."

Joonie did not know how to respond. Her aunt had not told her about a baby that had to be removed because it had died while inside her. Was this a second pregnancy? Or could there have been only one pregnancy, and that her aunt was confused?

Shortly afterwards, Billie Bob left. She stayed alone with her sleeping aunt in the house. Just after one o'clock the phone rang. It was her aunt's friend, Millie, calling from Manhattan to ask when they were coming for lunch; the turkey was on the table, and everyone was waiting for them. If they didn't come soon, they were going to miss the Easter Parade altogether.

"Auntie Laverne's not feeling well," Joonie said. "She's asleep. I think we won't be able to make it to Manhattan today."

"I'm sorry to hear that. We were looking so forward to meeting you. I invited a nice history student from campus. Maybe *you* would still like to come? I can send for a cab."

"Thank you, Auntie Millie, but I can't leave my aunt on her own. There's no one else here."

"Give her our very best regards. Hopefully we can get together next weekend?"

"That would be very nice. Thanks for calling. I'll pass on the message, Auntie Millie."

Joonie sat in the lounge listening to her aunt snoring in her bedroom. Outside the snow had melted and the trees were starting to turn green, promising an early spring. There was excitement in the air as a father and mother with three children tumbled out of their car, all sporting Easter outfits. Joonie was overcome with a feeling of loneliness. She hadn't left the house all day, and except for Auntie Millie's phone call, no one had called or come around. The house was quiet. Skollie was nowhere to be seen. Even the huge fluffy Easter bunny – intended as a gift for Bobby Jo – looked forlorn and sad sitting on the dining-room table. Except for the steady purr of the fridge in the kitchen and her aunt's groaning in her sleep, it was quiet as a cemetery. She understood now what her aunt meant by South Africans having a lonely time of it in the States. You could live in a city of eight million people and still be achingly lonely.

Joonie comforted herself with thoughts of Ma's love of hot-cross buns and her father's weakness for marshmallow Easter eggs. Her mother would have made her usual roast leg of lamb and potatoes and sweet yellow rice, full of juicy raisins, followed by her avocado-and-ice-cream dessert.

By three o'clock that afternoon she couldn't bear the loneliness any longer and went into the kitchen and phoned home. Her father answered. For a moment he could not speak so surprised was he to hear her voice.

"Hallo, Dad. How's everyone? I know it's an awkward time to call, but I needed to hear your voice. Say something in Afrikaans, Dad."

Her father laughed. "Ons mis vir jou, girlie. Everyone's well. Hang on a minute, I just want to close the door. Some of the family's here. You know what the Easter long weekend is like. How is everything going over there with you, Joonie?"

"Great, Dad. America's a really great place."

"Really? Your mom misses you, you know. And Ma. She's changed since you left."

"How's Ma changed?"

"I think she thinks she's not going to see you again."

"She'll see me again, Dad. Let me talk to her."

"She's having a nap."

"Ma's having a nap with the house full of visitors? That's not like Ma. Is there something more going on, Dad?"

"Nothing's going on. Your grandmother's sixty-five, don't forget. You leaving robbed her of her little adventures. She's bored."

They talked some more about the family and then her father said that there had been a visitor for her a week earlier. Hilary, she thought. She had written a letter to Hilary a week or two ago, telling her about her job, and the handsome Greek boy at Billie Bob's shop who had befriended her.

"Was it Hilary?"

"No." He paused. "It was Blair."

The breath caught in her throat. "Blair?"

"I told him you were in New Jersey. He seemed shocked."

"*He* seemed shocked? I'm shocked now, Dad. I've been gone a few months."

"He said he wrote you a letter explaining his sudden departure."

"I didn't receive it."

"That's because Ma didn't forward it to you. She's the one who answered the door. She didn't want you to be confused, she told us. She still has it."

"Ma has no right to keep it from me, Dad! Can you send it to me, *please*?"

"You want to read it?"

"Of course I do, Dad. I've never had an explanation as to why he disappeared like that. Did Ma read it?"

"I don't know. But you know Ma. She's Miss Nosy Parker. She knows how to open sealed envelopes without leaving a trace."

They spoke for a few more minutes, but she hardly registered what her father said. After she'd put the receiver down she sat unmoving for a long time. There was a thin thread of hope. She felt better, knowing that Blair hadn't just walked away from her. He had written her a letter, he had an explanation, he still cared. But she would have to wait for his letter before she could reply, lest he thought that she had received his letter already and had not cared to answer.

She woke up the following morning feeling cheerful and ready for the day, and went directly downstairs to check on her aunt. Auntie Laverne was still asleep and she noticed that only one side of the bed had been slept on.

"Is that you, Billie?"

"It's me, Verne – checking to see if you're okay. How are you feeling today?"

Her aunt opened her eyes sleepily. "I think I'll stay in bed. I feel tired."

"That's a good idea. Your friend Millie called yesterday; they were waiting for us, she said. She suggested we get together next weekend."

"We can go next Friday, it'll be fun. You'll like Millie. She reads Tarot cards, and quite accurately. Her sister Veronica is a bit stand-offish at first and hates South Africans who complain – so don't talk about how cold it has been here. They have this card game on Friday nights at the flat – seven of them. Reggie makes the stupidest jokes. The thing is, though, that you can't stop laughing. Ursula, of course, doesn't understand a word of Afrikaans, and hates these gatherings. Can you ask Billie to make me some coffee?"

"I'll make it for you."

"Where's Billie?"

"I don't think he came home."

Her aunt lay back on the pillow with her eyes closed. There was a look of quiet resignation on her face as she lay silent for a few moments.

"I knew it would happen one day," she eventually said. She sounded tired. "A married man's a married man. He never belongs to you even when he moves in. Everything a man does in life is for money and sex. I don't have money, and as for sex, I hate it, even though I'm only thirty-three." Blankly staring at the wall, she continued, "To be honest, it's a relief not to worry about him anymore."

"Don't say that, Verne. You don't mean it. Uncle Billie adores you."

Her aunt gave a sarcastic laugh. "Of course he adores me. Don't you adore Skollie? You put out her bowl of milk and her cat food and she won't scratch your face and pee on the couch." She turned on her side to face Joonie, accidentally exposing a pert breast. "With a married man it happens inch by inch – even if he is separated from his wife. He too can't let go all at once – so it will go on a bit longer, but eventually he will be gone. I was served with a notice."

She was surprised by her aunt's brutal clarity and acceptance, especially after her erratic behaviour of the previous day. Her aunt wasn't the dizzy, dippy woman her family thought she was. She could be very clear-headed and had accurately assessed her relationship with Billie Bob, as it turned out.

Joonie returned to work on Tuesday. Billie Bob arrived at the shop at the end of her shift and took the money and receipts from her. It was an awkward moment.

"You're probably wondering why I didn't return to the house yesterday."

"It's not my business, Uncle Billie."

Billie Bob pretended to study the receipt at the top of the little stack she'd handed him. It was a while before he continued, "I'd like you to know the kind of friendship we've had and I still hope to have. I looked after your aunt after she was released from hospital because no one had come to see her and she seemed very alone. I do love your aunt, but not in the way she wants."

"You've slept in her bed …"

"Yes, I have. She's a good woman and things happen. But I've been wanting to leave for a long time. I just couldn't. Just when things seemed to be going well with her, she would have a relapse and I would stay on. The relapses occur more often now and I can't carry on. My son bought a horse farm in Missouri a few years back. He wants me to run it for him. I've always loved the outdoors and wanted to sell up two, three years ago already and be near my grandchildren. Even if I wasn't married, your aunt doesn't want to move. Your coming to live with her has provided a way out for me."

She felt sad, but understood. "Things happen for a reason, Uncle Billie."

"I'm not abandoning ship, Joonie; it just won't be like before. I have the greatest respect for your aunt."

She didn't answer. He had respect for her aunt, yes, but he was nevertheless leaving. The thing her aunt wanted most was his company. She was happy with him around.

"About the store; I have someone who wants to take over the franchise in four months. By that time your baby would've been born and you can decide whether you want to continue to work here. The position will be open to you."

"Thank you, Uncle Billie. Could I wait and tell you later whether I want to keep the job?"

"Of course."

That afternoon after work she told her aunt about her conversation with Billie Bob. "He was very sincere, Verne, but if you don't want me to continue working for him, I'll quit."

"No. You keep your job, honey. Billie did nothing to you – and he's still a good guy. This day had to come."

Joonie felt sad and a little empty. She had also got used to him in the house. She admired her aunt's quiet acceptance of the situation. "You're strong," she said.

"You too, honey. You just don't know how strong yet. But we all have our limitations."

The next Friday afternoon she and her aunt caught a bus to Manhattan. The pills had kicked in and Auntie Verne seemed on top of the world, wearing a silky dress under her full-length coat and a purple flower in her hair. It looked incongruous with the faded hennaed hair, but Joonie said nothing.

They got out of the bus at Times Square from where they decided to walk the last few blocks to the apartment where Millie and Veronica lived. Joonie was mesmerised by the air of excitement: massive billboards, bright neon lights, yellow cabs filled with passengers in a hurry to get somewhere, girls in high heels and skimpy clothing hovering in doorways. They were car-less now with Billie Bob's departure, but with all the frenetic activity on the streets, they were happy to walk and be part of it all.

"If you think it's busy here on an ordinary Friday evening," her aunt said, "wait until the 31st of December when the countdown to the New Year starts in Times Square. Do you think you will still be here to see it?"

Joonie was all too aware of the passing of time. She'd been in America two and a half months already – which made her almost six and a half months pregnant. "I don't know. July's just around the corner when my baby's due, I promised to go back within a year, which gives me until the end of next February, at the latest."

"Will you really go back after the baby is born?"

"I have a return ticket. I have to."

"Your baby will be an American. This will be a great place for her to grow up. She'll have so many opportunities. You must think carefully."

"I know."

"Why not stay then? Martin next door is an articling student. We could speak to him and ask him for advice on how you can best obtain official permission. Maybe he can get you to see one of their lawyers. He's a nice boy, and clever too."

"I don't know if I want to stay permanently." She thought of Blair, and didn't want to meet any boys to further complicate her life.

"Didn't you come here for the opportunities America offers?"

"I came here to hide my shame – which was so stupid as everyone knows anyway."

"Are you sorry you came?" The sadness in her aunt's voice made Joonie look at her.

"No. I'm seeing the world," she said, deliberately light-hearted. "And as you say, my baby will be an American. You never know what that will be good for. How far to walk still, Auntie Verne? My legs won't carry my body much further."

"Not far. Four more blocks and we're there."

She shivered, regretting that she hadn't put on a thick jersey and boots instead of trying to be fancy with a thin dress under her coat and fancy shoes. But it was supposed to be spring. No, she doubted very much that she could stay in a country that was this chilly even during spring, not to mention the dreadful sub-zero temperatures of winter.

"Have you never thought of going home yourself, Verne?"

"I think about it all the time."

"What stops you?"

"Oh, many things. By the time I get to the end of the list, I don't want to go home anymore. Still chasing the dream, I suppose, whatever that is. The longer you stay away the more you remember the things you didn't have and still won't get in your own country, and you stay on. I should've left years ago."

"So go home now. You can start fresh. We can go back together. You're only in your thirties. You can meet a nice man there."

"That would be wonderful, hey, to know that I can resolve it all with a plane trip. I have too much invested here, though."

They arrived at the apartment, one of many ugly brown brick buildings with stairs running down the outside wall, and took a small elevator up to the third floor. Millie, a slim woman in her late thirties with straight hair to her shoulders and dressed in cream pants, opened the door. Joonie stepped into a tastefully decorated space with tinkling glass, wind chimes and wooden masks on the walls. These were not African masks; she guessed they came from the Amazon jungle, the exact opposite of the mishmash of trinkets in her aunt's lounge.

They hugged and shook hands. Millie was warm and friendly. "It's nice to finally meet you, Joonie. We've heard so much about you. Welcome to our little group."

Millie's sister, Veronica, was very different. Dressed in army fatigues, with cropped hair, she watched the visitors like a bald-headed eagle from her perch near the liquor cabinet.

"How many months to go?" she asked unceremoniously.

"Less than three." Joonie replied, looking her straight in the eye.

"Married?"

"No."

"My sister can be very direct," Millie said.

"Better than being a hypocrite," Veronica retorted, turning back to Joonie.

"This is Jennifer, my partner. Jennifer's from Grassy Park and has been here four years now. Millie and I come from Belgravia Estate."

Joonie was surprised by the freedom with which Veronica revealed personal details. She didn't know anyone who would, without being asked, own up to such a relationship to someone she had just met. She looked at the partner: red-haired and dimply, pushing fifty but dolled up like a sixteen-year-old in tight jeans and a clinging green sleeveless top, much too low for her massive breasts and ample arms.

"Hallo," she said.

"Hi. Nice to meet you, Joonie."

"And this is Kevin, my boyfriend," Millie introduced a man who, having had a few drinks already, immediately put his arms around Joonie and asked, "Can I offer you a sherry, Joonie?" About the same age as Billie Bob, he looked rather good with his spiky hair and crinkly designer pants.

"It's not good for her," a big broad woman in tight black stretch pants, sitting on the sofa, said. "I don't think you should have alcohol. I'm Susan, by the way. And this is my husband, Gavin." And she rested a podgy hand on the thigh of the handsome man with a crew cut and faint smile next to her. "Just don't touch my husband, Joonie."

Joonie laughed; she knew Susan was joking.

"Sherry, Joonie?" Kevin persisted.

"Okay, just a small one. I've never had sherry."

"Oh, you'll love it. It'll warm you up." He turned to look at the rugged guy in blue jeans and a maroon sweater sitting at the table shuffling cards. "Is no one going to introduce Deddy?"

"Deddy can introduce himself," Susan said. "He's big and ugly enough."

"Haai, shame, don't say that about Deddy," Kevin said jokingly. "Deddy keeps us in laughs."

"Deddy's his real name?" Joonie asked.

"No. His name's Reggie Philander. Reggie, meet Joonie. Joonie's here on a year's holiday."

Reggie nodded at her, his eyes flitting over her belly.

"Where's Ursula?" Veronica asked him.

Reggie continued shuffling and reshuffling the cards.

"Was there no one to look after David?" Millie asked.

"You could've brought him along."

"He's too hyper. He's on new medication."

"Reggie's son, David, is autistic," Millie explained.

She didn't know what being autistic was, and didn't ask.

Kevin started to pour a sherry for everyone. "Come, people, let the games begin," he called. "Can you play eleven-cards, Joonie?"

"Yes, but I'll watch a few games first. Am I allowed to play?"

"Of course you are," Kevin said.

Five people made themselves comfortable at the card table: Reggie, Gavin, Susan, Veronica and Millie. Reggie put the deck in front of Gavin. Millie lit a cigarette. Except for Reggie, everyone was smoking, even Auntie Verne.

"Explain the rules to her, Verne," Veronica said, putting down two bowls of peanuts and chips.

"Five people play at a time," Auntie Laverne said. "It's really eleven-cards, or rummy. The person on the left of the person who wins gets up and the person waiting to play sits down. A 'boem' is a set of four games – a dollar a game. For the fourth round we play for two dollars and you can't put out your cards until you win. If you accidentally put down your cards, or put down the wrong cards by mistake, you're out."

"Ons straf jou!" Kevin laughed. "We penalise you and you're out."

The five started to play. After watching three games, Joonie felt confident enough to join in. She had stood behind each of the players in turn and noted their style of playing and their different bluffing techniques. Reggie, Gavin, and Susan seldom put out their cards until the end of the game. They held on to their Jokers, memorised the cards put out on the table and knew what not to throw.

Susan would say she had a terrible hand when, in fact, she was waiting for only one card. Reggie would grumble when someone put out a set, complaining that he had been "kapped" – when in reality he had a winning hand.

With their eyes glued to the cards, the group talked about the people they knew back home. Veronica mentioned a school friend of hers at Athlone High by the name of Basil Sasman. A few seconds later, putting down a winning hand, Reggie turned sideways and gave a loud sneeze, "Siss, man!"

Joonie frowned. Had he sneezed or repeated the name Sasman? Reggie sat with a deadpan look on his face as he studied his cards. She realised from the sniggering at the table that it was a joke, silly, but also funny in a way she couldn't explain. Encouraged by the snickers around the table, he went on to make another.

"Who can make a sentence with the words attack and quarrel?"

No one said anything.

He continued, "This guy bought a 'tak' of grapes... and ate it 'korrel' for 'korrel'."

There was something ridiculously stupid about hearing such a Standard Two joke, but watching Reggie's expressionless face as he told it, Joonie found herself laughing against her will.

"Do you always laugh at his jokes?" she asked.

"Your 'he' has a name," Reggie said next to her. "Hello, Joonie, my name's Reggie."

"Hello, Reggie, my name's Joonie with a J O O."

"Tell me, Joonie with a J O O, can you make a sentence with the word, Cyril?"

"No."

"That's not how it starts," Veronica said.

"Okay. Knock knock."

"Who's there?"
"Cyril."
"Cyril who?"
"Cyriliddle closer."

She laughed. "Okay, that was good."

The card game ended at four in the morning. Veronica and Jennifer said goodnight and disappeared into their room. Susan struggled out of her seat and said she had cramps in her legs from sitting for six hours straight. Gavin helped her up, his face expressionless. Joonie wondered how they managed to have sex. Susan was so fat, one thigh alone could feed all the people in the block.

"Do you guys have a lift?" Reggie asked.

"No. We'll call for a cab."

Satisfied with the answer, he left along with Gavin, Susan and Kevin.

"You don't have to go home, Verne," Millie said. "There's a pull-out couch over there. You guys can sleep over unless it's too awkward for Joonie. It's slippery out there on the roads, and not too safe, not even in a cab. I can take you home in the morning."

"It's morning now," Auntie Laverne pointed out.

"That's what I mean. Stay a little longer. Maybe you would like some tea? I have some lovely strawberry tea I bought from a health-food shop, and a whole variety of other teas."

Millie's choice of tea didn't surprise her. "I wouldn't mind some, thanks."

"And you, Laverne?" Millie asked.

"Not for me, thanks. I'm just going to catch forty winks. We'll take a cab home later. I don't want you to drive all the way."

Her aunt lay back on the couch and was instantly asleep.

"Would it be cheeky to ask if you could read my cards? Auntie Verne said you were quite good at it," Joonie hesitantly asked.

"I read the Tarot cards. Not everyone likes them."

"I don't know anything about Tarot cards. I just think it's interesting to hear what people see in the cards and tell you about yourself."

"Have you asked someone to tell you about your future before?"

"Not a card reader; just an old woman Ma took me to see. She told me to have the baby."

Millie's brows rose in surprise. "So this is how you came to be here?"

"One could say so, yes. She saved me from making a huge mistake."

Millie fetched two big square cushions and led her into a small adjacent room. They sat opposite each other on the floor with feet crossed at the ankles. Joonie, happy to still be able to sit comfortably in this position, had a chance to look around while Millie took the cards out of a purple plush velvet bag at her feet. Joonie felt at ease, ensconced within the warm shades of the room: a plum-coloured Afghan rug hanging against a biscuit-coloured wall, a painting of a chocolate-brown child sitting in front of a mud hut, a bowl of gemstones on a small intricately carved table.

"Is this where you do your readings?"

"Yes. It's a little quieter at the side of the building. We're the corner apartment." Millie picked up the cards and gave them to her. "Shuffle them and put them in three piles."

The unusually long cards felt awkward in her hands and she shuffled slowly, dividing and setting them out into three piles.

"Now put your hand on one of the piles."

She rested her hand on the middle stack.

Millie picked up the cards and arranged them in a cross shape. She pointed to a card with a heart and three swords pierced through it. "This is the Three of Swords – not a card you really want to come up, I must confess. It symbolises betrayal."

Joonie stared at the card. She certainly felt that she had been betrayed, even if not in the conventional manner, and had a flashback of Blair with his arms around her on that day, telling her how in love he was with her.

"It can also mean abandonment or separation," Millie continued.

"The cards really say that?"

"Yes. If it doesn't currently apply to you, though, the card serves as a warning."

"It applies, don't you think – being away from my family? Separated and abandoned?"

"Not abandoned, surely."

"No, but I feel kind of left out sometimes; don't ask me why. The father of my child doesn't know that I'm pregnant. I made the decision not to tell him. I don't know if it was a good or bad decision. On one hand I feel that he should know, and on the other hand I'm afraid he might reject the baby and then I'll feel worse. A rejection of my baby will also be a rejection of me."

"Of course, there's also the possibility that he might want to be part of your life and your baby's – and then you would have another decision to make."

"Exactly. And I can't handle that decision right now."

"Do you want to talk about it?"

She considered the invitation to speak her heart, almost saying yes. "Not now," she said after a pause. "Maybe at a later stage. Thank you, Auntie Millie."

"Anytime. You have my number. If you have time off from work and you want to, we can have lunch next week. I can introduce you to some of my American students."

"That would be great, thanks again. I would like to know more about college here, and how to apply. Not that I will be here for very long."

In the cab back to New Jersey, a couple of hours later, she thought of everything Millie had told her. The cards had indeed been accurate, although she didn't much like them, and wouldn't try them again.

She and Auntie Laverne arrived at the house late in the morning to find a visitor waiting for them on the cold porch.

"Stavros!"

He got up from the slatted wooden chair, rubbed his hands vigorously together and hugged her. "I came back early." He turned to her aunt with a broad smile. "Hope you had a good time with your Cape Town friends."

"We did, thank you," her aunt replied.

"Have you been sitting here long?" Joonie asked.

"For about an hour. Billie Bob said you guys had gone to Manhattan last night to play cards. I figured you wouldn't be long." He looked at his watch and smiled. "I must say this must be the longest card game in history."

Her aunt glanced at her with a twinkle in her eyes that said Stavros was interested in her, and went into the house.

"I thought you were only coming back next week," she said.

"I changed my plans. I missed you."

She felt a little hot in her face. "You did?"

"Yes. I missed being around you. Hearing you giggle – not that you giggle enough, though."

It was the first outright compliment, the first move on his part. She didn't know what to say. She liked him too, but hadn't allowed herself to get foolish over the gift he'd given her before leaving for Greece. She was an unwed mother-to-be. No boy would be interested in a girl in her situation, and she wasn't used to boys like him. Stavros and she came from different backgrounds. Even Blair, who was white, had something in common with her – the culture and history of their country; they came from the same environment, they spoke the same language. Stavros was Greek, he was an American, a budding journalist, drove a Mustang – a car she'd only seen in the movies. He came from a wealthy family and she from a working-class family. She was outclassed by him, and with her big belly, out of consideration as a girlfriend. More so after he'd told her that no girl is ever good enough for a Greek mother.

"It's cold. Let's go inside. I'll make hot chocolate for all of us," she suggested.

"Do you want to go and see a movie later? There's a great Al Pacino film showing at the Edgewater Multiplex Cinema. It's a replay of *Dog Day Afternoon*, one of his best movies made two or three years ago."

"I'm a pregnant girl, Stavros. Why would you want to go out with me?"

She could see he was taken aback by her statement, but looking into her eyes he said, "I like you. I like your company. You're beautiful and intelligent and different from any other girl I have ever met."

She didn't know how to respond. He had a strong energy, she felt excited in his presence. Was it stupid to entertain the thought of falling in love? And was it possible to be attracted to two people at the same time? Blair was the father of her child; he would be a more suitable partner, but he was on a different continent, and there was no guarantee that he still felt the same way about her. The letter Ma had intercepted had not yet arrived. Did it make sense to consider friendship with a new guy when her heart still bled for another?

Stavros came to stand behind her where she stood at the window. She could feel his breath on her cheek as his body moved closer to hers. She looked out at the boys shooting hockey pucks into a net on the wet street. There were so many pros and cons, she thought.

She turned around to look at him. "Are you going to hurt me, Stavros?" It was a bold question, she realised, but she felt bolstered enough to ask it. She had nothing to lose.

"No."

"If you hurt me, I'll hurt you back."

He laughed, putting his arms around her. "You can't hurt anyone, Joonie. But that is what I like about you. You are brave and independent."

Two weeks later, I received the letter my father had forwarded to me. I remember Auntie Verne handing me the airmail envelope containing the letter. I read it with a rush of affection in the privacy of my room and could almost feel Blair next to me, his warm breath on my neck. I read how dismayed he was to discover that I had left the country. His father had booked a ticket for him to return to Johannesburg the same evening he had last seen me and he had been forced to leave in a hurry. He was accepted for the military training and whisked away to a training camp a couple of days later. He had called at the first opportunity. My mother had been nice to him on the phone, but had nevertheless told him that it was pointless calling again; I was gone. The letter had been written during a flight to Cape Town. He was still at Voortrekkerhoogte, receiving his basic training, but got compassionate leave to go and see his mother who had suddenly taken ill. He said that he was writing so he could leave the letter at my parents' house for them to send to me. Ma must have opened the door and taken the letter from him. The last sentence in the letter was in the form of a question: Is it over between us, Joonie? I'll never believe it.

I am fifty now, but I can still recall the thrill I felt when I read the letter and remember it word for word.

The letter had a strange effect on me, though. I found it impossible to answer. I had rushed to judge Blair and rushed to get on a plane and leave the country as soon as it could be arranged. What was I to do now? One guy hurt and disillusioned, and another filled with feelings for me I couldn't reciprocate?

So I did not respond. I did nothing. I just did not know what to do. What bothered me most was my own erratic behaviour. I had been with one guy seven months earlier, and was seriously considering moving into an apartment with someone else. I had said "I love you" to two people. I had slept with both of them. There had to be something wrong with my brain. The brain was the information centre of the body, where all plans are made. Does God forgive faulty thinking? I fretted. Could I be with Stavros, knowing Blair still loved me? I was confused. Knowing Blair still had feelings for me didn't mean that he would accept the child, I told myself, he might even think that the child wasn't his, and then I would have no one.

I wrote Hilary a long letter and shared my confusion with her. She wrote back and said not to feel so much guilt, and not to decide with my heart, but with my head, in favour of the baby. I reread Hilary's last paragraph a few times:

> *It's unfortunate that you didn't receive the letter before you left, because you might never have left South Africa, but the reality is that it didn't happen that way and Blair isn't with you. Stavros is. Your child will have all the benefits you left South Africa for in the first place.*

The thing is, I hadn't left South Africa for American benefits; I had run away.

So I put Blair out of my mind and continued my cashier's job at the corner store until my feet puffed up like baked bread and my stomach looked ready to burst. I kept a close eye on Auntie Laverne because I could only move in with Stavros if she remained stable. In June I turned eighteen. There was no big celebration, just a romantic dinner for two at a small Italian bistro where we had stuffed cannelloni and he had a bottle – and I a sip – of good wine, and he put a silver bracelet with charms dangling from it on my wrist.

Early on the morning of 5 July, just hours after she and Stavros had finished watching the American Independence Day celebrations on television, she was awakened by a sharp pain in her belly. She had been restless all night and wondered if it was a cramp or the beginning of labour. She listened to the traffic start up outside; it was not yet dawn. From the room on the floor below the spluttering sounds of her aunt's snoring drifted up the stairs. There had been no overnight visits by Billie Bob since their last meeting three months ago. On the carpet, next to her single bed, Stavros was sleeping on the floor. His face was buried in the pillow, his dark locks splashed across the side of his face. She sat up in bed and felt something warm gush out of her. She lifted up her nightdress. "Oh my God…"

She turned to Stavros sleeping on the floor. "Stav…"

He moaned in his sleep.

"Wake up, Stav," she whispered close to his ear. "I think I have to go to the hospital. Urgently."

He sat up immediately. "Are you serious?"

"Yes." She tried to stand up and gripped the side of her belly as she braced herself for another contraction.

He pulled on his jeans and a jersey over his shirt and helped her down the stairs to the bathroom. Her aunt appeared in the doorway. "What's going on?" she asked bleary-eyed.

"I have to go to the hospital, Verne. I had a feeling something was going to happen. I felt cramps all last night.

I hope you don't mind that I asked Stavros to stay here. He slept on the floor."

"The hospital? What are you going to the hospital for?"

"My water has broken. My hospital bag is packed; we're leaving in a few minutes. I just want to go to the loo quickly."

When she emerged from the bathroom, her aunt was back in her room, back in bed, judging by the closed bedroom door. She was surprised by her aunt's indifference, but she had more pressing concerns and pushed it to the back of her mind. Stavros was waiting for her with her coat at the front door. "It's really time?" he asked in amazement. "The baby's coming?"

"Yes. I had another contraction. I'm getting scared now."

He put his arm around her. "Don't be scared, Joons. Everything will be all right. You'll see. By tomorrow morning you'll be a mom."

"You think so? I mean I know what's going to happen, but I just can't believe it. I can't wait. I'm so excited, and scared, too, that it's going to hurt."

"You'll be fine. I'll be there waiting for you."

Outside in the car, it was dark and silent; spooky almost with the street lights reflected on the wet, slippery asphalt. A lone police car drifted along the wide road. Except for the flashing motel lights on the main road, New Jersey was in slumber.

"I wish my mother was here. One needs one's mother at a time like this."

Stavros turned to look at her. "I'm here for you, Joons."

"I know. I don't know what I would've done without you. My aunt acted strange this morning. I hope it's not one of her episodes coming on."

"Maybe she was just groggy."

"I hope so. She had always said she would come with me and hold my hand when the baby was born. And just now she acted like she didn't know I was pregnant. And she went back to her room and didn't say anything."

"Maybe it's too early for her."

They arrived at the hospital where a room had been reserved in her name. The nurse at the front desk took her details.

"Are you the father, sir?" the nurse asked.

"No."

"Whose last name will be on the birth certificate?"

"Mine," Joonie replied.

A contraction gripped her insides and she groaned with pain. "Jeez ... that was a big one. The pains are coming more quickly now."

"We'll soon have you settled in your room," the nurse reassured her.

They prepared her in the labour room. The nurse examined her, felt between her legs.

"I can't take the pain, nurse. Please ... can you give me something?"

"We're going to give you an epidural," the doctor said. "You will have to remain very still when the needle goes in. No matter how bad the pain, you can't move."

She sat up so they could insert the needle in her back, struggling to remain still as she felt another huge contraction coming on. Minutes later her legs felt like lead and she couldn't move them; there was no pain. The contractions had been reduced to a dull ache.

After about an hour the nurse told her she was fully dilated and that it was time for her to push. "Now!" the nurse said. "Count backwards and when I say push, you push. Ten ... nine ... eight ..."

Her face scrunched up as she took a deep breath and pushed.

"Another deep breath," the doctor said. "One big push and we're there. Now!"

She breathed in deep and gave one long agonising push, screaming for her mother.

The first cries of the baby rang through the air. She couldn't believe that she had done it – that it was her baby the doctor was busy with. She lay back exhausted, watching the nurse suction the nostrils and the teeny mouth and the doctor cut the umbilical cord. She was in a daze, high on the epidural, laughing and crying at the same time – for where she was, for the baby she had brought into the world, for herself and what the future held for the two of them.

The nurse weighed and measured the baby, wrapped her in a fleecy white sleeper, and put her in her arms. Joonie felt in awe of the greatness of God. God had never truly been a reality to her until now. She looked down on the tiny head all wet and waxy and accepted that it was really her baby. Had she produced this little human being with its ten toes and ten little fingers? She? Ungrateful and big-mouthed Joonie from Maitland? And what a truly awesome gift it was. Thank you, Lord, she said in gratefulness. Thank you for my little girl. She lifted the tiny hand. It gripped at her finger and held on to it. The tears ran down her face. Thank you, Lord. Thank you for looking after me and thank you for this wonderful, wonderful gift. Thank you.

Stavros came into the room where she would stay the night, until she was moved to her own room the following day. He bent over the bed and kissed her on her forehead. His face lit up with joy when he saw the infant in her arms. "Wow ... she's beautiful, Joonie. Look at this little rose.

How did it go?"

"Didn't you hear me screaming?"

"I did. I thought someone was throttling you," he smiled.

"You won't believe the pain. I was going crazy until they gave me the epidural. Now I can't feel anything."

He leaned over the baby. "I would like to hold her, but I'm afraid."

"Don't be. Just be careful how you hold her head."

Stavros picked up the baby. "She's beautiful, Joons. She looks like you. Does her father have light hair?"

It was the first time he made mention of the father of her child. "Yes."

"And blue eyes?"

"Both of us have."

For a moment he was quiet and she wondered what went through his mind. Surely, she thought, he wasn't jealous.

"You gave your last name as the surname of the child."

She was now wholly convinced that there was some anxiety on his part. "Whose name should I have given, Stavros? The father doesn't even know. He's in the past."

He straightened, and gave her an apologetic smile. "I'm being stupid," he said pensively. "Don't mind me. Of course you had to give her your last name."

"Can you believe it? She's just been born and she has a document in her name already. A birth certificate. She's an American citizen."

"You had two names for her. Which one did you give?"

"Bobby Jo. That will be her American name. Her nickname will be Bokkie, after the springbok, South Africa's national animal and emblem of our sports teams. I know she will be an athlete; maybe gymnastics or tennis. I liked playing tennis, you know. My parents couldn't afford my training, so I stopped when I reached matric – my final year in high school. Maybe Bokkie will be interested in the game. Oh God, I'm rambling on and on, I'm so happy. It must be that epidural they gave me."

He smiled. "I'm happy it all went well for you, Joons. It's amazing to hold her like this. Do you think she can have my last name one day?"

It was a big question and one that made her pause before answering. She knew what he was really asking; to remove Blair from her life. Should she say yes, and follow Hilary's advice, or say no and crush all his hopes? She was too excited over her baby to create any tension between them and replied, "Not before I'm nineteen."

"Really? You will marry me?" He leaned over the bed, baby and all, and gave her a whopping kiss on the mouth.

"I haven't met your parents yet, Stav. They may not like me," she reminded him.

He handed the baby back to her and sat down in the chair next to the bed. "My parents are divorced. My mother's the one that matters. No, she will not be happy about us. I must tell you now. I don't want to lie to you. But both my parents will expect me to marry a Greek girl. All that talk about culture and tradition – you know how it is. They step out a lot from the way things are done back in Greece, but they won't marry out of the culture."

She felt a deep disappointment, but hid it from him. "Is that why you haven't taken me to meet your mother yet?"

"Yes. I'm being honest with you. I didn't want you to be pregnant when you met my parents for the first time. They'll stand together on this. They know nothing about South Africa and the different people who live there. All they know is the repression they see on television. And the wildlife. They think wild animals run around in the streets. But when they see the baby they'll fall in love with her."

Joonie was doubtful. "They will see me as a girl who fell pregnant and latched onto a rich guy."

"I'm not rich, and there's no shame in having some spare change in my pocket. I work now, Joons. I don't have to go to my parents for anything. I love you. If my parents don't like you, that's fine. We'll be on our own."

"You mean you will defy them?"

"I'll marry the woman I want to."

He left after many assurances from her that she would try to rest after her ordeal. The nurse came in and took the baby to the nursery where all the other newborns were kept. Joonie's earlier happiness evaporated, she felt hollow and empty, as if a friend she had waited so long to see had come and gone. How could she not have figured out long ago that his parents would disagree with his choice?

That same night she got permission from the hospital to make an overseas call and spoke to her mother and father. They were delighted to hear the good news and congratulated her, happy to be grandparents.

"So we have a little American in the family now," her father said.

"Yes, Dad. A future gymnast, or a tennis player. She has long legs."

He laughed. "I don't want you to run up a huge bill for this call, Joonie. Look after my grandchild, and send us pictures. Soon, we'll see her in the flesh; you have six months left over there."

Her father's last words bothered her. How was she going to tell her family that she was thinking of staying on? Her situation had changed. There was someone in her life – someone who wanted her and wanted to take care of her and her child.

On the second day of her hospital stay, Millie, Veronica and Jennifer came to see her. They brought gifts and went mad over the baby and loved the name Bobby Jo. Joonie was so proud. She commented on how the baby had already filled out after its long stay in the womb, stroking her soft strands, hugging her as if someone was going to take her away.

"What did your aunt say when she saw her?" Veronica asked.

"She hasn't seen the baby yet."

"What do you mean?"

"She hasn't come to the hospital."

Veronica exchanged looks with her sister. "That's unusual, isn't it? I'm sure she'll come today."

For a few moments no one said anything. Then Veronica asked, "Is your baby's father white?"

"What do you mean is the father white?" Millie immediately retorted, irritation in her voice. "Is Joonie black? Joonie herself is white. The baby's not white just because the father is white."

"Joonie's not white. She only looks white."

"Oh, shut up, Veronica. You just want to be difficult."

Veronica laughed. "She's a knockout, Joonie. Whatever you had to go through, it was worth it. I wish I had a little girl like this."

"Thank you, Veronica. I agree: she's more than worth it." Veronica was brusque, she thought, but she had a good heart. She liked her. "Where's Reggie? He's not with you guys today?"

"Reggie's got problems at home. He's paying the price for a big mistake he made years ago. It's his own fault."

"Haai, Veronica," Jennifer cut in. "Joonie doesn't want to know the man's business."

"It's his fault, yes. He had an affair. What woman can

forget that? I don't like his wife myself, but I'm with her on that. I would kick his black arse out."

"Shame. You play cards with the man."

"I play cards with him, yes, and I like him, but he cheated on her. I'm on the woman's side. This shit happens when you're black and you want to try white. Stay with your own kind, I say."

"That's nasty, Veronica," Millie said. "He and his wife just aren't suited. Bangers and mash don't mix with viennas and chips."

They all laughed. "Why did she marry him then?"

"You know why. Anyway, it's none of our business."

Stavros arrived just as the women were getting ready to leave. She watched to see their expressions as she introduced them. They looked him up and down – from his long brown hair to his jeans and cowboy boots.

"Hmmm!" Veronica said. "I could change my orientation for a guy like this. You don't hang slangs, hey girl? You've been here a few months, and already you've met someone."

She blushed. The bantering was all in good spirit.

"What do you do, Stavros?" Millie asked.

"I've just started work as a journalist for a newspaper. I met Joonie at Billie Bob's shop."

"How's Billie doing?"

"Good. He's moving soon to look after his son's horse farm in Missouri." He turned to Joonie. "Did your aunt come?"

"No."

She didn't know if Millie and Veronica knew about the baby her aunt had lost, but thought her aunt's absence strange, considering how much she had looked forward to the baby's arrival.

Three days later she was discharged from hospital. It was strange and yet wonderful to walk to the car with Stavros holding the baby. It gave a real feeling of family and she felt her hopes rise again. This was what people got married for; to have children and be together through the tough patches in life, and Stavros had shown her how much he cared. She was going to be safe with him. Her child was going to have everything she needed.

The morning was hot. There was something very comforting being in an air-conditioned car with a baby in her arms.

"I'm a family, Stavros," she found herself saying.

"Am I not part of that family?"

"Of course you are, but for now it's all about me and Bobby Jo. It's a new experience. Look at her, so trusting, sleeping in my arms."

He smiled and turned his head to look at the sleeping infant in her arms. "She's not so red anymore," he said. "She's all smoothed out."

"I know. And the colour of her hair is more distinct now. I have to breastfeed her as soon as we get home. I don't have much milk. The nurse says it's like that in the first few days. She gave me a breast pump if I have difficulty."

They arrived at Auntie Laverne's house. There were two days' newspapers lying on the mat in front of the door. The curtains were drawn; everything seemed shut down, as if the occupants had all fled. She got a fright when they stepped inside and saw Auntie Laverne slumped on the stairway, the baby's cradle toppled over at the bottom of the stairs. Her aunt had put henna on her hair and the paste was starting to dry, making her look like a freak.

"Verne! What happened?"

"I tried to bring the cradle down."

"Why?"

"To put it in my room."

She handed the baby to Stavros and went to help her aunt up. "Bobby Jo can't stay in your room, Verne."

"Why not?"

She stared at her aunt. "What do you mean? How can she stay in your room?"

"I bought the cradle."

Joonie didn't understand. What did the cradle have to do with anything? Her aunt surely didn't think the baby was going to sleep in her room?

"She has to be with me, Verne. I have to breastfeed her. Have you taken your pills?"

"Why does everyone keep asking me if I've taken my pills? You're not here to check on me. Who are you, anyway?"

Joonie blanched under the attack. This was a different woman from the one who had welcomed her into her house five months ago. She looked over at Stavros. "Take her upstairs, Stav. I'll come now."

"You can't take my baby!" her aunt screamed.

Joonie's fear mounted. She had been in bed for three days. Her legs felt wobbly, and her aunt was out of control. "It's not your baby, Verne. You're mistaking Bobby Jo for someone else."

She shouldn't have said that. Her aunt grabbed one of the wooden giraffes on the living room cabinet and threw it at her. "It's my baby!"

She didn't know what to do. Her immediate concern was Bobby Jo's safety.

"I'm going upstairs," she said. "The baby's crying."

She left her aunt where she was standing at the bottom of the stairs armed with a vase she had grabbed from the table to throw at her, and went upstairs. Stavros was sitting waiting nervously for her on the edge of the bed.

"You can't live here, Joonie. The baby's not safe here."

"I know. What am I going to do? Auntie Verne has no family here, only me. She gave me a place to stay. She is my responsibility now."

"No, your baby is your responsibility. Think of her. I don't want you here for another night. You'll be too scared to go to the bathroom for fear of what she might do. Your aunt's a nice woman, but I think something's happened to her. Her actions are bizarre. You should call your family. The doctor may want to admit her to hospital. If she has no other family here, you and your father will have to make the decision. Speak to Billie Bob also."

"Billie Bob's taken himself out of the picture. He's moving to Missouri."

"I know, but he knows your aunt well; he used to stay here. He will know what to do."

It was good advice but not that easy to act upon. What could her parents do from Cape Town? Who was responsible for her aunt? Her family was back home. Billie Bob had absconded. She didn't want to be glib about it, but that's what had happened. She felt exhausted. She heard things being thrown around in the kitchen downstairs, but couldn't do anything while the baby was crying.

She took a deep breath where she sat next to Stavros on the bed and tried to relax. She was new to breastfeeding and already knew Bobby Jo could burst your eardrums with her screams when she was hungry. The baby found her nipple and greedily started to suck. Joonie smiled down at her. "Who's little greedy bokkie are you?" she cooed. "Joonie's? Are you Joonie's girl?" She looked at Stavros who sat next to her, watching her every move. "This is all so beautiful, Stav. I just wish I knew what was happening to my aunt. She's young. She can't be losing her mind at this age."

"I don't think you have to be old for something like that to happen, Joonie. But don't stress. Right now, just feed Bobby Jo, and make the call to your father and tell him what has happened."

It took almost half an hour to feed Bobby Jo. When she was sure the baby was fast asleep, she put her down on the bed and tiptoed to the bedroom door to listen. "I don't hear anything. I think Auntie Verne has gone back to sleep. I have to get to the phone. You stay with Bobby Jo, Stav." She opened the door and tiptoed quietly down the short passage to the extension telephone on the half-moon table against the wall.

She called the overseas operator and asked to be put through to her parents' number in Cape Town. Her mother answered the phone.

"Mom, I know it's after midnight there, but I had to call you."

"How's my grandchild there?"

"Your grandchild's fine. But I have a problem with Auntie Laverne. I've just come home from the hospital with Bobby Jo. Auntie Laverne chopped up the cradle and destroyed the whole lounge and thinks my baby is hers." Her mother sighed at hearing this news, almost as if she knew what she was going to hear.

Joonie told her the whole story, every now and then glancing over her shoulder, expecting Auntie Laverne to rush at her.

"I knew something crazy was going to happen. Laverne's never been right in her head. Did you call the doctor?"

"Not yet. I want to speak to Dad first. I don't know what to do, and I don't want to be responsible if anything goes wrong. She's been in hospital before, I've been told. Luckily a friend is here to help me." Her left hand holding the telephone receiver was shaking with fear.

"If you were here now, you wouldn't have had any of this."

"Maybe I had to be here, Mom. What would've happened to Auntie Laverne? There's no other family. She doesn't have a husband. The friend she had isn't around much anymore. Can I speak to Dad?"

"We miss you, Joonie," her mother continued, in a different, softer tone of voice. "Think about it. Ma's not well either. You've had the baby. Maybe it's time to come home."

"What's wrong with Ma?"

"Ma's leg's worse, she can hardly walk. The doctor also found she has high blood pressure. She's pining for you."

"Tell Ma I miss her, she must take her medicine. We'll see each other soon. Now can I please speak to Dad, Mom? I don't know what I'm going to do when Auntie Laverne wakes up."

Her father came on the phone. In a rush of words, Joonie explained the situation. Her father listened without interrupting, and then spoke calmly to her.

"Now listen to me, Joonie. Take a deep breath. First, how is the baby?"

"The baby's fine, Dad. Just a hungry little girl."

"Listen to me now. This is something your mother and I have always talked about; what we would do if something happened to Auntie Laverne with us so far away. And there it's happening. Do you know the name of her doctor?"

"Yes."

"Call him up and explain the situation to him. Ask him to make a house call – tell him that you have a new baby, and you don't know what to do."

"What if he says she has to be admitted? She's worse than the last time. It's beyond just giving her a pill."

"If she must be admitted, she must be admitted. That's why I want you to call the doctor right away and call me back. Don't worry about the cost of the call – make it reverse charges. Let the doctor do what is best and call me back with his number. I'll speak to him. I'll speak to Auntie Olive also if it's necessary for one of us to come over there."

"Auntie Olive? Do you two speak again after all these years?"

"She's my sister. One can't hold a grudge forever. We made up on Ma's birthday in March when we took her for lunch to the Bismillah Restaurant up Wale Street in Bo-Kaap. She likes their samoosas and custard tarts."

"And Uncle Lionel?"

"No, to that stinker I won't speak. But back to your problem. Make that call and get back to me. You've just had a baby, you have to take it easy. After this is all sorted out, I want you to come home."

She didn't answer.

"Joonie?"

"I heard you, Dad. I can't talk about it now."

"What do you mean you can't talk about it now? Don't tell me you didn't mean what you said."

"I've met someone."

"You've met someone?"

"His name's Stavros. He's Greek. We're just friends right now, but it's ... developing."

"Developing?" He laughed. "Well, I'm happy that you have a friend and that you're not alone; just don't rush into anything. I don't want you to get hurt. And come home as you promised. Is he someone who will come and live in this country?"

She couldn't answer that question as she herself didn't know what she wanted to do. "I have to go, Dad. It is a bit of an emergency here. I'll call the doctor and call you back after I've spoken to him."

She hung up and went back to the bedroom where Stavros was watching over Bobby Jo, sleeping peacefully on the bed. "I spoke to my father. He wants me to call the doctor right away."

"That would be the best," Stavros agreed.

"It seems quiet downstairs. Maybe you should go and take a look while I make the call."

Stavros disappeared down the stairs. She looked at the ring he had put on her finger a week earlier over a feta-cheese-and-olive pizza at Joe's Trattoria. A friendship ring, he had said, until the real one came. Was she ready for such a commitment? Speaking to her father always forced her to examine her own behaviour, and the truth was that she was reckless and emotional and did things on the spur of the moment and then regretted them afterwards. She did not want to make a mistake again. And she had to be honest with herself at least, if not with Blair. She was attracted to Stavros, but the friendship that had developed between them wasn't of the same intensity and grit as the one she'd had with Blair. Blair wasn't rich, he didn't have a university degree, but despite their different colour classification she and Blair were cut from the same political and emotional cloth. Stavros was half American.

Stavros returned to tell her to come down and see what the place looked like. She went downstairs with him and saw her aunt asleep on the couch, a big stain on the velvet from the henna on her head. Horrified at the mess, she looked around. The cradle had been smashed with a chair, which was also in pieces, and broken figurines, dishes and jars of jam and preserves littered the floor. It was as if a gale-force wind had blasted through the house and destroyed everything. She carefully stepped over the pieces of jagged glass towards Stavros who was standing at the window. He was peering outside as if he could not bear to look at her aunt.

"This is wicked," he said. "And quite mad. I'll clean it up. I don't want you bending down and picking up things. Call the doctor. Let's take the opportunity now while Bobby Jo's asleep."

She looked for the doctor's number in the small telephone directory her aunt kept on her bedside table next to the lamp, found it, and called the doctor. After he listened to her describing her aunt's behaviour, he said he would arrange for an ambulance to transport her to the hospital.

"I'm calling Billie Bob," Stavros said. "After all, he was her friend all the years. It would be helpful to have him here now."

"Hasn't he already gone to Missouri?"

"I don't think so." He dialled Billie Bob's number and found him at home. He explained what had happened. "Billie Bob said he would come right away."

Billie Bob did as he promised. His eyes widened when he entered the front door. Slowly moving his head from side to side, he assessed the situation and said it was the worst he had ever seen his friend. He and Joonie tried to get her aunt to the bath so they could wash her hair at least, but she wanted no one to touch her. Finally, the ambulance arrived. Auntie Laverne was put onto a gurney and loaded into the ambulance.

"A member of the family has to come along," one of the paramedics said.

Joonie and Stavros exchanged looks. "I've just had a baby," Joonie said, "but there's no one else to admit her, so I'll have to come with."

"I'll take care of the baby," Stavros said.

"I can't leave her. She has to be breastfed. We don't know how long all this is going to take." The baby travelled with Joonie in the back of the ambulance. Billie Bob followed in his car.

At the hospital they waited almost three hours for tests and scans to be done. Joonie was exhausted. The baby slept in fits and starts and needed to be in a crib. At last, the doctor came to where they were sitting in the waiting room and explained that her aunt would have to undergo a series of tests and would be hospitalised for two days at least. He couldn't say for how long exactly. If she didn't improve with medication, and it turned out that she had dementia, she would have to be transferred to a nursing home where she could be cared for.

It was with a heavy heart and a weary body that Joonie left her aunt in the ward.

"What will you do now, Joonie?" Billie Bob asked on the way back to the house.

"I will have to stay here in New Jersey, I guess, until I know what my aunt's situation is."

He escorted her and the baby back into the house, which Stavros had cleaned up in the meantime. "I'm sorry that you had to be here for all this, Joonie. It was good knowing you." He remained standing at the front door. "Don't stress too much about this; things will work out. This was a bad time for this to happen. Anyway, I have to go. I'm leaving for Missouri next week and there are so many things to attend to beforehand. If I don't see you again, best of luck."

He turned to Stavros. "And you be good, Stavros. Look after her. You met in my shop. I feel responsible for you both. I'll be in touch before I leave to see how things are."

Joonie swallowed at the lump in her throat, "Thanks for your help, Uncle Billie. Sorry, I'm too tired to get up.

Good luck to you too, and good luck at the farm."

There was an awkward moment when Stavros came back after seeing Billie Bob off at his car. She sensed he had something on his mind, but he didn't speak immediately. The day had been dramatic and stressful with first her bringing a new baby home, and then her aunt's sudden madness. They both were in need of a few minutes of silence.

"I thought you were moving in with me, Joonie."

"The house can't stand empty, Stav. And now that she's gone, it's safe for Bobby Jo to be here. There's a lot for me to think about."

"You don't have to stay here to think. My apartment's just six blocks away."

"I know, but not tonight. I'm longing to go to bed. Any minute now Bobby Jo will be awake again. I hope you don't mind."

He looked disappointed, but seemed to understand how stressed out and fatigued she was. "I found the letter, you know."

She half heard him. "You found the letter? What letter?"

"The letter your boyfriend wrote you."

She sat up, squinting at him. "What are you talking about?"

"Blair. Your baby's father. You didn't tell me the truth about him."

She realised that he was referring to the letter her father had forwarded from Blair. She had put it in her bag. A bag was private property. It wasn't his place to look in her bag without asking. Was he snooping into her diary also?

"What is the truth?" She tried to keep her voice even. "I don't know what you're talking about. Is this because I'm too tired now to go to your place tonight? It's been a hard day, Stavros. That letter is old. It was left with my grandmother. My father forwarded it to me months later."

"I thought we had no secrets."

"It's not a secret. Let's talk about it, then. I left South Africa without him knowing. He found out afterwards. He wrote a letter. My grandmother intercepted it. My father forwarded it to me. No secrets, Stav. Where did you find the letter anyway? Were you scratching in my bag?"

"Oh, you kept it in your bag, did you?" he laughed.

"Should I have kept it in my bra?"

Her remark made him laugh. They bantered a bit, but something in his tone made a little warning bell go off in her head.

Hi Dad

Bobby Jo is three months old today. You won't believe how utterly gorgeous she is. She is smiling now and sleeps with her face on the mattress and her bum in the air. She's just too precious for words. We have met our next-door neighbours, who also have a baby, and the wife and I went to the park with our babies for a little picnic on the grass. The weather is cold this time of the year and October arrived with quite a bite. Autumn is called "fall" here – I suppose for the falling of the leaves – and the streets are covered with yellow, red, and orange leaves – too beautiful, bitingly cold, but still bearable to go out for walks with Bobby Jo bundled up like an Eskimo. It's amazing how once you have a baby, you want to spend every moment with her.

Hope you're all well and that Ma's doing better. And thanks for helping me sort all this out. You will be pleased to know that Auntie Laverne's in a nice place where there's good medical care, big lawns, and where she has her own room. Stavros and I visit her, and sometimes she knows who we are and says she wants to get out, and sometimes she asks what our names are. There's no way she can live on her own anymore. It's dementia. Apparently the birth of my baby unsettled her and the doctor suspects that she must've suffered some trauma related to a baby in her past. Now her memory comes and goes. The doctor told me that she sometimes thinks she's back in Cape Town. The lawyers are taking care of everything. The house has been sold and the money put in trust to pay for her care.

It's sad, Dad. She was good to me. I feel bad that I couldn't look after her. Maybe you should come to New Jersey and see her before something happens – which brings me to the hardest part of this letter. I hope you won't be too disappointed. I know that I've promised to return by the end of next February, when the ticket is to be used, but I have to think of myself and Bobby Jo now. Stavros has asked me to marry him on New Year's Eve, which is just a little over two months away. Marrying him will give Bobby Jo a father and me a place to stay. I'm not selling out, Dad, or doing it because I have no one here. I'm doing it because I don't want a repeat of what happened with me and Blair. That's why I'm writing instead of calling, so you all can have a chance to digest this. I am not America crazy. I am just thinking of my child. I want the best for her. There are things here that make me feel alien and out of place, but there are other things also that give me hope. They say America is a melting pot of cultures, and of new beginnings. There're all kinds of people here; everyone wants to stay. Stavros, being

an American citizen, will make it easy for me to get papers. I hope you understand. I have registered for a BA degree, part-time, majoring in English. Classes started two weeks ago, because here the semester begins in September. It is a night course so I am home with Bobby Jo during the day. Stavros looks after her at night. He's good with her. He loves her like his own child. How can I want more, Dad? I'm continuing my education. I'll become independent. I'm not making silly decisions. I know what you're thinking, but give me some credit for how far I've come. Hug Ma and Mom for me. I will call you at the end of the month.
Lots of love
Joonie

She read the letter twice before folding it. As she was putting it into an envelope, the apartment door opened behind her. It was Stavros carrying a bag of groceries and a bunch of flowers, a big smile on his face. He came over to where she sat, sealing the envelope, and leaned over and kissed her.

"Oh, I must've done something right," she said. "I'm getting flowers."

"It's not for you. It's for my other girl. How's my bokkie?" he asked, using one of her favourite expressions and looking towards the cradle they had repaired and set up in the living room.

"Your other girl's fine. Fast asleep. This girl wants you to do her a big favour and mail this letter, if you don't mind. I wrote to my father. The calls were getting too expensive."

"We're going to have supper at my mother's house tomorrow night," he said as she handed him the letter.

135

She looked at him with raised brows. "You are taking me into the lion's den?" Her mouth curled into a curious smile. "Well, what do you know. Finally. The great Greek mystery will be revealed. You did tell your mother that I have a baby, didn't you?"

His answer wasn't immediately forthcoming, and he didn't look directly at her. "I did, but I told her you had been raped."

Her face turned red, and for a moment she couldn't speak. "Raped? Oh my God. How could you tell her something like that? Bobby Jo's not a rape baby, Stavros. Are you ashamed of me?"

"Of course not. I just didn't know how to tell her."

"Why didn't you tell her the truth? I won't go there under false pretences. I won't have anyone looking at Bobby Jo and me as victims, pitying us. You told me your mother was your mentor. Tell her the truth. I had a relationship. He went into the army. He didn't know I was pregnant. We had long-term plans. Do you know what rape conjures up in someone's mind?"

"I'm so sorry," he said, his face ashen. "You never told me much about your child's father."

"That's because I want to forget him."

"Want to – you still think of him?"

"How can I not think of him? I have his child. It's important how people see us. It wasn't rape. He's a decent guy."

"So decent that he left you pregnant?"

The words hovered like a thick cloud between them, and for an instant she hated him.

"You don't know the circumstances."

Bobby Jo woke up and started to cry. Joonie walked over and lifted her out of the cradle. She heard the front door close and knew that Stavros had left the apartment.

She held the baby tightly for a few seconds, then breastfed her and put her back in the cradle. She thought of the letter she had just written to her father. She wanted to change it, but Stavros had taken it with him to post.

She switched on the television and sat down on the couch. People moved on the screen, she heard voices and laughter but nothing registered. She felt hurt by his words. He had changed his tune, she thought. He had met her as an unwed mother-to-be. She had questioned his involvement with her at the beginning of their friendship, but he had said it did not matter to him. Now he was embarrassed, throwing it in her face. What was she to do? She had just written a letter to her father telling him she was going to marry Stavros; now she felt uncomfortable at the thought of being with someone who was so possessive of her. She felt stifled. She needed breathing space and time on her own to be able to think clearly. His constant presence and her dependence on him boggled her mind.

She got up and went to the bedroom and threw herself face down on the bed. She had heard more than once Ma tell her mother or some visitor to judge a man by his actions, not his words. "If a man whispers sweet nothings in your ear, that's nice, but it's usually because he wants something or he's acting out of guilt for something he's done or still planning to do. Does he pay the rent? Does he fix the dripping tap? Is he the last one to go to bed and pull a cover over you? That's the person you want. Not someone who's an oil painting and doesn't know how to treat you."

The telephone rang. She answered it. There was silence on the line, no one replied. Eventually the phone clicked off in her ear.

It was after midnight when her sleep was interrupted by the sound of crashing glass. She sat straight up in bed, her heart pounding. She got up to investigate. Stavros was taking off his boots in the living room. Behind him a glass lay shattered on the kitchen floor.

"It's late, Stavros. Where were you all this time?"

His voice slurred. "I went out drinking with my friends. I'm sorry for what I said to you earlier. I don't know what came over me. I was out of line. I hope you can forgive me."

She took a while before she spoke. "I don't know. What you said was true. I was naïve to think that I could come here, have a baby, fall in love, and live happily ever after."

"But it happened – you fell in love and we're getting married. When people love each other, they can work it out. It was a stupid comment. I regret it." He walked her backwards into the bedroom, trying to coax a smile out of her. "I love you, Joonie. I step out of my skin sometimes. I don't like it, but I love you."

"What do you love about me, Stav?"

"I love the way you laugh, the way you look. You're naughty. You're fresh, but also naïve. You scratch back. You speak your mind. And I love that you're South African. You love me, don't you?"

"I like you a lot – when you're not always doubting or questioning me."

"You *like* me? We're supposed to get married in a few months."

"Like is better than love, my grandmother always said. People who say they love you still hurt you. People who like you don't have an agenda and like you from the heart. Which one do you want?"

"Love."

"Okay. I will love you then."

"Do you want to know what I did tonight – before I went drinking? I went to see my mother. She's been calling me at the office. She wants me to meet this Greek girl she knows who works in the building next to where she works. We had words. I told her that she was stifling me, that I'm not her husband; I'm her son. She wasn't going to pick a wife for me. It was all right when I was little and she picked out my clothes. I'm grown up now."

Joonie was surprised that he had confronted his mother, and glad too, but still thought it rude to speak to a parent like that. "That's a bit harsh – no?"

"I was angry. I reacted – the same way I handled the conversation about your ex-boyfriend. I left her house and went drinking with my friends. Having said all of that, are you ready to meet her tomorrow night?"

"Yes," she agreed. "I'll even buy her a box of chocolates."

The following evening she wrapped Bobby Jo in the white blanket with the silver ribbon Stavros had given her at Easter and took extra care with her own appearance, putting on a simple white blouse and black skirt, and low heels. She pulled her hair back in a ponytail and with her finger put on a dash of lipstick.

It took thirty minutes to drive to the short cul de sac lined with huge trees and with Cadillacs parked in the driveways. The house was old and large with creepers hanging down the brown brick walls. The porch with clusters of rocking chairs and plants stretched all the way around the house.

"This is Teaneck," Stavros said with pride. "We lived in the Bronx until I was about ten years old and then moved here. It's very quiet."

An old man in a light coat sitting on a rocking chair had got up when he saw the Mustang pull into the driveway and stood waiting.

"Should I carry Bobby?" Stavros asked.

"Please. Who's the man on the porch?"

"My grandfather. I'm named after him."

Joonie followed Stavros up the three steps leading to the porch.

"Hi, Grandpa," Stavros said fondly, giving his grandfather a kiss on the cheek and a hug. "This is my friend, Joonie. And this is her baby, Bobby Jo."

The older Stavros stepped closer to shake her hand and to peek inside the soft fluffy blanket. "A boy or a girl?"

She liked the old man immediately; he smelled of Old Spice, the aftershave her father used, and seemed friendly and kind. "A girl. Her name's Bobby Jo."

He looked enquiringly at his grandson.

"It's not my baby, Grandpa," he laughed.

"I didn't think so," the old man grinned. "She's too beautiful."

They continued to the front door. "Do I look all right?" she asked.

"You always look great. I particularly like that cheeky schoolgirl look."

A long brown car drove up. Joonie turned to look and was surprised to see the car park behind the Mustang in the driveway. "How many people are coming for supper?"

"Just us, as far as I know."

The front door was opened by Stavros's mother. Joonie had expected a plump woman with heavy eyebrows, wearing an apron over her dress, but his mother was narrow-hipped and tall, in tight-fitting beige pants and a russet-coloured top, her reddish-brown hair in a short bob.

"This is Joonie, Mom," he introduced her.

"Hello, Joonie," his mother smiled, extending a manicured hand with red fingernails. "I'm Aspasia. I've never heard the name Joonie before. Is it South African?"

"It comes from the names, June and Junaid. My father

had wanted a boy and wanted to call him Junaid. My mother wanted June. When I came out a girl, he made up his own name, Joonie."

Aspasia laughed. "Really? And your baby?"

Joonie opened her mouth to respond, but the front door swung open and an older man and woman, dressed in pants and warm jackets, came inside. They were accompanied by an olive-skinned young woman with long dark hair and pouty lips, wearing killer stilettos, and the conversation was lost. Aspasia introduced them. The man and woman were Stavros's uncle and aunt, Michael and Xenia. The young woman's name was Maria. Joonie assumed she was Greek.

"I thought, seeing that we were having supper together tonight, Stav, that I would invite Uncle Mike and Aunt Xenia, and a friend of theirs, Maria, to join us."

Joonie looked at Stavros. It was clear that he was taken aback. He had wanted them to be alone with his mother. His mother, however, obviously had her own agenda. Was it his mother who had called the house the previous night and hung up?

Aspasia led them into the dining room. "Why don't you sit here, Joonie?" she said, pointing to the chair closest to her. "And you, Dad, next to Joonie. Michael and Xenia, you guys sit next to each other on that side with Maria. Stavros and I will sit at each end of the table. You can put the baby down, Stav. She isn't going to run away."

Joonie felt slighted at the way her baby was dismissed.

"Whose baby is it, by the way?" Xenia asked.

"It's Joonie's baby, Bobby Jo," Stavros answered. "It's not my baby, in case you're wondering, Auntie Zee."

"I'm sure it isn't." There was an undeniable edge to her voice.

Joonie felt like a fool sitting there, resenting the money

she had wasted on the expensive box of chocolates she was still clutching in her lap.

She looked up at Maria, on the other side of the table, and caught Maria looking at her. Maria, she thought, wasn't feeling too comfortable either. She was there to be introduced to the young Stavros, but had arrived to find the young Stavros taken. Possibly she hadn't even been told that Stavros would be there with a girl. Aspasia was a shit-stirrer, Joonie thought; she liked a little malicious fun.

"So, Maria," Aspasia said, "I believe you're new in this country. How do you like it?"

"I love the States. It has so much to offer. It's a dream come true for me. Back home, girls like me dream of a chance like this."

"Are you working here?"

"Trying to. I'm an actress. I had a small part in a movie back in Athens. Unfortunately, the production ran out of money and the film was never completed. I've gone to a few auditions here, but no luck so far. It's extremely hard, and there's always someone who's better than you." She turned to Stavros. "What do you do, Stavros?"

"I'm a journalist for the local newspaper."

"Oh." Maria's eyes brightened. "Is it hard work?"

"I like it, so it's not work for me. I cover entertainment. I also review books."

"It sounds interesting. You must know a lot of people in the field then. Maybe I should take your number and keep in touch." She glanced at Joonie as she reached for her bag.

"I have it. I can give it to you," Aspasia said.

Only Joonie's eyes moved. She felt completely ignored. And hurt that Aspasia would offer to give her son's telephone number to a girl who had clearly been invited to take him from her.

"I've just started," Stavros said. "I don't know these people personally. My first assignment was to interview an author who grew his own marijuana in big pots on his patio. I'd never heard of him."

Joonie looked down at her hands with a little smile. She had to give him a star for withstanding the temptation. She wondered if he would've been that distant if he had been there on his own.

The telephone rang. Aspasia answered it. "Call for you, Stavros. It's your boss. He says he's been looking for you."

Stavros answered the phone in the hallway, out of earshot. He talked for a few minutes, and came over to Joonie.

"My boss wants me to cover a breaking story – a young actor found dead in his apartment – apparently from a drug overdose. I have to go. I'm sorry."

"What about me?"

"I can't take you home right now. It's on the other side of the city and King Street, where I have to be, is just a few blocks from here. If I can get there immediately I can get a scoop. The cops are already on the scene."

"I know it's your job," she whispered, "but you invited me here for supper and I'm having a horrible time. Please, I want to go home."

"I can't take you now, Joonie. You'll have to wait until I get back."

"Okay, get Bobby Jo for me."

He looked at the faces around the table. They were aware of the tension. He went to fetch the baby.

She got up from her chair. "I'm sorry, but I have to go too." She put the box of chocolates on the table. "I never had a chance to give this to you, Aspasia." She thought to hell with it; she wouldn't call her Mrs Dukakis. Mrs Dukakis had invited her over for supper and treated her kak by completely dismissing her and inviting another girl for her son to meet.

"But we haven't even had the first course yet," Aspasia objected.

"I know, but unfortunately I cannot wait with my baby until Stavros gets back." She put on her coat and took Bobby Jo from Stavros.

"Where are you going?" he asked.

"I'm hailing a cab. I'm going home."

"You can't go out there in the dark by yourself. You don't even know this area."

"Why don't you call a cab for me then?"

"For God's sake, Joonie, I'm not going to be long. Why don't you just wait?"

She drew Bobby Jo's blanket over her head, walked to the front door, opened it and stepped out in the crisp night air.

The old man caught up with her at the pavement. "Please ... let me give you a ride home."

"I'm so sorry for being rude, Mr Dukakis. Please forgive me for leaving like this. I just felt very uncomfortable in there."

"I know," he said. "Not a good idea to have invited Maria. But this is the way of Greek mothers and their sons, especially one with only one son. A Greek mother wants a Greek girl for her boy, and even then a Greek girl is sometimes not good enough." He smiled kindly to let her know he wasn't speaking ill of his daughter, just wanted her to know that he understood how she felt.

"Thank you."

"Will you let me take you home?"

"Thank you, Mr Dukakis. I would appreciate it."

Stavros came home late that night and came straight to the bedroom where I was sleeping and smacked me in the face with the back of his hand, so hard, that I fell out of bed.

"You little bitch! How dare you embarrass me in front of my family!"

I came out of my sleep in a daze, not knowing whether I was still in a dream. I didn't recognise him. He was like a raging wolf looming over me, his hand poised to strike me again. I tried to get up. He pushed me back with such force that my head knocked against the bedside table. "Stop it!" I screamed.

But he was punching me, completely out of control. The baby howled. He let go of me and went to the living room and brought her back with him. "There, feed your child," he said, and thrust her upon me like she was a broken doll. As God is my witness, if I'd had a gun, I would've shot him full of holes.

That night I found out the hard way that a man can be good to you, even love you, and turn on you at the same time. You don't know that when you're young. No one's told you. Your head's in the sky. You have your own lofty ideas about relationships with the opposite sex. You mistake possessiveness for love. The sting of that first slap never goes away and that first slap is the warning most of us ignore.

The next morning I woke up black and blue in the face. I waited for Stavros to go to work. I didn't know what to do or where to go. I could've called Millie in Manhattan to give me a place to stay, but didn't want anyone to know, especially not someone with connections back home. All I knew was that I had to get away, get back home. It was not a wish anymore, it was imperative. Out of desperation, I finally called Billie Bob in Missouri. Uncle Billie was shocked to hear what had happened, but couldn't help me except to give me advice. "The best thing you can do, Joonie, is to go to the South African embassy in Manhattan and explain your situation. Ask how you can take your child with you, and go home."

It was good advice, but I was stuck. The money I had arrived with had been swallowed up by medical and other living expenses over the past months. At the very least I needed two or three hundred dollars for cab fare to the embassy and the airport and for a visa if the baby needed to have one, and for other small expenses. I had a few nickels and dimes of my own for a box of tissues for my tears, but no real money to enable me to escape. It was 7 October; Would I even be able to get a booking at such short notice? How was I going to live in the apartment with Stavros and plan my escape without him suspecting something? And how was I going to pay for everything?

That night I waited in a state of agony for him to come home. My mouth was swollen, my head ached, but I fried sausages and made a salad to make sure there was something for him to eat.

He arrived home early and came to sit at the living-room table where I was feeding Bobby Jo. It was as if nothing had happened between us. He was calm and caring, a different guy from the maniac who had beaten the snot out of me the night before.

"There're no words to describe how I feel about what I did to you, Joonie," he started. "I don't know what got into me. I was just so angry at you for not understanding. I lost control. I don't lose control easily, but no one had ever done anything like that to me. You embarrassed me. You were stubborn and refused to wait. You spoiled everyone's evening. Why, Joonie? Why did you do it?"

I listened to him talk. I was far away from accepting meaningless words. The bruises on my face and arms reminded me of where I was and what I had to do. At the same time I knew that I had to answer his questions and behave normally. So I said the words he wanted to hear – yes, I forgive you – and didn't mean one syllable of it.

That night he wormed himself into me for sex. I had to put on a smile and pretend. He didn't know that the more the promises poured out of him, the more betrayed I felt. All I could think about was the sting of his open hand on my face and the way he had almost tossed Bobby Jo in my lap. Did he think I would forget? It would've been better if there was no exchanging of bodily fluids. I hate the very slobber that comes out of men.

So I played the game. Women can play the game without fear of discovery; a few groans, a few grinds, and it's all over. I remembered something Ma had once told a woman who was complaining about her womanising husband. "Jy kry net lekker vir 'n bietjie, Elizabeth, dan's dit alles oor. Laat hom gaan." You just feel good for a little while, then it's all over; let him go.

The next day, I made a trip to the South African embassy while Stavros was at work and to my delight found out that Bobby Jo could be put on my South African passport, and that they would rush the application due to the special circumstances. I was told I could pick up the visa in four days' time. Back at the flat, I phoned South African Airways and was greatly relieved to get a booking for 20 October.

Three days later I said over breakfast that I was going to the hospital to visit my aunt as I hadn't seen her in a long time. Stavros was glad to hear that I wanted to go out on my own, and gave me fifty dollars for a cab. I dressed Bobby Jo up in a pretty pink dress and white leggings, and feeling a little guilty for taking his money, I took a bus to the home where my aunt had been moved to and saved twenty dollars in fare. I must admit that I was tempted to take the whole fifty and not go and see her, but I didn't have the heart not to visit Auntie Laverne one last time.

I was shocked when I entered the ward. The roots of her hair had grown out and she looked a sad, pathetic figure with half her hair its natural brown and the other half a garish red. As soon as she saw the baby in my arms she said, "They took my child, you know," speaking with the voice of a little girl. Bobby Jo's presence seemed to stir up memories and she kept on about the baby that someone had taken from her. After a while I wondered if there was any truth to her ramblings. There were so many versions of a baby she had lost, where would she pull them all from? I dug into my bag for the Hershey's bar I'd brought along to eat, removed the wrapper and gave the chocolate to her. She wolfed it down and said, "I'm hungry. Do you have more?" I sat with her until she wandered off to someone across the room and forgot about me.

I don't know how I managed thirteen days in close proximity with Stavros without him suspecting anything about my plans and preparations. On the evening before my scheduled flight, I served him a glass of red wine with his meat and potatoes, and then another glass, and another. He liked wine but we seldom drank it at home. The three glasses made him feel drowsy and he dosed off and soon he was snoring on the couch. I was desperate. If I didn't find money in his clothes I would be forced to approach Millie and I didn't want to do that. When I was certain he was fully asleep, I felt around in his jacket he had slung over the back of a chair and found fifty dollars. His wallet was on the night table and I discovered an additional four hundred dollars tucked in behind his social insurance card. I removed two hundred and left the rest. I had two hundred and fifty dollars now; added to my own money it came to two hundred and ninety dollars in all. My overnight bag was packed and hidden under the bed. The previous day already, I had washed all Bobby Jo's clothes, spinning them dry.

The following morning I got up as usual and served him porridge. He asked if we didn't have eggs. "Sorry, I've forgotten to buy some," I said. The truth was that I didn't want to spend an extra dollar from the little money I had. He asked if I could pick up his clothes at the dry cleaners. Yes, I said, and took the fifty dollars he gave me. I waited at the window. As soon as his Mustang had disappeared down the street, I called my father and told him I was coming home.

I had left this call for last as I was still asking myself if it was the right thing for me to leave. Dad was surprised to hear that I had changed my mind and excitedly told me they would all be at the airport to welcome me back. They had all been upset by my letter, he said, which had reached them only two days earlier.

I hastily packed the last of my things. The suitcase could hardly hold everything. My actions were jumpy. I didn't know how I was going to manage Bobby Jo, who was a lot heavier now, my suitcase, which had to be booked in, the stroller and my overnight bag. It was my last hours in the apartment. I was scared I would forget something and not be allowed on the plane. I also didn't know if I should leave Stavros a note. In the end, I couldn't leave just like that and wrote a few words on one of the last few empty pages left in my diary, telling him that I was sorry things hadn't worked out between us and that I had gone home. I tore out the page and left the note on his side of the bed. Then I called a cab and prayed that Stavros wouldn't come looking for me – we were booked on an overnight flight that only left at seven in the evening.

I arrived at JFK International Airport shortly after three in the afternoon. After paying for the cab and tipping the porter, who had stacked all my luggage on his trolley, and pushed it to the ladies' toilets, I had sixty dollars left. The toilets had a changing room for babies. I stayed in there for three hours, feeding Bobby Jo, eating a sandwich I had prepared at breakfast time and more or less counting the minutes. I dreaded that an airport official would come up to me and ask what I was doing and take me away. By six, no one had come and I folded up the stroller, put it on top of my suitcase and overnight bag on the trolley, and awkwardly pushed it with my right hand, while carrying Bobby Jo on my left arm.

An airport employee came up to me and asked if she could help with the baby. I thankfully accepted. She pushed the trolley to the SAA check-in counter, with me in her wake, clutching Bobby Jo to my chest to steady my nerves. Bobby Jo squealed with pleasure, almost as if she understood she was going somewhere new. The girl behind the counter checked my ticket and passport and asked where Bobby Jo's ticket was. Bobby Jo was travelling on my passport, I told her. I still had to pay the fare, she informed me.

This was a shocking surprise. I did not expect that one had to pay for an infant. "How much does it cost?" I asked.

"You have to go to the reservations counter, ma'am,"

she said. "Can you help her get over there fast, Mary?" she asked the airport employee who had ushered me to her. "We're boarding in half an hour."

"But why can't she sit on my lap? She's only three months old and won't require an extra seat."

"It's an extra passenger, ma'am, and extra space with a bassinette is provided. If you want to get on this flight, you'll have to hurry. There're just three seats left."

Mary helped me to the reservations desk and explained the situation to the clerk. The cost for Bobby Jo was two hundred and fifty dollars. Sweat broke out on my face, I felt hot and panicky. I had sixty dollars to my name. Where was I going to get the rest? Even if I were to call Millie or Veronica, they wouldn't arrive at the airport in time.

I turned to Mary and asked her to help me get back to the check-in counter with my luggage. By now a long line of passengers were queuing up to check in. I would have to go to one of them and beg; there was no other way. I looked at the people standing in line, mostly white South Africans who had come on a holiday to the States. I gathered this from the casual clothes they wore and the takkies. Near the end of the line an Indian man and his wife and two children stood waiting with their overnight bags. I glanced at a luggage tag and, turning my head slightly, I read the address. The family lived in Rylands. It was an Indian area in Athlone. I knew where it was. Surely, I thought, they wouldn't turn me down.

Bracing myself, I walked up to the family. I had never begged in my life. "Please, sir," I said to the man. "I'm in a desperate situation and wonder if you can help me. I'm booked on this flight, but my baby was born here three months ago and she doesn't have a ticket. My ticket was booked in Cape Town in January already and we didn't realise that I would need a ticket for her as well. I am short of a hundred and ninety-one dollars to buy a ticket for her."

I held my breath as the man stared at me impassively. His wife turned her head away and bent down, pretending to attend to one of the girls. "I'm not a beggar, sir," I said as calmly as I could, well aware that my desperation and my track pants and top might not inspire much confidence. "And I know it's very forward to ask a stranger for this kind of money, but I'm in a terrible fix. Can you please help me out? My father will pay you back as soon as we arrive in Cape Town. I'll give you my name and our telephone number. We live in Maitland. I will personally bring the money to you."

He was shocked by my request, and for a moment didn't say anything.

"This is a most unusual situation, young lady. You are not asking for money for a cool drink, you are asking for a hundred and ninety dollars. It's a lot of money in rands."

"I know."

"I don't know," he said, glancing at his wife, who was now looking for something in her handbag. "In Maitland you live, you say?"

"Yes, off Voortrekker Road."

His wife looked up and nudged him. Their eyes connected.

"We have a daughter living here, Ramesh," she said. "Maybe our daughter will seek help from a stranger one day and the stranger will help her."

The man turned to look at Bobby Jo, now asleep in my arms. "I will trust you, young lady."

"You can trust me, sir. We are travelling on the same plane. My father will be at the airport. Maybe he will have this amount of money on him."

"It's all right," he said. "I trust you."

He gave me the money and a business card with both his work and home telephone numbers. I thanked him and his wife profusely, and rushed back to the reservations desk, poor Bobby Jo bobbing up and down in my arms as I ran. By the time I had bought the extra ticket, the last of the passengers were disappearing down the passage that led to the plane. The gate was kept open an extra few minutes, specially to allow us to board.

Only when I sat back in my seat and Bobby Jo was handed to me by the stewardess who strapped her in on my lap and I felt the vibration of the engines revving up, did I feel safe. America had indeed spat me out.

The flight back to South Africa was a bitter victory. She hadn't triumphed, not in the way she had wanted to. She had left South Africa out of shame and for opportunity and had met a handsome Greek and had been beaten by him. What reason was she going to give her parents for not marrying him after all? They had heard how good-looking he was and how well he treated her. Dare she tell them the truth? Sitting back in her seat, staring blankly out the window, her hand resting lightly on the sleeping Bobby Jo, she wondered how Stavros had reacted upon arriving at the empty apartment. It was a wicked thing to have done, she thought, and she felt guilty. Still, he shouldn't have lifted his hand to her. She had opened her big mouth in front of his family and allowed her Maitland manners to come out, but she hadn't deserved to be beaten out of her sleep like a dog.

She dozed off with Bobby Jo on her lap, woke up, fed and changed the baby twice, drank and ate what the stewardesses put in front of her, but each time fell into troubled sleep as soon as she put her head back. She awoke with a jolt when she heard the PA system come on in the plane and the pilot's announcement that they were landing at DF Malan Airport in twenty minutes and that they should fasten their seatbelts.

The plane started to descend. Her nose, hot with tears, was pressed to the small window as she sighted Table Mountain in the distance. The mountain had a soothing effect. It was like a loving mother waiting patiently for her child to come home. There was no mountain like it anywhere else – especially when the clouds unfurled and spread over its flat top and "laid the table". She was minutes away from feeling that familiar South African sunshine on her face. It was going to be good to be home.

When she stepped into the arrivals hall, all of her extended family were waiting for her: her father and mother right in front; cousins and aunts swarming around them; even Hilary was there, with another school friend of theirs, Elaine, in tow, as well as some of the old Grassy Park neighbours. They surrounded her like a swarm of bees, all cooing over Bobby Jo, who, strapped in the stroller, was not fazed at all. Joonie had changed her outfit an hour or two before they landed and her baby girl looked like a little princess in her white smocked dress with pale pink ribbons, a dress she had bought herself weeks ago for Bobby Jo's christening. The christening hadn't taken place, and she decided that she would let her baby wear this outfit as well as all the clothes she had received as gifts rather than save them for later and have her outgrow them all. She hugged her father first, and noticed immediately that her mother had got thinner, and that Ma wasn't there.

"She's beautiful!" her father said. "How she's grown since the last pictures you sent us!"

Auntie Olive bent over to pick her up. "What a gorgeous child, Joonie."

"Thank you. Can she just get used to all this excitement, Auntie Olive? Please. She's had a hard time travelling; she's very tired."

Auntie Olive stepped back with a hangdog look on her face. "Okay," she agreed. Beryl and Charmaine stood excitedly waiting their turn to pick up the baby.

"She's just too poenankies, Joonie – so oulik. She looks like a white child," Beryl said.

"She is mos a white child," a neighbour replied. "Her father's white. And Joonie herself can pass for white. Kyk daai kind se hare – amper silwer."

Joonie felt claustrophobic and wanted to get Bobby Jo home, but she spotted the Indian man and his family near the cigarette kiosk and turned to her father. "Dad, you see that man and his family over there? He helped me out at JFK. Do you have any money on you?"

"How much do you need?"

"A hundred and ninety dollars. I'll tell you about it later."

"I don't have dollars. Let's go and talk to him."

Leaving Bobby Jo in the care of her mother, she walked with her father to the family who had spotted her also.

"This is the gentleman who helped me out, Dad. If it wasn't for him, I wouldn't have been on this plane."

"Mr Singh," the man introduced himself, smiling and leaning forward to shake hands with her father. They talked for a few minutes before her father asked whether he knew how much his daughter owed him in South African currency. Around eight hundred rand, he said. Her father took out his wallet; there was only three hundred rand in it.

"Will this be all right for the time being, Mr Singh? I can deliver the rest to you on Friday, the day after tomorrow, if you give me your address."

"No problem. My address is on the card I gave your daughter. I have a spice shop in Rylands. It is easy to find."

When they arrived at the house, it was buzzing with church people her mother had invited, many of whom she didn't know. Ma was nowhere to be seen and the house seemed strange: noisy and too full of people. She had gotten used to silence and small parties of people. Bobby

Jo started to squirm in her arms.

She excused herself and headed with the baby for her grandmother's room, hoping to be able to spend a few minutes alone with Ma. She opened the door. Ma's bed was neatly made, with her customary bowl of yellow daisies on the bedside table. But Ma wasn't there. Joonie looked around the room. It felt empty – not empty of furniture, but empty of spirit. She opened the wardrobe. Nothing was in it except for Ma's small jewellery box sitting on one of the shelves, with a thick brown envelope on top.

A strange feeling came over Joonie. She lay Bobby Jo down on the bed. When she straightened up, her father was standing in the doorway. He came into the room and sat on the bed. He patted the spot next to him, indicating that she should also sit.

"How could you not tell me, Dad?"

"We didn't want to upset you. You were busy trying to sort out Auntie Laverne, you had a new baby. That was more than enough to deal with. I was actually planning to call you, but then you called to say you were coming home, and we decided to leave it until you got here."

"What did she die of?"

"The doctor said old age, but I don't think so. She missed you. She knew she wouldn't see you again. The last words she spoke were about you – to tell you that you are the best grandchild, and to give you the jewellery box in her wardrobe."

Joonie smiled through her tears. "*She* was the best, Dad. I loved and admired her. She gave good advice, and she was adventurous. Did you know Ma took me to an old woman last year who told me to have my baby and take her away?"

"A fortune teller?"

"Sort of."

Her father smiled. "I'm not surprised. Your grandmother would try anything if she thought it might work. And it worked, didn't it? We might not have had Bobby Jo with us now. Oh God, what a mistake that would've been. Rest in peace, Ma."

Her mother and Auntie Olive came into the room. "I'm sorry you had to find out like this, Joonie," her mother said.

"It's okay, Mom. I understand why you did it. Maybe it was better for me not to know. Dad said Ma left me her jewellery box?"

"Yes. It's in the wardrobe. Don't take it out now. We have a full house. Everyone wants to see you and the baby." Her mother leaned over the sleeping infant and put her finger in the little hand. "She's such a beautiful child. I'm so glad you didn't give her up."

She smiled at her mother. "My stubbornness for once was a good thing, eh Mom?"

"It certainly was for the best."

There was a knock on the door, and more visitors crowded into the room. In the distance she heard the phone ring.

"Do you want to take the baby to your room?" her father asked. "I made you a sturdy little cot and put a mattress in it. It will be good for her until she's a year old."

"Oh, Dad," she hugged him. "I am so happy to be home."

Hilary came into the room. "International call for you, Joonie."

"Ooooh," her mother cooed. "It must be the Greek boyfriend."

"Oh, there's a Greek boyfriend?" Auntie Olive asked. "What a lucky girl. Maybe overseas *is* better for you."

"Don't put ideas in her head, Olive," her mother said. "We've just got her back."

Joonie went to take the call in the kitchen where the table was being laid by people with familiar faces, some of whose names she couldn't remember. She could smell leg of lamb roasting in the oven. Plates of custard tarts, lemon meringue and a chocolate cake with a white chocolate collar lined the counter.

She answered the phone.

"Joonie?"

"Stavros ..." His deep voice was unmistakable.

"I don't believe I'm talking to you."

"How did you know I was here?" In her mind she could see him standing in the kitchen leaning against the wall, sorry for what he had done.

"I had a feeling you would do something like this – just not this drastic. Do you hate me so much that you couldn't tell me you wanted to go?"

She motioned to her mother to take the visitors into another room. They traipsed out after her and Joonie pushed the door shut before saying, "I don't hate you. I was afraid to tell you. And would you have understood if I told you I wanted to come home? Put yourself in my shoes, in a strange country with a baby, no job, no money, and no family to go to, depending on someone I am scared of and feeling indebted to."

"You mustn't feel obligated to me. We could've talked. I bitterly regret what happened. It was horrible, and the last thing I want is for you to be scared of me."

"We can't undo what happened, Stavros. I was rude in front of your family, and you hit me – hard, and brutally. Maybe we should've talked before that."

"I know. Hindsight is twenty-twenty. I was so angry at your impatience and the way you behaved. But hitting you wasn't a solution. It will never happen again. We can go for counselling; just come back, we'll work it out."

He chuckled. "In fact, after the shock of discovering you gone, I was furious, of course, but I couldn't help but wonder how you pulled it off."

She sniggered also, to her surprise. "I had to beg a man for money to pay for Bobby Jo's airfare. Can you believe it – a complete stranger?"

"I'm so sorry for what happened, Joonie. Do you think you can forgive me?"

Someone turned the knob of the kitchen door and Hilary entered with Bobby Jo, but immediately backed out again. Her baby hadn't slept since their arrival and was irritable and after a second or two, Joonie said, "I forgive you. But I have to go. I've just arrived here half an hour ago. The house is full of people. And Bobby Jo needs to be fed. I'm sorry it didn't work out, Stavros. You were good to me. Please excuse me, I can't talk to you now. Bye."

The visitors started to move back into the kitchen. She looked around; supper was about to be served. No one looked at her, but she could tell from some of the expressions that they had caught the last of her conversation.

"Was that Stavros?" her mother asked, moving closer.

"Yes. He wanted to know if I arrived safely."

"He's not missing you already, is he?"

"He is."

"You still didn't tell us about the Indian man who helped you out," her father said.

She wondered how much she should tell them. "I needed money for Bobby Jo's ticket. I didn't realise that I had to pay for her until I got to the check-in counter; I thought babies sat on your lap." She smiled at her own naivety.

Her father steered her and her mother out of the kitchen and asked, "Stavros didn't have money?"

"He was gone already by the time I went to check in. I'm very grateful to Mr Singh and his wife and would like to give him back the balance of the money as soon as possible. I'll give it all back to you, Dad."

"And the Greek boyfriend? What is happening there? We get a letter to say you are getting married and then a phone call two days later to say you're coming home."

"Do you mind if we talk about it another time, Dad?"

"I don't mind."

"You love him, don't you?" her mother asked.

She adjusted her jeans, looked at her mother silently, then lowered her eyes.

"Good," her mother said. "We don't have to worry about you leaving again."

"My child's American, Mom."

"What does that mean? You're South African. Your family's here. It won't be the first time a child grows up without a father."

"Did you grow up without a father, Mom?"

"No."

"Me neither, so we can't talk. I'm not looking for a father for her; she has one, even if he doesn't know."

The first few days back in Cape Town were dizzying. Friends and family popped in at all hours, unlike in New Jersey where people made appointments to visit. Between feedings and nappying and visitors, Joonie was too exhausted to think of going out.

The second week of her stay, her old school friend Elaine came by late one Friday afternoon to see the baby, and invited her to go with her and her boyfriend, Mark, to a jazz club in Athlone that evening. "You look tired,"

Elaine said. "Maybe your mother could babysit and you can have a break."

Her parents were only too happy to look after their precious grandchild. She had not had much time to herself, even with help, and they were glad that she was going out; they were besotted with Bobby Jo – to the point where her father would come home from work and if Bobby Jo was sleeping he would make strange-sounding noises over the cradle so she would wake up. Joonie knew her mother and father wanted her to be as comfortable and happy as possible so that there would be no reason for her to return to America.

"Have you taken a look yet at what Ma's left you?" her mother asked, watching her and Elaine doll themselves up in front of the mirror.

"No. I first want to get used to her not being around. On one hand it's good to be home, but on the other hand there're just so many memories. I can't believe she is gone from our lives. For ever."

"Memories can't be wished away, no matter where you are. You're eighteen. You're beautiful. You have your whole life ahead of you. You mustn't rush into anything, Joonie."

Joonie picked up her bag, kissed the baby on her forehead and her mother and father on the cheek. "See you later."

"Have fun," her father said. "Don't be late."

"You'll change Bobby Jo's nappy if she cries, won't you, Mom? She doesn't like to feel wet."

"I changed your nappies, didn't I?"

"And last thing, no one is to kiss Bobby Jo on the mouth."

"We kissed you on the mouth and nothing happened."

"I grew a baby, Mom."

Her mother burst out laughing. "You grew a baby because you didn't listen to us. Go on, then, and behave yourself."

They got into Elaine's mother's green Beetle. Joonie had a sudden urge to see the place where it had all begun. "Can we go down to the corner shop?" she asked Elaine.

"You need something?"

"No. It's just a whim I have. I've been here almost three weeks and I haven't been to the shop yet where I met my baby's father."

"You met him here, in Maitland?"

"Yes. His mother lives on the next street. He lives with his father in Johannesburg, but at the moment he's in the army."

"You're not in touch with him?"

"He doesn't know he has a child."

"But you still want him?"

She didn't answer immediately. "I don't want to complicate his life."

"But you did love him – I mean, you didn't just…"

"I did love him, yes. Very much."

She watched Elaine as she turned the car around and drove to the shop. "Stop," she said and got out, her heart beating a little faster. The owner smiled when he saw her come into the shop.

"Do you remember me, Mr Ali?"

"Of course. You live just down the road. You went to America at the beginning of the year."

"I did." She opened her purse. "Can I have two KitKats, please?"

He handed her the chocolate bars.

"Thank you. Tell me, the guys who used to hang around the shop here – do you still see them?"

"One or two of them, yes."

"Which ones?"

"Not the one you are looking for," he smiled. "I haven't seen him lately. Only his mother comes to the shop sometimes. Apparently, she's not well."

She thanked him and got back into the car. "I'm ready for the party. Let's go."

She had never been to a club. She had been to a few restaurants with Stavros in New Jersey, but no place where there was dancing.

The club was in the back streets of Rylands. Dozens of cars were parked in the parking lot next to The Galaxy. Loud music could be heard in the street.

"The place looks full," she said to Elaine.

"I told Mark to keep our seats. He's bringing a friend along, Wasif."

"A Muslim guy?"

"Yes. You'll like him. He's a lot of fun, and a great dancer. You won't be able to stay in your seat with the kind of music they play here."

She looked around at the women in short black dresses and high heels. "People are dressed up. We're in jeans."

"That's okay. We look smashing."

"Is Mark a steady boyfriend?"

"We see each other on weekends. It's the only time he has; he's a medical student. He's twenty-four."

"Wow. Your parents don't mind you dating someone that age?"

"He's going to be a doctor, right? That's a big prize."

"True," she laughed. "Parents want looks, colour and money. A doctor's high on the list."

"Don't forget hair. Heaven forbid you come home with someone with tight hair."

"It depends how tight."

"There're degrees of tightness?"

"Oh yes. If a girl child has ten little plaits and bows in her hair, that's tight. If you can't separate the hair to put in a bow, that's tight with no hope," she explained to Elaine's amusement.

She followed Elaine inside the club, having to squeeze past people standing in the passageway while trying to get used to the thick haze of smoke. At least the music was familiar – an upbeat Bee Gees number, "Staying Alive", was playing. The floor was packed with dancers. Almost immediately, Elaine spotted Mark in the crowd. He came over, a tall, thin guy, with glasses and dressed in a suit. He looked like an accountant. Elaine introduced them.

"Hallo," he greeted her with a nod of his head. "I've heard a lot about you." He had a wart on his bottom lip.

"I hope good things," she said, not sure he could hear her above the noise.

"Yes, of course."

He was a proper kind of guy, well mannered, and led them to a table where they had to squeeze in next to other people.

Elaine had hardly sat down when she said she wanted to dance.

"I'm too tired," Mark said. "I've just come off a twenty-four-hour shift. Why don't the two of you dance?"

"Two girls dancing?" Elaine asked.

"Why not?" Joonie said, feeling the beat of the music, and wanting to get on the dance floor. She had never been to a place like this but had done enough dancing in front of the mirror, and before she left for the States with friends at home parties. For a moment her thoughts flashed back to the party Hilary and she had arranged during their matric year and the forgettable hunk she'd had on her arm that evening.

Elaine looked at her and at the dancers. "Okay. Joonie

and I will dance. Will you order us something to drink in the meantime, Mark?"

"What do you want?"

"Coke and ice."

"And you, Joonie?"

"Do they have sherry here?"

"They have everything. Should I get you a glass?"

"Yes, please."

They walked onto the floor and like most other dancers spun one another around for the first number. When the first bars of "Greased Lightning" sounded, she started to imitate Olivia Newton-John, snaking and slithering around Elaine. Her friend took a while to get into the swing of things, but soon they were the centre of attention. Other females joined them. The song came to an end and immediately another one started. Joonie danced and danced, feeling free and unencumbered in a world of her own. She was taking Elaine by the hand and twirling her when a tall good-looking guy with cropped hair and tight jeans came over and with a smile separated the two of them and started to dance with her. He was surprisingly good, taking both her hands and leading her in a dance she had never tried before. At one point, he leaned her over backwards, so far that her hair almost touched the ground and she thought she would topple over.

"Trust me," he said. "And don't let go of my hands."

She trusted him, trying steps she had only seen other people do. When the dance was over, he led her back to where Mark was waiting and without a word disappeared into the dancing crowd.

She was breathless. Her drink had arrived, and she took a long swallow. Elaine came off the floor and sat next to her. "That was great dancing, Joonie."

"Oh," she said, shimmering with delight, tilting her

head back, swallowing the rest of the sherry in one gulp. "I'm having such a good time. I want to dance some more."

"Be careful. That's Gideon Hall. He makes the girls giddy with his antics on the floor, but he's a serial heartbreaker. Mark's ordering you another sherry. Okay?"

"Okay." She looked over at the dancers. She saw Gideon lead another girl onto the floor. She tried not to look at them. Next to her Elaine and Mark tried to have a conversation, with little luck; they were seated just a few metres away from the loudspeakers.

"I don't think Wasif's coming," Elaine said. "He's a nice guy, but unreliable. We can dance again if you like."

"Sure."

Joonie felt someone touch her arm. She turned to see Gideon standing next to her. "Can I dance with you tonight?" he asked, holding out his hand.

It was as if he had waved a wand over her and turned her into a dancing queen. The marathon began; one song after the other, to a point where people cleared the floor to give them room for their moves. Gideon was daring, taking big chances with her – until her hands, sweaty and slippery, slid out of his grip and she landed on the floor. Flat on her bum. People clapped. Gideon twirled around and helped her up. Emboldened by the applause, the sherry, the intoxicating atmosphere, she got up laughing, taking his hand again.

It was a mad, magical night. When Gideon finally led her back to her table, she flopped down in her seat like a rag doll.

"It's one o'clock, Joonie," Elaine said next to her. "Mark needs to go back."

"Of course. I didn't realise the time. Sorry! It was a great night, Mark. Thanks for having me tag along."

She liked Mark. He wasn't an oil painting, as Ma would have said, and he'd danced only once, but he was good company and a nice guy.

As much fun as she was having though, her thoughts had flitted back and forth to Bobby Jo and whether she was alright. It was the first time Bobby Jo had been away from her for five hours, and the first time in decades her parents had handled a baby. She had prepared a bottle and hoped the feeding had gone smoothly.

They left the club. Walking to Elaine's car, she noticed Gideon standing nearby, chatting to some guys. She looked in his direction. He smiled, nodded at Elaine and Mark and joined them.

"What's your name?" he asked her.

"Joonie."

"Mine's Gideon. Can I see you tomorrow evening?"

"Why?"

"Why do guys ask girls out on dates?"

"To play the big bad wolf with little Red Riding Hood?"

He grinned. "You're very cheeky for your age. How old are you?"

"Eighteen."

"I'm twenty-four. Are you going to give me your number?"

"Are you date-worthy?"

"Jis! I like you. Do you always answer a question with a question?"

"Are you always this persistent?"

"Yes. It's what you want, isn't it?" His green eyes glittered in the dark. "Do you have a boyfriend?"

"I do. Do you still want my number?" she asked, wondering what he might say if he knew she had a four-month-old baby.

"Yes, please."

She looked in her bag for her pen. He held out his hand and she wrote her number on his palm.

"I'll call you," he said and walked off.

Elaine looked at her in wonder when she got into the car. "Jeez! I've never seen anything as smooth as that. You're very brave to give him your number. You might fall in love."

"Fat chance."

"What do you think of Mark?"

"He's a nice guy."

"But not your type – right?"

"Not my type, but he's the kind of guy you don't have to worry about. I go for the bad boys. Mark's solid." She put on her safety belt. "I had a great time, Elaine. Thanks."

Gideon called three days later and asked her to go with him to a movie. She said yes. He picked her up at her parents' house in Maitland, and came in to meet her family. Bobby Jo was blissfully asleep when she ushered him through to the kitchen. As he sat with her parents in the kitchen drinking tea, talking about his work as a draughtsman, she took a good look at him, something that had been impossible in the club. She was struck by his calm demeanour – unlike his antics and gyrations on the dance floor the previous Friday – and the respect with which he listened to her parents talk.

Gideon liked painting and drawing and seemed knowledgeable about the political situation. The conversation was so interesting that her father didn't want them to go out.

"I don't mind if we stay here and –" Gideon was saying, when the baby cried. He stopped mid-sentence.

"That's Bobby Jo," Joonie said. "She's four months old and I have to feed her."

He looked perplexed, but said nothing. Later, when he said goodbye to her at the door, he asked whether she was married.

"I'm not married. I fell in love. I trusted. I got hurt."

"And you don't want to be hurt again."

"No. I'll take a course in becoming a spinster if I have to."

He laughed. "You just say that. All girls your age dream of the perfect guy to father their children. They start worrying about it long before their first training bra."

"You're right," she giggled. "And when the guy comes, he's not the right guy. I didn't dream of having a baby at this young age, though."

For two weeks she and Gideon talked every day on the phone. The first Friday they went back to The Galaxy, the next Saturday they went dancing at another club; the second week they also went to a movie on the Tuesday. That Sunday, they took Bobby Jo out to the beach where Gideon sat with her on his lap. He showed a different side of himself to the one that made the girls on the dance floor swoon. Her mother was happy that she had made such a nice friend. She liked Gideon. He had the right looks, a good job, and was firmly settled on South African soil. Her father didn't say much.

The relationship was fast and furious, and on their fifth date, a Monday night, she had sex with Gideon in the back seat of his car on Signal Hill. Only after their torrid roustabout on the beige leather seat, did she berate herself for her stupid and reckless behaviour. She hoped that her actions weren't going to cost her. When Gideon called her the following evening, she said she had a massive headache and wanted to go to bed early. She offered a different excuse each time he phoned. She liked Gideon a lot and she knew he would make a good husband, despite his reputation, but she was too young to get married. She could also not swear that she was over Blair.

One morning, she woke up with nausea and malaise, and stayed with Bobby Jo in her room the whole day. She was burnt out, she told herself; too much had happened over the past few months. Deep down, however, she knew the truth. When the same feelings of morning nausea recurred day after day, she knew that she was pregnant. She said nothing of her condition to her parents. She wasn't going to have the same conversation twice and wasn't going to agonise over what to do next; she was just going to set her mind to it and have an abortion – and act as if nothing was wrong.

Christmas and New Year came and went. She went to see a doctor, who scheduled a procedure for the middle of January. Two days after making the appointment the phone rang at ten o'clock at night. She was in bed, Bobby Jo was asleep in her cradle; she knew instinctively who the caller was.

She got up and went into the kitchen and picked up the receiver. It was Stavros.

"How are you, Stavros?" she asked, trying not to sound irritated.

"How am I? I'm frantic. I don't hear from you. You're not returning my calls. I want you to come back. I miss you, Joonie. You've been there almost three months."

"I can't come back."

"What do you mean you can't?"

"Don't ask me to explain. I just can't."

"Did something happen?"

She didn't answer.

"Did something happen, Joonie? I want to know."

"I don't want to talk about it."

"What is it?"

"I can't tell you."

"You *must* tell me."

She looked at the receiver in her hand, and put it down softly in its cradle.

Her mother came into the kitchen in her nightgown. "Who was that?"

"Stavros. I told him I'm not going back."

"I didn't know that was still going on – but you did the right thing. Don't feel bad that you've told him. He's too far away. Get back with Gideon. He's a nice boy. Stick with him."

Joonie turned to go back to her room, but felt restless. She needed someone to talk to and wanted to call Hilary, but it was too late to call her friend at that time of the night, especially since she'd neglected her of late. If only her grandmother were alive, she thought. Ma would've helped her make sense of her life.

The phone rang again. She sighed and went back to the kitchen. It was Stavros again.

"I want to know what happened," he said.

The words popped out of her mouth before she could stop them. "I'm pregnant."

"What?"

"You heard right."

There was a long silence. "How many months?"

She was too agitated and upset with herself to respond kindly. "It's not your baby, Stavros."

The phone clicked off in her ear.

Her mother's footsteps sounded in the passage. When she re-entered the kitchen, Joonie was still standing with the receiver in her hand. "Did he say something to you?" her mother asked.

"Who?"

"Gideon."

"It wasn't Gideon, but if he should call, tell him I'm not here."

Her mother frowned. "Where will you be?"

"I'll be here. I just don't want to see anyone."

"He is anyone now?"

"He is anyone, someone, no one. Not so many questions, Mom. I don't feel good."

She left her mother in the kitchen staring after her and went into her grandmother's room. She took the big brown envelope and the jewellery box from the shelf in the cupboard where they had been waiting ever since she came back. The brown envelope was thick and bulky. She lay down on the bed and opened it.

Wads of one-hundred-rand notes, held together with elastic bands, stared back at her. She was moved. Her grandmother had always skimped on things for herself, yet she had left her a small fortune. How much was it? She was too stunned to count. She removed a sheet of paper from the bottom of the envelope and read the few short sentences written in pencil:

> *I've saved this money for you, Joonie, for university. It's yours now, seventeen thousand rand. Spend it wisely. Buy your little girl a new bright red bicycle with a bell when she is big enough to ride.*

The tears welled up in her eyes. She knew the story of the red bicycle her grandmother dreamed of as a child. Ma's friend, who was in the same class as her, had had one and Ma had paid her with sweets for a ride. When the sweets ran out, Ma would do things for her friend, like allow her to copy her homework, just for Ma to be able to sit on the bike for a while and ring the bell.

Ma's family were so poor they sometimes only had porridge and chicken livers for supper. Compared to her grandmother's childhood, Joonie's was a picnic in the park, and she was lapping it all up like a spoiled brat, being reckless and irresponsible. She didn't deserve her grandmother's largesse.

She put the money back into the brown envelope, and opened the wooden box. It contained three exercise books with handwritten notes. The first two appeared to have been written a long time ago. The handwriting started out with an awkward scroll in pencil, to a studied kind of writing, in ink, in the last book.

She opened the first book. There was a single entry in, dated 11 June 1925:

> *My father came to see the school principal today and said he was taking me out of school. He didn't say why, but I know. My mother has another baby coming, and I have to help with the work in the kitchen. The boys change their school shirts every three days. There are five of them. My mother is big now. She can't bend over and do the washing anymore. I don't know when she's going to stop having babies.*

Joonie read the entry over and over again. There was nothing else written in the book, but perhaps the empty pages said more than a pencil could record. It spoke of a life of soap blocks and dirty nappies.

She picked up the second book. There were no dates but, judging by the handwriting, it appeared to have been written a few years after the first book. Again Ma had written in Afrikaaans.

> *When I was sixteen, Lawrence came to ask my father if he could marry me. I sat on the chair in the dining room in my Sunday-school dress, feeling embarrassed in front of my aunts who had all been alerted to what was about to happen. My mother had had two more pregnancies since my brother Charlie's birth a year earlier, but these pregnancies mysteriously disappeared. I don't think my father knew they even occurred. I was home during the day and knew what went on. My mother was a sickly woman who couldn't do her own grocery shopping*

from having a baby year after year, and I listened at the bedroom window when her friend Elizabeth came to visit. Twice that year there were screams of pain and bowls of hot water being carried back and forth, and lots of towels with red stains which I had to wash the same day. Much as I dreaded what my father was going to tell Lawrence in his skinny suit and polished shoes and watery blue eyes, I hoped he was going to say yes so I could get out of the house.

My father asked me to my face if I was pregnant. I was embarrassed and wanted to say no, but knew that my condition would soon show, and said yes. He looked at Lawrence and me with a disappointed look on his face. Get married, he said to me, but you and Lawrence will stay here for a year. You will help your mother as before.

I now had an extra load of washing to do, extra potatoes to peel, and had to sleep with Lawrence in the back room and night after night feel his hands on me. Seven months later Joe Michael was born.

Joonie continued reading, unable to put the slender little book down. She was astounded by her grandmother's hard life as a young girl, and her resilience. And the fluency with which she wrote. The pages were filled with details of her father Joe's childhood and the birth of Olive, who had followed ten months after Joe, and Laverne, the late baby, born when Olive was in her teens already. It was as if her grandmother was right there with her in the room, telling her all these things.

Joonie reached the last page:

Lawrence bought Laverne a blue tricycle for her fourth birthday. The tricycle seems to be the only

> *thing that pleases Laverne. She is not like Joe, who is a happy boy, and Olive, who is about to turn thirteen. She doesn't play with her older brother and sister and has a temper. Lawrence says it's just normal behaviour. I don't believe it. I can see when a child has that streak. Last Christmas she stood on the dining-room table with a broomstick in her hand and hit the lamp shade above her head until it broke and the glass splintered all over the flowers and place settings.*

She put the book down. There was one more booklet to go, but she needed to prepare something to eat before Bobby Jo woke up. Her grandmother had packed a lot of information into the thin little book; for the first time she now understood many things – also why her grandmother had taken her to the old lady in Retreat. Her grandmother herself had got pregnant as a young girl and hadn't wanted her to make a mistake. Her grandmother wanted her to do something with her life and not squander it in a kitchen having baby after baby. The seventeen thousand rand was to help her reach that goal.

Was every woman's story the same, she wondered? And would Ma have married Lawrence if she hadn't found herself pregnant? She doubted it. Ma let her inherit the box of secrets for a reason – Ma considered her worthy of her faith in her not to disappoint.

Later that night, when everyone was asleep, Joonie opened the last book. It also had only one entry, in the form of a short letter to her.

> *Dear Joonie*
> *Laverne had a baby when she was fifteen years old. She was a beautiful child, the fairest child born in*

> the family. No one knew who the father was except me. He was a white bus conductor. Laverne had met him on the Klipfontein Road bus and got off with him at the depot in Mowbray. That's what she said. She didn't do well with the birth. It unhinged her and she ended up in Valkenberg Hospital with a stick between her teeth to prevent herself from biting her tongue. The doctors said she would be in hospital for a long time. The social workers came to the house to talk about placing the baby into a foster home. Your father, who had just turned thirty and married to your mother, didn't want the baby to leave the family and took her into his home. When Laverne was released from hospital, she had no interest in the child. The baby remained with your father. That baby was you, Joonie.

She stared at the writing on the page. It was a preposterous mistake. Had she misread or misunderstood something? She read the paragraph again. And again. And it was still there; that last, unbelievable sentence: *That baby was you, Joonie.* There was no mistake. She was Laverne's baby. But how could it be? How could her aunt be her mother? She wanted to go to the kitchen and ask her mother if it was true, but was so stumped by the letter she sat back with the book in her lap until Bobby Jo's cries jolted her out of her stupor.

At supper that evening, her father noticed her silence. "You're quiet tonight, Joonie."

"I have lots of things on my mind, Dad. I read Ma's letter. It's disturbed me."

He quietly put his knife and fork down. "A letter? Did Ma write you a letter? What did she say?"

"I don't want to talk about it tonight."

JOONIE

The telephone rang. Her mother answered.

"Hi, Stavros. Yes, she's here." And with that she passed the receiver to Joonie, and left the kitchen. Her father followed her mother into the living room.

"Hi."

"You shocked me yesterday, Joonie, and I'm sorry I hung up on you. But I was so shocked. I mean, how can this happen twice?"

It was her turn to hang up on him. He called back immediately.

"I don't care what you did, Joonie. I've thought about it. I don't want to know who he is, or how it happened. You did all this because of what happened between us. I caused this to happen. Please just come back. We'll work it out."

She tried to remain calm. "How will we work it out? It's not something you'll ever forget."

"You'll have an abortion. We'll go for counselling. We all make mistakes. I love you too much to let you go. Just come back. We'll forget about it. I want you and Bobby Jo in my life. We've known each other for a year, Joonie. Think of all the good times we've had. I fucked up big time. Haven't you ever made a mistake?"

She was strangely subdued. "Many, and still making them. Let me think about it."

"What's to think about? I'll book your tickets on South African Airways. I'll make them one-year return tickets. You can pick them up there."

"Call me tomorrow. I don't want to do anything rash."

She replaced the receiver, not quite sure what to do next. Her parents came back into the kitchen. She looked at them. "Did you guys look through the stuff Ma left for me?"

"No," her mother replied.

179

"I didn't think so. If you had you wouldn't have given it to me. Right, Mom?"

"What are you talking about? I hate it when you speak in riddles."

"What is it, Joonie? What is this letter you mentioned earlier?" Her father gave her a very concerned look. "Speak."

"Ma left me some money to go to university and also three little books with handwritten notes. She wrote some really serious stuff. I don't know if I can believe it."

"What did she say?" her mother asked, swallowing hard, as if she was still eating.

"She wrote that Auntie Laverne had a baby with a white bus conductor when she was fifteen years old. I was the baby. Is that true, Dad – that the aunt who everyone said is cuckoo and out of her mind is my mother and you are not my real parents? It's a helluva thing to have kept from me if it's true."

Her father blanched. He sat stone-faced at the table. "It's true." He glanced at her. "We didn't want it to come out like this. There was no right time to tell you. No time is the right time to tell a child that the parents she's known since birth aren't her real parents. We didn't want to frighten you by telling you as a little girl. Then when you got older, we thought we'd left it too long, and kept putting it off. Even Ma couldn't find the right time to tell you directly."

He cleared his throat and after a while continued, "Auntie Laverne had you when she was fifteen, yes. She became deeply depressed after the birth and became harmful to her own child. They have a name for it, I forget what it is. She was put in a psychiatric ward and we had to make a decision. We didn't want you going into foster care and other people taking you. Your mother and I couldn't have children and we decided to adopt you – and would've adopted you even if we did have kids. But there were problems doing even that as we had to wait for Laverne to get better and sign the papers. She never was stable long enough for her to be granted custody. The bottom line is that she could not be alone with a baby."

"I know."

"How do you know?"

"When I came back from hospital with Bobby Jo she thought Bobby Jo was her baby. She had told me a story once about being pregnant, but in her story, the baby was never born. Now I understand why she carried on like that."

The unpleasant memory transported her back to New Jersey, to the house with the smashed cradle on the staircase, the baby crying, Stavros and Billie Bob trying to help.

"Still, you owed it to me to tell me, Dad," she said quietly. "I lived in her house, put her in hospital, and didn't know it was my own mother who was slowly losing her mind. A good time to have told me was when I went to America. You let me go, knowing I was going to my mother's house and not my aunt's. And she never gave any clue that she knew. Do you know what she said to me when I went to see her to say goodbye? They took my baby! They took my baby! Over and over she repeated herself. I didn't know what she was talking about. I'm angry, Dad. And I'm sad."

Her father got up and came to sit next to her. "You will always be our child, Joonie. That doesn't change. You came to us when you were five days old. We took you because you were my sister's child and my sister needed to get better before she could have custody of you. She never got better – not completely, or not sufficiently for you to be safe with her. And I did what I thought was best; I brought my sister's child into my home and took care of her. And so did your mother over there. Isn't that love?"

"It is, Dad, and I understand why you did it. But what about my real mother wasting away in a hospital in America? I would never have left her there if I'd known she was my mother."

"Have you considered that maybe if you brought up the whole thing with her now, that it might be too traumatic for her and that she might go mad?"

"She went off anyway. She tried to take Bobby Jo from me. She went berserk. I can see now why she believed Bobby Jo was her child. I don't even know what to call her. And what do I call you?"

"We're Mom and Dad, same as always. That's what you call us. And you will find the right words for your mother the next time you meet."

"You know that I can't stay on here now that I know."

"You must do what you feel is best," her father said. "God knows what your trip to America was good for. The Lord works in mysterious ways."

"What about Gideon?" her mother asked.

"I don't know."

"He could go with you."

"I don't love him, Mom. I'm going for a walk around the block to clear my head. Need anything from the shop?"

"A packet of Stuyvesant's," her father said.

She went into her room and took eleven hundred rand from the money her grandmother had left her. She handed her father a thousand rand. "I don't know how much you had to pay that Mr Singh, Dad, but here's a grand. Thanks for helping me out."

"You know, Joonie, everything happens for a reason. You had some time with your mother, even though you didn't know at the time that she was your mother. You must take comfort from that. Things happen to us and we don't know why they happen. I think your trip to America prepared you for the trip you must make back there – to look after her or to bring her back."

"I don't think bringing her back is an option, Dad. Not in her condition. But I want to spend time with her, ask her things, tell her who I am."

Her father smiled. "Despite all your tricks and devilry, you have some good in you."

"A lot of good, Dad. Now, let me go to the shop. I'm taking Bobby Jo with me. It's still light outside."

"Don't be long. It will soon be dark."

Pushing the stroller quickly down the road, she, instead of turning left to go to the shop, turned right and headed for Voortrekker Road. She walked along the main road until she came to a telephone booth. She called Hilary. Hilary was glad to hear from her and could tell that she was calling from a public phone. "Why didn't you call me from home?" she asked.

"The phone's in the kitchen. I don't want my parents to know. Can you come with me on Wednesday? I have something I have to do and I want you to come with me. I want to go to Medipark on the Foreshore."

"What for? Are you sick?"

"No. Don't ask too many questions. I won't know the answers."

"Oh God. Don't tell me you're pregnant!"

"I need you to look after Bobby Jo for me for a few hours. You could go and have coffee somewhere."

"Have you seen a doctor and made an appointment?"

"Yes. It's scheduled for this coming Wednesday. I'll tell my mother I'm spending the day at your house with Bobby Jo."

"Okay," Hilary said, clearly bowled over by Joonie's news. "I didn't know getting an abortion was that easy, and that it was legal."

"I don't know if it's legal. But the doctor seemed to know why I was there – I had to go and see him to explain my situation, and I just said I was throwing up and feeling nauseous in the mornings and maybe I needed a scrape. The word abortion never came into the conversation. He examined me and told me I was pregnant and told me to come this Wednesday at nine o'clock."

"So he understood why you had come to him, then?"

"I suppose so."

"Hell! I can't handle all the stuff happening with you. You didn't do this with Bobby Jo."

"Bobby Jo was a love child. I don't regret her one bit. But I don't know whose child this is. I don't want to go through any paternity tests or have there be talk of it. If I'm eight weeks pregnant, it's Gideon's child – we had sex once. If I'm three months, it's Stavros's."

"Hell, Joonie ..."

"I know, it sounds like I'm an unstable throwaway slut."

"Are you going to ask the doctor how far along you are before he starts the procedure?"

"Of course. I'm not going to live the rest of my life not knowing who the father was." After a short pause, she added, "Or maybe it's better for me not to know."

"I would want to know if it was me," Hilary said.

"There you've answered my question. We want to know these things. Listen, I can't talk longer. I'm on a public phone. Are you able to come with me?"

"Yes."

"Thanks, Hilary. You're a real friend. Meet me outside Cape Town station at nine o'clock."

She said goodbye and hung up. She walked back the way she had come and continued past their house to Mr Ali's café. She felt overwhelmed. There was her mother in a nursing home in New Jersey; there was Stavros wanting her to come back; there was Gideon also, the serial heartbreaker who had spent all his free time with her and didn't know why he was being avoided now. They had had super times together and she liked him, found him physically attractive, irresistible in fact, but she wasn't in love with him.

She saw one or two neighbours as she passed their houses and showed off Bobby Jo to them. They congratulated her on having such a beautiful child. She thanked them for their kind words and continued down the street, feeling better for having talked to Hilary.

There were a few customers in the store but no one she knew. When it was her turn to be served, Mr Ali came from around the counter to look at Bobby Jo. "All praise to God. You have a beautiful child, Marsha Allah."

"Thank you."

"Will you let me give her a gift?" he asked.

She smiled at his generosity. "Thank you, Mr Ali, but you don't have to."

"I want to. It's nothing big." He went back behind the counter and took out two tins of KLIM milk powder and put them on the counter. "For when you run out of milk," he said.

"That's very kind of you, Mr Ali. Thank you." She bought her father's cigarettes, some fresh rolls, cheese, lettuce and chocolates, put everything in the carry-all under the stroller and left. Her breath caught in her throat when she stepped outside and walked straight into Blair – with a short army haircut.

"Oh my God ..."

"Joonie!" He seemed not to know what to say and grabbed hold of her and hugged her. "I don't believe this is you. I never thought I would see you again. I heard you'd gone to America."

She was caught by such surprise it took her a moment to respond. "I did go. How are you?"

For a few seconds they were both at a loss for words, him just holding her. Then he noticed the stroller. He let her go and bent down to look at the baby. "Whose baby is this?"

"Mine."

"Yours?" His expression changed and he turned slowly to look at her – his eyes asking the question he dare not ask with words.

"How old is she?"

"A few months."

"How many?"

She didn't answer.

He looked from her to the baby. "What is her name? She's beautiful."

"Thank you. Her name's Bobby Jo."

There was an awkward moment as they looked at one another. His expression was wistful as he leaned over the sleeping baby and touched her hair. "I don't know what to say, I'm so stunned meeting you like this. Are you back?"

Right there she made up her mind. "I've been here for about four months. I'm leaving again."

The smile in his eyes faded. "Oh. Are you married?"

"No."

His face became drawn. "I didn't run out on you, Joonie. I wrote you a letter trying to explain. The day we last spoke my father called and I had to get on a plane the same evening. You never wrote me back."

"I didn't because I didn't receive your letter. Only later

I discovered that you had been to my house and were looking for me."

"Do you want to know what happened?"

She wanted to know, desperately, but was afraid of being confused even more. "I have to go, Blair."

He seemed hurt that he was being this quickly dismissed. "Can I pick her up?"

"She's sleeping, maybe another time."

"When?"

"I don't know. Listen, I've got to go." Against her will she started to push the stroller, trying to come to grips with her feelings. Seeing him so suddenly was all it took; she still loved him.

"I want us to talk, Joonie."

"There's nothing to talk about, Blair. My life's in enough of a mess. It's too late now."

"It's never too late. I've never stopped loving you."

She got ready to move on. "I must go, Blair." She started to walk away faster.

"I still love you, Joonie," he called out after her.

She walked on, her legs feeling wobbly, her face red. She hadn't expected that she would run into him. What was he doing here? He was supposed to be in the army. She was out of breath when she reached their front gate. She went straight to her room, put Bobby Jo in her cot and returned to the kitchen to make a call. Her father was no longer there, so she put the cigarettes on the corner of the table where her mother was now rolling out pastry.

She dialled Stavros's number. He answered after a few rings.

"Are you sleeping?"

"Yes," he said, brightening at hearing her voice.

"Do you still want me to come back?"

"What a question."

They talked for a long time. Ten minutes later she replaced the receiver, and almost immediately the phone rang again. It was Blair.

"I want to talk to you, Joonie."

She was relieved that her mother had left the kitchen in the course of her conversation with Stavros. "There's nothing to talk about, Blair," she said. "I'm going back to America."

"Can I come around to see you?"

"No."

"You don't know what's gone on in my life."

"You left without saying anything to me. It's too late now."

"Is she my baby, Joonie?"

The question was in her face before she could blink. She looked at the receiver in her hand and put it down and in a daze went back to her room. She stared at the sleeping Bobby Jo for a long time.

Soon after her father arrived home, he and her mother came into her bedroom. Her suitcases were open on the floor; she was folding things.

"Can we sit down?" her father asked.

"It's your house, please."

Her parents sat on the bed. Her father looked about him; there were piles of clothes everywhere.

"What are you doing to yourself, Joonie?"

"I'm going back to the States, Dad."

"To Stavros?"

"Yes."

"Why?"

"Why not?"

"I thought you liked Gideon. You've been out almost every night with him. It seemed like you were both heading in the same direction."

"I'm not in love with him. I missed home. I came for a holiday. I'm going back."

"You were not supposed to go there for good. You promised us."

"Things happen."

"What happened? In the space of one year you've been involved with three guys."

Her face reddened.

"Did something happen that you're suddenly doing this?"

"Something happened, yes. My mother's in a mental institution in another country and no one told me about it. I probably would never have found out if it wasn't for Ma's letter. My going back will be better for the family."

"How will it be better for us? You have us all in turmoil with your back and forth."

"Is that what you want to talk about, Dad? About me chopping and changing? I know I'm only eighteen, but I'm a mother now."

"Then you must act like a mother and not take your child on a merry-go-round."

She felt properly chastised and knew they were right. When her parents retired to their room, she went to the kitchen and called Hilary. "Listen, Wednesday's off. Don't come to Cape Town station."

"You've decided to keep it?" asked the only person she could confide in.

"No. I'm not having it done here," she said under her breath. "I'm going back to the States."

Joonie looked out at the snow-covered city of New York as the plane swooped down on the runway and felt deeply depressed. The people at home seemed far away. She had regrets about everyone she'd hurt and regretted that her regrets always came too late. She was fickle and irresponsible and had not even told Gideon of her plans when she sat next to him in the movies on Tuesday night. What would it have cost her to tell him? What would it have cost her to tell Blair that Bobby Jo was his child? And why had she come back? Stavros had been good to her, helping her with her aunt, helping her with Bobby Jo, but he had also raised his hand to her. Had she so quickly forgotten? Had she come back to have a place to stay while she sorted out her aunt and have an abortion, terminating a pregnancy only Hilary – and Stavros – knew about? And what did she call her aunt now? Auntie Laverne, Mom, or just Verne as she had insisted when she arrived here almost exactly a year ago? She felt tender and differently towards her birth mother now.

Joonie disembarked from the plane with a big sling bag, two overnight bags and Bobby Jo. It had been rough travelling by herself with a baby. The bassinette provided by the airline helped, but with the turbulence in the air, she had kept Bobby Jo on her lap for most of the journey.

A flight attendant helped her into the terminal. Stavros was waiting for her outside the arrivals hall with a trolley. His face brightened when he saw her and Bobby Jo, but she felt nervous and wary, acutely aware of the turmoil inside her. A flashback of Stavros striking her made the heat rise up to her face, but it passed. He hugged her and kissed Bobby Jo on the tip of her nose and handed her a warm jacket to put on. He was always thoughtful, she thought; she hoped their life together would be peaceful now.

"Can you hold Bobby Jo for me, please, while I put this on?"

"Only too happy to," he said, throwing an extra blanket over the baby. "I missed you so much, Joonie, and I missed Twinkle Toes," he said, handing Bobby Jo back to her, kissing her face and hair as he did so. "Promise me you won't leave again."

She was careful with her words and tried to keep her voice even. "I can't promise anything, Stavros. I can only promise to try."

He put Bobby Jo in the stroller, for her to push, and pushed the trolley with her luggage. Like a family, they walked to his car. Joonie was touched when she noticed the baby seat he must have bought specially.

They were no sooner settled in his car, Bobby Jo strapped in on the back seat, than he asked, "Did you see the father of your baby while you were there?"

Her spirit sank. They hadn't even reached his apartment and he was starting with his questions. She turned her head to look out the window and answered matter-of-factly. "I ran into him two days before I left."

"Oh. I didn't think you were going to say that you did. What did he say about Bobby Jo? Does he know it's his child?"

He was looking so hard at her that one wheel hit the curve as they exited the parking garage.

"I didn't tell him, but he knows. How can he not know looking at her? I'm sure he's figured it out."

"You seem like you want him to know."

She resented the accusation in his voice and deep down felt she had made a mistake to return. "Would that be a crime?" she asked, turning her head to look him straight in the eye and then at the oncoming traffic, slowly getting used to travelling on the right-hand side of the road again.

"He might ask to be part of her life."

"He might. I don't know. I managed to evade him for the rest of the time."

"Why evade him if he doesn't mean anything? Or maybe he does mean something to you still."

How dare he talk to her like this, she thought. She had just spent seventeen hours in a plane coming back to him. She was sorry now that she had, and angry with herself for persisting in thinking that he would change. He wasn't going to change. It wasn't that he was lying when he made all those promises, he just didn't have it in him to change. He had no idea how his possessiveness affected her.

Still, she kept her voice under control. "This was a long trip, Stavros. Please. I don't want to get into a whole thing about Blair. I came back to you, didn't I?"

"Don't you want me to be Bobby Jo's father?"

It took extreme effort to control her irritation. She was tired from the trip, depressed that she was back. "If we stay together, yes. I know you love her and think of her as your own."

"If we stay together? You mean this is a trial period?"

"Oh, Stavros, I feel so cross-examined, man, like you're waiting for me to say the wrong thing."

He seemed oblivious of the struggle going on inside her. Weighing her words, she continued, "I don't know if this is a trial period. A horrible thing happened between us. I want to be sure I'm doing the right thing; just like you would like to be sure."

He said nothing and was forced to concentrate on the road. The snow came down in thick wet drifts against the windshield, making it hard to see. She looked down at her hands in her lap so he couldn't see her face. She had returned from brilliant sunshine and stepped straight into a heavy grey bog. She felt boxed-in and trapped in the claustrophobic space and the smell of polished leather inside the Mustang. What was she doing here back in his car? What madness had made her come back? She was so weary, she felt like ending it all right then. She opened the door, not wide, but wide enough for her to hurl herself out.

"What are you doing?" Stavros asked in alarm.

"I can't breathe."

"Then open the window, not the door. This is the highway, for heaven's sake. It's dangerous. Look at all the trucks on the road."

She blocked her ears, kept her right hand on the handle of the open door and leaned outward, watching the ground as it sped by underneath them. The question for her wasn't: should she jump? It was: could she stay in the car and *not* jump? She was in the grip of something she had little control over. She could see it now: her body flung onto the icy asphalt, trapped under the cars behind them, bones crunching, leaving a crimson ribbon of blood. She wouldn't even know what had hit her. There would be no pain.

She closed the door and curled up on the seat. She was shivering with shock, realising what she had almost done. She bit on her lower lip to keep her teeth from chattering. "Can you take me to the hospital, Stavros?"

"What's the matter with you, Joonie? That was a crazy thing to do."

"I have a pain in my chest. Can you take me to a hospital?"

"Of course, I'll take you. Did I cause this now?"

"No," she lied. Continuing the same line of conversation would drive her mad.

"What happened? You're trembling."

"I don't know."

Stavros left the car in the parking lot in front of the Holy Cross Hospital and went with her to the Emergency entrance. Her legs felt restless and she felt jumpy and nervous and could not stay in her seat. Getting more and more agitated, she paced up and down with Bobby Jo in the stroller, waiting for her turn. At one point she felt so anxious that she asked Stavros to look after the baby while she went up to the nurse's station and warned them that something was going to happen to her if they didn't see to her right away. "My face feels flaming hot," she said, her voice hoarse, "and I have difficulty breathing."

The emergency ward was full, she was told. Her anxiety increased. She didn't know if she wanted to sit or stand and kept moving around. Mercifully, Bobby Jo remained fast asleep with Stavros rocking the stroller back and forth. She was convinced that if a doctor didn't check her immediately she would drop to the floor and pass out. Her breathing became faster, her heart pounded in her chest with fear.

Finally, a doctor who was attending to another patient, noticed her condition and called her over to a curtained cubicle where he took her blood pressure and listened to a jumble of confused sentences as she tried to explain why she was there. On the other side of the bed a nurse was making notes.

"Your blood pressure's rather high. Can you tell me what happened?"

"We were driving home from the airport, and I became suddenly afraid. It was all too much for me coming back.

My mother's in a psychiatric ward here. Then there's my boyfriend. His mother. My baby. A whole lot of things. I became anxious, I couldn't breathe. I opened the door while my boyfriend was driving; I needed air. My boyfriend wanted me to close it, but I didn't do it immediately. I just had this crazy impulse to jump from the car and end it all."

"You wanted to end your life?"

"No. I just didn't want to deal with everything. My life was completely different back home."

"Have you had these thoughts before?"

"No."

"Because I can commit you if I think you're a danger to yourself. And to your baby."

Calmer now that she was in a doctor's hands, she said, "I'm not a danger to anyone. It was just a whole lot of things coming at me all at once. My aunt's in a mental facility here. I just learned recently that she wasn't my aunt, but my mother. My parents kept this from me my whole life. It threw me completely. I'm still not over the shock. The main reason I came back was for her. I can't just leave the woman who gave birth to me to rot in a mental institution. I also came back to Stavros. That's my boyfriend," she added. "I thought we could work things out."

"Stavros is the guy out in the hallway with the baby?"

"Yes."

"Is he the father of the baby?"

"No."

"Can I ask why you broke up?"

She hesitated. "He became violent. I escaped and went home."

"Where's home?"

"Cape Town, South Africa."

"South Africa's a long way from here. You mean when you say you escaped, that he didn't know you got on a plane and left?"

"That's right."

The doctor nodded his head. "You have a lot of things going on in your life – far too much for a girl your age. I would suggest that you go and see a psychologist to talk about this. It's clear to me that you don't belong here and that you'll be happier in your own country. Think of your child. Think about yourself. A man who abuses a woman will do so again. Your child will be motherless if anything happens to you. What you experienced in the car was a panic attack. You can't die from a panic attack, but you must take heed of it. You experienced anxiety because of all the stress in your life."

On her way out of the ward, the doctor stopped to talk to Stavros. "Look, she had a panic attack. She's feeling better now, but she's basically depressed. I don't want to give her medication for anxiety; she can become dependent on them. The best thing for her is a one-way ticket home."

Stavros was silent as they drove to the apartment. She felt bad, almost as if she had betrayed him. He had been good to her, taking her back, pregnant with another man's child. Another man wouldn't have done what he did.

At home, he helped her to bath and settle Bobby Jo, then came to sit next to her on the sofa. "I didn't know you hated it here, Joonie. If you really can't stand being here and it drives you to having these dark thoughts, I'd rather let you go."

She was surprised, especially after how hard he'd tried to get her back. "I won't go," she said, "but please take it easy with me? I have to tell you about my aunt. I didn't want to tell you on the phone. I learned in Cape Town that Auntie Laverne is really my mother and not my aunt."

"What?"

"There's a lot we have to talk about, Stavros. When Joonie's a year old I want to go back to college. I want to study, perhaps complete that BA degree I started last September. I want to work. I need to have my own money and not be so dependent on you."

She told him nothing of the money her grandmother had left her. She had no bank account yet that she could put it into as she had no papers as a citizen, but would find a good hiding place for it. She hated being deceptive, but one thing Ma had always told her she now believed in wholeheartedly: never tell a man everything, even when you're lying next to him in bed.

"I want to talk about my pregnancy as well. I want to have it terminated. I want to have it done as soon as possible."

"Whatever you want, Joonie. Being my wife will give you independence too; you will have citizenship. I think you can apply for that after being married to me for two years."

"You still want to get married?"

"Don't you?"

"Let's talk about it in a few weeks. Let me first settle in again. I'm not feeling great right now. I really want to give our relationship a chance."

I have very little recollection of events after that conversation, except that I woke up in a hospital bed a few days later, with a pad between my legs. I was in a daze. I felt empty – empty of the life that had been scraped out of me, and empty of spirit. Back in Stavros's apartment I went to bed and didn't get up for two weeks, except to feed and change Bobby Jo. Fortunately, she was a sweet, healthy infant, happy to quietly lie or sit up in her cot when she woke and to amuse herself with the row of colourful rubber animals I had strung above her head. She was making cooing sounds, letting us know she was there; if there was ever a period in my life when I was afraid that something terrible might happen to me, it was then. It was Bobby Jo who kept me going. I kept thinking of my responsibility towards her. I loved my child. I didn't bring her into the world to leave her behind for others to rear, I kept reminding myself. But it was not easy to fight what was going on in my head and expel every demon that made me feel weak. On top of it, a new, additional fear quietly developed: that my mother's dementia might indeed be passed on to me.

It was in this fearful, panicky state that I made the trip to the nursing home where my mother Laverne resided. I didn't know what I would say to her or even if I would tell her who I was, but knew as I walked down the shiny corridor, with Bobby Jo in the stroller, that I wanted more definitive answers than the last time. Was my mother going to be in the home forever? Was there any hope of

JOONIE

taking her to a home in Cape Town?

The nurse at the desk told me that Laverne Johnson had stopped speaking, and that the one thing she had looked forward to, her food, was no longer of interest to her. She was incontinent and no longer sat in the communal hall. I would find her in her room, she said.

Feeling apprehensive, I softly knocked on the door. No one answered. I opened the door. She was sitting on the bed in a nightgown staring out the window. I was shocked by the deterioration of the past four months. Her hair was cut short like a boy's. She didn't turn when I entered, but moved her head slightly at the sound of the rubber wheels of the stroller on the polished floor. She looked much older than her thirty-odd years.

"Auntie Laverne?" I said.

There was no response. I sat on the single chair in the room, wondering what to do. It was clear that I didn't have to ask the doctors if her illness was terminal. Her arms were thin, her eyes sunken, her skin an unhealthy hue. Her breakfast stood untouched on the tray.

What did someone with an advanced state of dementia think about, I wondered. Did she have thoughts at all?

I moved my chair to sit in front of her and took Bobby Jo out of the stroller and held her in my arms. "Auntie Laverne," I said, holding my infant up to her. "This is Joonie ..."

I don't know what made me do it; it was a stupid thing to have done, but at the sight of the baby, my mother covered her face in her hands and rocked back and forth, emitting a sound such as I'd never heard before. Not loud, but animal-like and keening. I feared that I might've stirred up something long repressed inside her and that she would go berserk. But she didn't. Her rocking slowed. Her moaning stopped. She turned her head to look at Bobby

Jo, whose face was pink and eyes were slitty from having just woken from a deep sleep. Her thin hand reached out for the baby. I let her touch Bobby Jo.

"It's your baby, Mom. Don't cry anymore. It's Joonie."

The tears pearled at the corner of her eyes. I put the baby in her frail arms, holding my arm under hers so Bobby Jo wouldn't drop from her hands. She moaned like an injured puppy, grasping the baby to her chest. And then I felt her arms weaken and I put my child back in her stroller. I helped my mother get back in under the blankets. She was my mother now and I could say it. I kissed her forehead and went out with my baby and told the nurse at the desk that my mother was sleeping.

The next morning the doctor called to say that Laverne Johnson had passed away.

After the funeral, attended by Billie Bob, Millie, Veronica and the rest of the card-playing friends, Stavros took all of them to a Persian restaurant for chello kebab. The restaurant was quiet and intimate and had the right ambience to toast a woman who had led such a tumultuous life. Joonie told her mother's friends the story of her grandmother's legacy and how she had discovered that she wasn't Laverne's niece but her daughter. They listened in disbelief and afterwards showered her with praise. "God works in mysterious ways," Millie said. "You were inspired to come to America. Had you not come here you might never have known the truth."

"The truth can be crippling, though, Auntie Millie," she said, looking down at Bobby Jo on her lap. "One isn't always ready for it." She found it easy to admit this.

"I know, but better than not ever knowing, right?"

"Right."

"Your mother was a loner. I knew her all the years and never knew she had a daughter. She never spoke about it."

"I didn't know either," Billie Bob mused, shaking his head in wonderment.

"I don't think she herself knew," Stavros said. "There was no indication of it."

"How could she not have known?" Reggie asked. "She had had a baby."

"I think she became confused," Joonie said. "I was taken away when I was just a few days old. And the brain can do miraculous things. It suppresses memories you don't

201

want. That's what I think, anyway." She remembered the confusing story about her birth mother having been four months pregnant and forced to have an abortion. Was that the truth? – that another baby hadn't been actually born but done away with? It didn't matter now.

"Anyway, God is good," Millie said. "Billie Bob couldn't stay forever. Laverne would've been alone. You came here and you had some time with her. You buried her. Lessons are learned by all of us. Maybe in the years to come you will learn a lesson from this too. What are you going to do now?"

She glanced at Stavros. "I'm going to stay home until Bobby Jo turns one and then further my education. I'm looking at some college material to see what I want to study. Last September I briefly enrolled for an English literature course, remember?"

"What are you thinking about?" Reggie asked. "Do you have any idea?"

"Well, when I was little, I told my parents that I wanted to be a lawyer, but really, deep in my heart I wanted to become an actress. I didn't even mention it to my parents as I knew they wouldn't approve. The stage and acting in movies is not a real job, they would have said, and I'm not going to kid myself that I have what it takes."

"I think you have what it takes. Why don't you study Drama now? You're the right age to get into something like that. I was an extra in a movie once; it's fun being on a set, and I know some people I can put you in touch with," Reggie offered. "I think you have the personality for it. And guess what? They have sherry at the wrap-up parties."

She laughed, remembering the night she'd played cards with them and had sherry for the first time. "I don't know. You read so many stories of what wannabe actors will do to get cast in a film."

"You can take Bobby Jo with to auditions. You can't do that when you go for an office interview," Reggie half jokingly added.

Stavros scowled. "Joonie's not looking for fame. It's a loose and heartbreaking business. She's right not to be interested."

No one said anything, not even Veronica who was so outspoken. The drinks arrived. Stavros found her hand under the table. "I've got something for you, Joonie. I hope you'll like it."

She was a little disturbed by what he had just said, giving the others an inkling of the state of affairs between them, but she decided not to make an issue of it and leaned over to look as he opened a small velvet box and lifted out an antique gold necklace with a heart pendant.

"It's a family heirloom. It was my grandmother's."

"Yoh!" she exclaimed. "I didn't expect this."

He put it around her neck while the others looked on. "You're going to be nineteen in a few months, but I wanted to give this to you today."

"Oh thank you," she hugged him. "It's beautiful."

"That's a beautiful necklace, Joonie. You're a lucky, girl," Veronica said. "Do you have an older brother, Stavros?"

They all laughed.

Stavros raised his glass, "Here's to Joonie and Auntie Laverne."

"Joonie and Auntie Laverne!" they all said, holding up their glasses. "Cheers!"

That night at the apartment, Joonie stood naked in front of the mirror in the bathroom admiring the gold pendant against the tawny texture of her skin. There was a soft knock at the door.

"Can I come in?"

She opened the door. She was feeling gracious towards him and wanted to show her appreciation of the gift.

"You're just utterly beautiful, Joons," he said, putting his arms around her.

"Thank you. Do you want to come to bed?"

"You've never asked me before. I must be doing something right."

She was surprised herself at her generosity towards him, and wondered how she could slip so easily from one emotion to the next. She had been sincere when she said that she wanted to give their relationship an honest chance. She wasn't happy at the way he had reacted to Reggie's suggestion that she try her hand at acting, but she would leave that discussion for another time. They both had lots to learn. She had always valued good looks, but good looks meant nothing. It can't pull a blanket over you at night; you can't eat good looks; good looks can't pay the bills at the end of the month. Good looks only help in the bedroom, and that night they helped a lot.

Dear Joonie

I got your address from your mother. I hope this letter finds you well and not too shocked to hear from me. I've thought a lot about our running into each other at the shop that day and repeatedly asked myself what the chances are that one goes home to your mother on compassionate leave and runs into the one person you've been looking for for almost a year. It was surely God, the Arranger, who inspired me to come down that weekend. I believe in such things, Joonie, and so I am writing to you in the hope that you will reply. If you have stopped loving me, please write to me and tell me so that I can put you out of my mind. We are older now. We have experienced some things together and some things on our own. You have a baby. I know now that Bobby Jo is my child. She has my eyes and my hair. I have photos of myself as a baby and we look the same. I also remember the day your grandmother was taken to hospital and we made love for the first and only time. If Bobby Jo is five or six months old now, you couldn't have conceived her from anyone else other than me. Am I right, Joonie? Am I asking too much? If you don't love me, I won't bother you again, but I would still like to get to know my child. I will not write more until I know how you feel. I would love to have a picture of her. You can write to me c/o the P.O. box on the back of the envelope. It is not easy communicating from the so-called operational area, and I can only mail and receive letters when one of my friends goes down to Windhoek to fetch special army supplies.

You are still my bokkie.

Blair

P.S. My mother is not well, but the doctors can't work out what is wrong with her.

She picked up the photograph he had enclosed. He looked fit and strong in his camouflage green-and-khaki uniform, a rifle slung over his shoulder. She was reminded of the disparity between them; he a symbol of white South Africa, she ... What *was* she? Despite the accoutrements, though, she recognised the naïve and tender guy she had known and fallen in love with.

She read the letter again, slowly, savouring all its nuances and meanings. There was no question about her feelings for him, but her feelings had almost been destroyed by his sudden disappearance a year earlier and not hearing from him afterwards. She had not wanted to speak to him at Mr Ali's cafe because she was still dealing with feelings of rejection and grief. Also, she feared that he would see Bobby Jo and want a relationship with her, or worse, not want the mother, but only the child.

More importantly, there were the gross apartheid laws that she didn't want to expose her child to, which, in fact, made it impossible for them to live together openly. She couldn't imagine Bobby Jo having to travel in a separate section of the bus or the train just because she was not considered white. It happened nowhere else in the world. And how could white people assume that they were different and better than people of colour? The time in America had opened her eyes. Here there was opportunity for anyone with determination to succeed. Her father liked to say that money was the root of all evil, but she had also learned that while that might be so, one nevertheless needed money to survive. She had huge plans for Bobby Jo. The money her grandmother had left her was going to be used to develop and hone whatever skills her daughter might have a propensity for. Was she going to take off again? Stavros had helped her through a pregnancy, he had made her first months in the country comfortable, he had taken her back despite her having left him and returning pregnant with another man's child. He had put a family heirloom around her neck in preparation for the ring that was to come. Could she break her own promises to herself, and leave him again? How far would she take her vengeance for the beating she'd received? And was it vengeance or just a fickle heart? She had discovered that it was possible to have sex with a man she didn't love. Didn't it make sense then to stay and not hurt anyone and provide the best opportunities and home life for her child?

She didn't have any answers, but knew that if she wrote

back to Blair and they spoke, that all her good intentions would fly out the window. Only Blair had made her feel like that; not Gideon, and not Stavros.

She folded up the letter into a small little block and hid it in one of her old bags in the closet.

It wasn't long before the cracks began to show in our cosy little set-up. It wasn't a big thing that had started it, merely a suggestion that we join Millie and the gang to play cards.

"What do you want to play cards with them for?" Stavros asked. "Am I not enough for you?"

What a question. Of course he wasn't enough. Where was my interaction with other human beings? I couldn't stay at home all day with Bobby Jo who was starting to crawl, watching *As the World Turns*. A soap opera on television could not make up for my own world turning monotonously in a one-bedroom, walk-up-to-the-first-floor living room strewn with toys and a small kitchen. There were no friends dropping in. We didn't even see Stavros's family. And I was not even nineteen yet! I needed to dress up and be with other people too. Like any normal person I needed some diversion now and then.

"Of course you're enough," I said, "but I'm bored."

"We can play cards."

"It's no fun with just the two of us. Why don't we go?"

"Is Reggie going to be there?"

"Of course. The game's not the same without him. He's the joker."

"You like him, don't you?"

"I like all of them. They're South African, Stavros. It'll be good for me."

"And for me?"

"You will have fun too."

"I don't think so. I can rent us a movie. Or we can go out to the movies. Everyone is talking about *Apocalypse Now*. And you like Marlon Brando, don't you?"

He'd forgotten about Bobby Jo, and he missed the point, but I didn't want the discussion to turn into something else and relented. I hated it when he became insecure. It had been flattering at first, but not anymore. I prepared tea and chicken salad sandwiches and took it into the living room and switched on the television.

"I want to go out tomorrow night."

"Tomorrow it will be a year since we met. Wait till you see what I have for you."

"I thought the necklace was my birthday present."

He smiled. "Come and sit on my lap and I'll tell you." I went over. He pulled me down towards him. "It starts with the letter C, a capital letter C, has doors and white-walled rims."

"What? You bought me a car?"

"It's an old convertible Cadillac, with an overhauled transmission and the original leather seats. I think it will suit you."

I didn't know what a transmission was and imagined it to be an engine. But it was the most unbelievable gift, too good to be true. He had always been generous; still, this was over the top. I hugged him again and again.

"You'll have the keys two days of the week."

My spirit sank. There were restrictions. It *had* been too good to be true. "You mean I have driving privileges, but it's not my car?"

"Not yet."

"You know what, Stavros, keep it. If you can't give me something I don't have to give back, I don't want it."

He threw the keys over to me, and laughed. "I was just kidding, Joonie. What's the matter with you? You have wheels now to take Bobby Jo for her check-ups and to go out shopping. I don't want to hear anymore that you need to get out. Go out during the day. How's that for a surprise?"

"Is that Stavros speaking? Stavros Dukakis?"

"It is he, yes. Come here, you vixen."

The sex lasted long into the night, and for a few months – except for an unpleasant visit by Aspasia, during which she discovered I was taking driving lessons and having difficulty obtaining a licence and made a snide remark about immigrants coming into the country and trying to marry innocent guys for citizenship – life had its brighter moments despite the drudgery of being cooped up in a flat with a young child all day and having to cope with a jealous boyfriend at night. Stavros had connections at the Department of Motor Vehicles and for two hundred dollars wangled a driver's licence for me, which was legal in all respects, except for being illegally obtained with a bribe. I had never driven a car before and this was a long, sexy vehicle with a hood that folded back, allowing my hair to blow in the wind. I was over the moon.

For three consecutive days Stavros took me to an empty parking lot and taught me how to drive, and made me learn the rules of the road. He repeated the lessons a week later. After that, he specially took a day off work and supervised me driving to a residential area where traffic was light after the morning rush, and then onto busier roads, and finally, the next weekend, onto the highway. When I proved to him that I was confident enough and could concentrate and manoeuvre the car properly and obey the road signs, he let me go out on my own.

Because it was my first time driving, it was easy to start out driving on the right side of the road. But finding my way around was like a tourist trying to find his way out of Mitchells Plain. I got lost several times during my first attempts driving around Cliffside Park alone with Bobby Jo strapped in on the back seat, and in doing so discovered quaint little places where we could shop and have pancakes with maple syrup and fresh cream. Bobby Jo liked these outings, and would rub the cream all over her face.

I took things slowly, driving only to the supermarket and pharmacy at first, becoming more familiar with my surroundings in the process. Finally, I felt confident enough to pass through the toll plaza and take the highway over the huge bridge that crosses into Manhattan, to visit Millie and Veronica. I couldn't believe that I had actually found the street and the place. It was a huge experience for me and my first real achievement in the big city. New York had scared me in the beginning with all its cabs and people and hustle and bustle on its streets.

With a car I could go where I pleased during the day when Stavros was at work. I visited Millie and the gang on Tuesday afternoons when Stavros always came home from the office meetings after eight. We played cards, with Bobby Jo crawling around the flat to everyone's delight. In the course of these visits I met some of Millie's students from the university, and soon I was more determined than ever to enrol when the new semester started in September. To cover myself at home, I told Stavros about some of the visits to Millie but didn't tell him it was a regular thing. I made sure that there was a good hearty supper when he came home so I wouldn't be accused of driving around all day and neglecting my domestic duties.

One night, I informed him that Millie and Veronica were giving a party to which we had been invited.

"I don't really want to go," he said. "When I come home I just want to relax with the two of you."

"Don't be such a wet rag, Stav. It's a party, not a card game. There'll be other South Africans there they'd like to introduce me to."

"Why do you need more friends?"

"Because I'm far away from home and I need to have some friends. You have your Greek friends. I would like to socialise with people from my country too."

"You're getting that way again," he said.

"What way?"

"That thing you do with your mouth. You're defiant."

I laughed to myself. Was he only noticing now? Still I didn't want an argument and tried to be more giving.

"Okay, I won't go," I said. "We'll stay home and look at old pictures of your mother."

"Don't be nasty."

"I want to go out, Stavros."

"No."

"Well, if you don't want to go, can I go?"

"You mean drive all alone to Manhattan at night? Not an option."

"Well, what options do I have?"

"Stay home with me, and tomorrow I'll take some time off work and we can go to Long Island. There's someone over there I want to talk to for a few minutes."

I had heard about Long Island and would have loved to spend the day out with him, but I had already planned to go with Millie to the university where she worked, to check out the night courses and to enrol. I had converted some of my money – which I had brought into the country illegally of course as one was not allowed to take large sums of cash out of South Africa at the time – to dollars with the help of Billie Bob, who said he didn't mind buying the rands; he had some business deal going and they would come in handy. With Millie's help I would enrol as a foreign student and study Drama. A lawyer Millie knew would help with the paperwork so I could study legally.

"I planned to go out with Millie tomorrow. I'm enrolling for a Drama course at Millie's university."

"Why Drama? You're listening to your friends again. Why not study Nursing or something like that?"

I suppressed an hysterical giggle. Was he serious? "I'm not interested in nursing. I won't be any good at it," I said as evenly as possible.

"You want to be famous then?"

"No. I want to do something I'm interested in, and I'm interested in Drama."

"You didn't think of Drama until your friends put it into your head."

"Is there anything wrong with that?" It was on the tip of my tongue to add that the girl his mother tried to interest him in was trying to get into movies and that that had been fine with Aspasia Dukakis.

He got up and put on his jacket. "I'm not in the mood for this conversation now. I'm going out."

I stared at the closed door for a long while. How easy it was for him just to get up and go. I heard a murmur from the new playpen we had bought in which Bobby Jo could take naps and knew she had woken up. I changed her nappy and fed her, remembering all those responsibilities my parents had talked about. At home, with all the built-in babysitters, I would've been happy and free to go out. I felt sorry for myself, hateful towards Stavros, and was about to go to bed when I received an unexpected call.

"Hi Joonie, it's Reggie Philander. Sorry to call you so late."

"No problem, Reggie. This is a surprise."

"I know. Millie asked me to give you a call and tell you the party's off. One of her students died in a car crash and she's busy with the family. She's postponing to next Saturday."

"Okay. I wouldn't have been able to come this week anyway."

"Then I'm glad the party's postponed."

"You are?"

"Yes. I've never really got to know you. Do you want to do coffee or lunch sometime this week?"

"I'd love to. I'll have to bring Bobby Jo, though."

"Of course. Where do you want to go?"

"I don't know many places. I live near Cliffside Park."

"Why don't we meet in the park then? You can follow me in your car. I know a great place where they have really thick foamy cappuccinos and carrot cake."

"That sounds wonderful. It'll be so nice to sit and chat."

"I know. One can't really talk at cards. They want me to be funny all the time."

"And you are. You make me laugh. Will Monday at noon be okay, or will you be at work? I can't meet you at night."

"Monday at noon is fine. I'm a building contractor. My time's my own."

I was so starved for conversation with people from back home – or anywhere else, in fact – that I couldn't wait for Monday to arrive. It was a sunny day and I dressed Bobby Jo warmly in a jacket and a hat and tucked her in the car seat. Even though the park was within walking distance, I took the car in case Stavros came home in the afternoon and found me gone with the Cadillac still in the garage.

I was sitting on the park bench with Bobby Jo in her stroller watching children at play on the grass, when I saw Reggie approach. I looked at him properly for the first time. He was tall with broad shoulders and looked good in jeans and a green windbreaker. We hugged, like people do back home, and kissed each other on the cheek, like they do in the States.

"It's nice here, you know," he said. "I'm on the other side of the river, not far at all, but I've never been to this park."

"I come here almost every second day. Bobby Jo loves it. The fresh air exhausts her and afterwards she sleeps longer than usual."

"She looks like you, you know."

"You haven't seen her father. They have the same double crown and blue eyes."

"What colour are yours?"

"People think they're blue, but they're actually grey."

"I don't know anyone with grey eyes."

"And I don't know any building contractors, so we're even."

He pushed the stroller over to his Honda, which was parked quite close to the Cadillac.

"Holy Toledo!" he said. "It must be some rich bird driving that."

I must admit it felt good being mistaken for someone with money. "It's mine, and I'm not rich."

"Yours?"

"It was an anniversary gift from Stavros. Our relationship is a year old."

"Well, isn't that nice. But you must be wary of Greeks bearing gifts," he joked.

It was funny the way he said it and I laughed, but it was also far from funny as it was the very thing that was crippling me. I would've appreciated the freedom to choose for myself far more than receiving all the expensive gifts, which only made me feel all the more beholden to someone who was possessive and jealous.

We were silent in the car driving to a small Italian restaurant where the specials of the day were listed on a board outside. "We can have lunch if you like. Their prawn pasta's very good."

"Thanks, but if I eat now I won't be able to eat tonight. I'll just have that thick foamy cappuccino you promised me."

"Deal."

The place was comfortable and homey, with a plump Italian woman serving us, and just the right ambience for conversation. Over cappuccinos and carrot cake, I found myself open up in a way that was unusual for me. I think it was because Reggie was male and not likely to gossip. He was both sexy and fatherly, a good listener, and not in a rush to list his accolades in an effort to impress. And he was interested in what I had to say. I liked that. I was needy of attention and found it easy to discuss bits of my life with him. He was tall, and there was something about his strong arms that made me feel safe.

"So are you happy living here, Joonie?"

"I am happy here, but also not happy."

"Okay," he said cautiously, raising his brows in surprise. "Want to talk about it?"

"Can I answer that with a question?"

"Yes."

"What do you do if you have a child, you're far away from home, and you live with someone you don't love?"

Reggie took a moment before he responded. "It would be easy to say, leave, but it's probably easier said than done."

"It is. One can never say never, and one should not ever take things for granted. I never thought I would stay with someone out of necessity."

"Is that what you're doing?"

"In a way, yes."

"Why did you come back?"

"Oh, for a whole lot of reasons. My child's future. My own shame. I also discovered, as I told you all after the funeral, that my aunt was really my mother and I came back for her as well. I'm glad that I did. She went to her grave in peace."

"Does Stavros hurt you?" he asked, not looking at me.

It took me some time to answer. "Sometimes."

"Verbally? Physically?"

"Both."

He looked at me curiously, nodding his head.

"I know what you want to ask, Reggie. The answer's yes. And no, I'm not going to stomach it, not for long. Now I want to know about you. You don't bring your wife to the card games."

He looked out at the children playing on the swings. "She only plays bridge." He laughed awkwardly. "We'll never be able to bridge that gap. I married for the wrong reasons – you know that need to marry a white woman to prove something to yourself? You prove nothing, and the glory, if you can call it that, only lasts for a short while. The main reason, however, is my son. He's a lovable boy, but sometimes he has seizures and is hard to handle. He speaks in rhyme, bangs away at the piano, and wolfs down his food. He understands what you say, but you can't reason with him. His mind's wired differently. His mother can't handle him by herself. He needs constant care. One of us always has to be home; Friday nights are my nights out. Saturdays and Sundays are hers."

"Well, that seems fair."

He took some time with his response. "When you're a parent you do things you might never have done otherwise."

"And if you should meet someone you loved?"

"I'll cross that bridge when I get there. So far it hasn't happened. Perhaps it's for the best."

"Don't say that. You never know what might happen. Perhaps you and your wife will find that magic again – or maybe you'll meet Twinkle Toes."

"That's a good one."

"Do you sleep in the same bed?"

"Yes."

"So we are in the same boat, then: necessity."

"I guess so," he laughed, and got up and paid the waitress. On the way back to the Honda, he continued, "We know each other's secrets now, Joonie. That makes us friends."

They were the best words for me at that time; a friend without obligation.

I arrived home at four in the afternoon to find Stavros waiting stiff-lipped for me in the living room. I could tell by the pull of his mouth and the fact that the television was off that he was angry about something.

"Where were you today, Joonie?"

"I went shopping."

"All afternoon?"

"What is this, Stavros? The third degree?"

"Were you out shopping all afternoon?" he repeated.

I knew then that he knew. "I stopped by the park to give Bobby Jo some fresh air."

"And that's it? You didn't meet anyone?"

"I speak to people who talk to me."

"How about Reggie?"

"I ran into him there."

"Don't lie. His red Honda was parked two cars behind yours. I came to see if I could see you, and I did – talking to that dickhead. And then you took off and got into his car. Am I wrong? How am I doing so far?"

I hated him for forcing me into a corner. "You're not wrong. He took me to have coffee. We talked."

"You talked? Why do you have to go with a strange man to talk? Isn't he married? And don't you have me to talk to? Put the baby down."

I nervously put Bobby Jo back in her playpen, bracing myself for the worst.

"Why are you shaking? Do you think I'm going to hit you?"

"Yes."

He gave a supercilious smile. "I'm not going to hit you, Joonie. Hitting you doesn't work. Give me the car keys."

"It's my car."

"No, it's not. It's in my name."

He ripped the keys from my hand. "Now take off that necklace; you're not worthy of it. I made a mistake to give it to you."

"*You* made a mistake? *I* made a mistake! Do you think you can buy me?"

"It seems that I can."

The statement was like a blow to my heart and crueller than what I knew was going to happen next. He came over and tried to get the necklace off my neck. He struggled to undo the clasp. It was a delicate gold chain, and as he pulled on it, hooking it into my hair trying to get it over my head, the chain broke and the pendant fell off.

"Now, look what you did! You'll have to earn it back," he said, coming to stand in front of me where I had landed on the chair, pushing my face into his crotch. "You can start by giving me a blow job. You do that, don't you, Joonie? It's part of your bag of tricks."

"Fuck you!"

The first strike was swift, with the back of his hand,

across my cheek. He took off his belt and lashed me with it. The tip of the belt caught my mouth and blood came gushing out, staining the front of my dress.

I grabbed an ashtray and threw it at him. The ashtray thumped against his head and he went stumbling backwards. He knocked me to the floor, and punched me in the face, several times until I passed out. When I came to, the room was darkened and he was dragging me into the bathroom and into the shower. He had Bobby Jo's pink plastic cup under my mouth to catch the blood dropping from my nose in big clots. The water rushed over me. My head felt as if it had been hit with a hammer, I couldn't breathe through my nose or see through my left eye, my mouth was filled with sweet-tasting blood. I sat crumpled up under the hot spray, my white dress turning crimson, leaving a pink residue around my feet. Next to me, he was crying like a helpless child, "Oh, God, what did I do … I'm so sorry, Joonie … I don't know what got into me."

My rage was such that if I'd had an axe in my hand, I would've struck him with it. In that moment of clear and present danger, I understood why some women killed.

"Take me to the hospital, please," I said.

"I can't. They'll call the police. They'll arrest me."

For what seemed like hours, I sat under the shower, too weak to move. I was wet and bleeding, I could hardly talk. He'd thought the shower would wash the evidence away and revive me, but it didn't. He walked me to our bed and propped me up with pillows so I wouldn't choke on my own blood. For two days he sat at my bed, feeding me chicken-noodle soup from ready-made packets, tending to the bruises on my face. He was terrified that my nose might be broken, but his gods were with him. The cartilage in my nose had shifted, but it wasn't crushed.

The beating did something to me that had never

happened before. It made me silent. Silence is a good thing when there's imminent danger. You don't have to answer questions; the other party feels guilty and won't retaliate. It gives you time to recover and to plan. The next move I made had to be the right one, and the right move was not to do anything while I was angry. I also had to take my status in America into account. I wasn't a citizen and couldn't go to the police for help for fear of bringing myself to the attention of the Immigration authorities. More than anything, I didn't want my parents to know that I had once more made a mistake. My return home would have to be out of want, not out of need.

The day after the beating Stavros's mother phoned to invite us for supper. That was the last place I wanted to be – for Aspasia to see her son's handiwork on my face and say the wrong thing, and for me to strike back. "I can't go," I said.

"She wants you to come. She wants to make up for that horrible night at her house."

"Can't you see what my face looks like? Must I go out like this?"

"Here, she wants to talk to you."

In the end, I took the receiver from him. "I can't come, Aspasia. I don't feel well."

Aspasia was unconcerned. "Try to come. It will just be us. I'm making some lovely lamb chops with mint. Stavros likes lamb."

"My face is swollen and bruised."

"Oh, come on. No one will see. Why is your face swollen?"

"Your son hit me."

"You two are fighting again?"

I replaced the receiver and gave Stavros a look that dared him to say something to me.

As the weeks passed, I watched him come and go, stocking up the cupboards with my favourite teas and other food, leaving new gifts on the living-room table, which I looked at and put aside. Nothing moved me. I felt like a dead fish. A hard and unforgiving me emerged. Millie and Veronica called a few times to invite me for supper, but I decided to stay in Stavros's apartment until my plans were in place. I also put Reggie off when he called, knowing how shocked he would be if he knew the consequences of our meeting in the park. I wasn't ready to go yet and wasn't going to flee with nothing in hand. I was going to enrol for a one-semester Drama course; it would be long enough for me to know if I wanted to pursue an acting career when I returned home. My sixteen thousand rand, after payment to Mr Singh, had dwindled to nine thousand, and I wasn't going to pay rent elsewhere when I didn't have to.

So I stayed put and while I waited, I played the role of a subservient wife and kept the peace. I ironed his shirts; I sat on the couch at night and watched the news with him; I went out for coffee and supper to restaurants and pretended a happiness I didn't feel. I let my birthday come and go without a word to him. At night, when he turned to me in bed, I fucked him in a cold-blooded and furious way just to get the job done. The sex was actually a release as it was the only outlet for my rage.

On a particularly summery day, weeks later, with the sun shining brightly outside, and my child fast asleep on a blanket on the floor, I took out my writing pad and wrote the letter I had wanted to write so many times before.

Dear Blair
I am only writing to you now because I wasn't going to write you at all and needed time to organise

things in my head. I have made some poor decisions over the last year, and I am paying the price for that now. No one is to blame; only me. When you left so suddenly for Johannesburg that time, without telling me, and I discovered that I was pregnant, I was shocked, and took the easy way out – coming to my aunt in America. My aunt turned out to be my mother, and ended up in a psychiatric ward where she died soon after I returned from Cape Town. I came back to America after I found out her real identity and was in time for her death. It turns out that I was adopted by my parents when I was five days old. My father wanted to take care of his sister's child and not have her – me – grow up in someone else's home.

There is so much to tell you, I don't know where to start. I have been selfish along the way. I did not answer your letter because I did not know how I wanted to deal with you after I admitted to you that Bobby Jo is your child. She is an adorable baby, and is almost a year old now. When I ran into you at Mr Ali's café, I was completely shaken. I hadn't expected to see you again. The question I had had on my mind all these months was answered when I couldn't look you in the eye. And I couldn't do it because my heart was thumping in my chest. I couldn't find the right words to say. I was also afraid that you might've changed towards me and I couldn't stand it if it were true. When you wrote to me the second time, I was assured of your feelings for me, but I wasn't sure of my feelings for you. So much time had passed.

I so desperately want to come back, Blair, but there's just so much going on in my life right now.

Maybe we can write to each other and re-establish our friendship? You know I will never deny you contact with Bobby Jo. I would be happy for her to have her father in her life.

I am sending you this picture of her sitting in her high chair. Look at her dimples; they're just like yours. Isn't she gorgeous? I call her Bokkie when she's especially sweet.

I hope your mother gets well soon.
Joonie.

Five weeks later, I received a letter back. The mail always arrived at about ten in the morning and I was careful to read the letter in the bathroom with the door locked, even though Stavros was at work that time of the day and I was alone with Bobby Jo in the apartment.

Dear Joonie
This is the happiest day of my life, hearing from you – and the picture of Bobby Jo is just beautiful. I knew when I saw her that she was mine. Don't ask me how. It's not just the hair and the eyes. And it's not the dimples. I wouldn't have reacted to her the way I did if there wasn't something about her that just drew me to her.

So how are you, Joonie? You wrote back, but did not say whether there is someone else in your life. Is there? Are you happy? Will you come back to South Africa? I will regret forever how a phone call I didn't make on that fateful night caused this rift between us.

Is it possible to have your number? I want to hear your voice. Please write back to me as soon as you can, and send me a picture of you too. I want lots of pictures. It is tough and lonely out here in the bush where we're presently deployed. I can't tell you where we are. It might also be difficult for me to call, but I will do so. There are no telephones where we are. I am planning to leave the army at the end of October, after my two-year stint is over – there are only four months and two weeks left!

I have learned some valuable skills and should be able to find a good job. Army life is not for me, and neither is sitting in an office. I have grown up. I know what I want to do now. I am moving down to Cape Town for a spell when I leave here. My mother was diagnosed with cancer and is not well. This can be our chance, Joonie. My mother's not the same anymore. I want to please her, of course, but you will come first in my life. If someone were to ask me to describe the word love, I couldn't do it. I just know that I want to be with you – watch you tie your shoelaces or put a ribbon in your hair or give that little giggle when you've done something naughty. Are you still naughty? Do you still love me? Can you see yourself with a wildlife ranger on a game farm?

Please write to me soon and send me your number. I want to know the whole story of your aunt; sorry, your mother. I was completely floored when you wrote that she was your mother. How can something like that happen and you don't find out for eighteen years? I was also sad to hear of your grandmother's passing. Mr Ali told me. She was a lively spirit. I liked her. May she rest in peace.

I love you, Bokkie. Please write a long letter and tell me everything.

Blair

I cried into my hands after reading his letter. He still loved me. He still wanted me. How could I have been so mindless and stupid to think that returning to America would be better for me and Bobby Jo? Reading his letter reminded me of the sweet, simple times we'd had in my mother's kitchen doing my homework, stealing kisses in the living room, horsing around on my bed. Blair's nature was completely different from Stavros's. I had never feared Blair.

For weeks she read his letter every day and clung to every word as she waited for the next one to arrive. Fortunately his unit had been withdrawn from the bush and was now stationed in Grootfontein and once he even managed to call her from the post office. He was sensitive enough to call at six o'clock South Afican time, when he knew it would be midday in New York and Stavros away at work. They talked for a long time and she was red in the face by the time the call finally ended. It was slightly easier for him to write, but the letters always arrived in twos or threes as he had to wait for a friend to collect supplies from Windhoek to mail them from there. Bit by bit the stories came out about her aunt, her life with Stavros, his possessiveness, his changing moods. It took a second call before she told him about the beatings. It was the first time she heard him be really cross.

"Why are you still living with him?"

"I have no choice now."

"There's always a choice. Do you need money?"

"No."

"Then what is the problem?"

"When I leave here I have to be completely out of his reach. I can't move to another place. He'll find me. You don't know the kind of rage he's capable of. When you meet him for the first time you'll think he's just the greatest guy. People like him. They don't know what a monster he can be. The Drama course I want to take ends next April. It's only one semester. I'll leave then, with some kind of diploma. He's not going to bully me out of here."

"Lose the battle and win the war, Joonie. Leave. You can always take up acting back in Cape Town."

"No. I'm not running. I've run too many times."

"I have a nasty feeling about this. This guy's dangerous. Is it worth staying on for a Drama course?"

"It's worth it for me. I've accepted what he is and nothing he says will change how I feel. I'm over the discovery that men disappoint, and that people can love and hate at the same time. I don't love anything about him. I've run away from him before and I did it clumsily. This time I have to be smart. I want to do the Drama course so I can have something to show for my time here – sort of like a souvenir from America."

A week before her Drama course was due to start, she asked Stavros if he wanted to come with her to orientation where new students were going to be shown around and given a general rundown as to how things worked on campus.

"What time is orientation?" he asked.

"It's this coming Saturday morning at ten. I thought if you came along we could take Bobby Jo too."

"I have an outstanding article I have to finish. Why don't you just leave her here and I'll babysit?"

"You'll do that?"

"Yes. It's her nap time at ten anyway. I can get some writing done and you won't have me in your hair along with all those wannabe actors."

"That'll be better then. Thanks."

Saturday morning arrived. She got up early to wash her hair and get ready. She never expected that she would be excited to go into an educational environment again. Her childhood dreams weren't so foolish after all, she thought.

It was only a one-semester course, but it would introduce her to the acting experience. And she was glad to have a morning off. She had forgotten what it was like to be free. She hadn't seen Millie and Veronica in ages; they'd given up on her, accusing her of always making some excuse for not visiting.

There was only one hurdle; how to get Stavros to give her the car keys. She decided on the simplest route. She went out to the bakery on the corner before he got up, bought crispy blueberry croissants and served them to him with fresh coffee.

"I'm leaving, Stavros. Can I have the keys to the car?" She knew she was taking a big chance.

"I'm going to sell the car. I don't want anything happening to it."

"Oh." She was genuinely surprised. She had thought that in time he would give her the car back. "I'm going to be late if I go by bus."

He looked at her, considering. "Oh, what the hell. They're in the second drawer in the bedroom. Go ahead."

She picked up her bag. "Can I keep them?"

"I just told you I'm going to sell the car."

"Until you sell it, I mean."

"Yes. You can use it on Saturdays to go to your class. How long are you going to be?"

"A few hours. I'll bring barbecued chicken for lunch."

"Sounds good."

She kissed Bobby Jo, said goodbye and left. She arrived at the college twenty minutes later and realised with a start when she entered the building and saw no people in the orientation room that she had gotten the date wrong. Orientation was only the following Saturday. How could she have made such a mistake? She had so much looked forward to the morning. What was she going to do now?

If she went to visit Millie, who didn't live far from the college, and came home three hours later, he might balk at giving her the car again the following Saturday.

She stopped at the restaurant, bought barbecued chicken and fresh rolls, and returned home.

She parked the car outside the block of apartments and walked up to the first floor. She had her hand on the door knob and was about to turn it when she heard a shrill laugh. She stood for a moment listening; the sound had definitely come from inside. She opened the door. Stavros's jeans and cowboy boots, a pink dress and panties and high heels were scattered on the floor. Bobby Jo had fallen asleep in the playpen.

Her breathing became faster. There was a girl in the apartment; she could tell by the sounds coming from the bedroom that they were having sex. She felt sick in her stomach. What should she do? She stood in the passage peeping at them through the crack between the wall and the door. The girl turned. Joonie paled when she saw that it was Maria, the same girl she had met at his mother's place the night of the ruined supper.

In a state of numbness she tiptoed back out of the passage and stood in the living room. She stared at the reddish brown boots he had bought in Texas and loved so much. She walked over, squatted and peed all over the boots and the clothes. She took a corner of the dress and wiped herself. She hadn't made a sound. Bobby Jo was still fast asleep. She picked up the chicken she had bought and tiptoed out as quietly as she had come in.

She got back into the car and drove off and stopped at a public phone booth a short distance down the road. Her legs felt jittery, as if she was going to fall to the ground and faint. She dialled a number. A woman with a British accent answered the phone.

"Can I speak to Reggie, please?"

"Who may I say is calling?"

"Joonie." She wanted to explain who she was, as she didn't want to cause Reggie any grief, but was too weak to muster the strength to continue. While she waited she could hear a child screaming in the background. Reggie came on the phone.

"Am I calling at a bad time? I hope this doesn't cause trouble for you."

"No trouble at all. What's up?"

"I need help. I'm at a public booth on the street."

"Let's meet in the park. I'll see you in ten minutes."

Reggie arrived, happy to see her after such a long time. One look at her, though, and his smile vanished. He listened in amazement to what she had to tell him. "I don't know what to say," he said. "I've never heard anything this bizarre. You peed in his boots?"

"Yes."

He laughed. "Well, you know what he's going to do now."

"Not really. I think he's not going to say a word about it. I've caught him in the act. How is he going to admit that – or even bring it up?"

"But he knows it can only be you. That's an awful chance you took. He might not give a damn whether you knew about Maria or not. You peed in his holy boots."

She laughed too. It was a helluva thing to have done, she agreed, but she was feeling strangely liberated, knowing that she had caught him with his dick in his hand. What could he say to her now? He was a skunk, and a pretender and she felt no guilt at all. If he wanted a silent war, well, she was a master at it.

"So how are you going to go home? Do you have to? I could talk to my wife; we have an extra room you can have."

"I don't want to impose on any of my friends. I'll go home at one and just pretend I've come from college. I don't care if he knows; he will know anyway that it was me. Who else would've had entry to the apartment and done such a thing? He's not keen on me doing Drama. Now we'll see who can act."

"This all sounds very dangerous to me."

"I know. That's why I called you. I just wanted you to know these things in case something happens to me."

"Nothing will happen to you."

"I know, but just in case. I know I'm being melodramatic, but I have no family or friends here who have my details back home if something happens. So I want to give them to you. Would you mind?"

"Of course not. But you're scaring me, Joonie. Maybe you should go to the police."

She ignored him. "I also want to know if I can keep a few things at your house. I want to buy a suitcase and some other things I want to send off before I leave."

It was on the tip of her tongue to tell him what had happened after she saw him the previous time in the park, but decided against it. Now was not the time.

"No problem," Reggie said. "I will drive you to the airport too when the time comes. You're making the best decision to go home. Do you still think you should stay for the Drama course?"

"I don't know. Maybe getting the date wrong for orientation was a message from God, or a sign that I should cut my losses and go."

"It may very well be. We get help from Higher Up, but we don't always take the cue. Think of your safety, and the safety of Bobby Jo. Do you want to leave your child with a babysitter who's beaten you up – even if he says he loves the child – and especially after you've peed in his boots?"

"No. And it was a big pee, let me tell you. I made sure the inside leather got a good soaking."

He laughed. "You're a wicked little minx, Joonie. I think a girl like you will give any man a heart attack."

It was her turn to laugh. "You think so?"

"No. I just wanted to hear you laugh. I knew a girl like you back home when I was still in high school; leader of the pack, lots of balls, but a powder puff on the inside."

"That's me, yes, a big chicken, and downright stupid at times. But there's a good me also. I always give people the benefit of the doubt, and I don't hurt people unless they hurt me first."

"You offer the other cheek."

"Yes – even though I'm bleeding inside. And then I get them."

There was an edge to her voice that made him glance at her. With a calming hand on her arm, he said teasingly, "Vengeance is mine, sayeth the Lord."

"The Lord isn't in my shoes. And don't use His name in vain."

He became serious again. "I'll call you tonight to see if you're okay. Will that get you into trouble?"

"I don't know. But please call."

She arrived home shortly after one. She knew as soon as she opened the door and saw the wet boots and jeans on the floor that there was going to be war. Bobby Jo was standing up in her playpen, crying.

Stavros, with black boots on, was standing at the window with his back to her, ignoring the child's crying. He turned suddenly and walked up to her, grabbing her by her hair, twisting it so hard that her head was jerked backwards.

"Did you think, you little bitch, that you could come

from the jungle and piss in my boots? Who the fuck do you think you are!"

She let out a blood-curdling scream. He let go of her hair and kicked her in the back. She smashed into the opposite wall. He grabbed her falling body, spun her around and punched her in the gut. She collapsed to the floor in a heap. He kicked her in the stomach with the sharp point of his black boot. "This isn't Africa, you cunt! What right do you think you have in my house! You're a fucking slut! My mother was right about you. You're here because you want citizenship. Well not with me, baby. Not with me!"

She tried to get up. He kicked her back down. Her head knocked into the corner of the coffee table behind her and started to bleed. Still, she managed to pull herself up.

"Help!" she screamed. "Help!" Out of the corner of her eye she spotted the Indian woman who lived in the apartment next to theirs, standing at the door looking on in horror.

Stavros was unaware of the woman's presence. He punched Joonie in the face and she went reeling backwards into the playpen. Bobby Jo was screaming at the top of her lungs, trying to hold onto her with clumsy little hands. She heard banging. People were disturbed by the noise. She climbed out of the playpen, leaving Bobby Jo red-faced and screaming, and ran into the kitchen. He was right behind her, flung his arm around her neck, holding her head in a vice under his left arm. She grabbed the carving knife from the counter, twisted it sideways, and stabbed him with all the strength she had left. His body fell away from hers and collapsed in a bundle on the floor, blood pouring from a wound in his gut.

The police arrived and found her sitting next to the body with Bobby Jo in her arms. It was a homicide, one of them said. She didn't know what the word meant exactly, but knew that it had to do with murder and with her. She was surrounded by cops in uniform and others in suits. Stavros was lying on his side, his right arm still over the gash where the knife had gone in, his eyes half-closed, his lips open in a faint smile. The smile frightened her. It was a dead man having his last say. But there would be no last say. Already the body was cooling and the eyes looked like glass.

She sat shaking on the floor until the Indian woman helped her up. She was overwhelmed by voices and the coroner who had arrived, inspecting the body and asking questions. Stavros was referred to as "the vic" or "the stiff" or "John Doe", although John Doe didn't apply as he wasn't an unknown. She felt unsettled and deeply remorseful. She ached all over; her head swam with thoughts of guilt. Stavros would be alive if he hadn't met her. If she hadn't come back. She's the cause of everything. She left him and came back. She increased the chances of him assaulting her again. He was an offender. She's taken his life. She's destroyed his mother. Robbed her of grandchildren. Caused two families to grieve. Her father was right. Money *was* the root of all evil. She had started it all with extorted money. How could ill-gotten money reap any good?

Two detectives and a female officer arrived. The Indian woman said that she had seen everything and would give a statement. The detectives took Joonie – all the while clutching Bobby Jo, who was curiously quiet ever since she had picked her up, to her chest – to hospital, where her bruises were photographed and attended to. She needed two stitches under her left eye. Accompanied by a female detective, she was driven down to the precinct where a social worker took Bobby Jo from her and she was interrogated for three hours by a Detective Logan, a big black guy with a shoulder holster, and two other cops in uniform.

"Why can't I have my child with me?"

"Don't worry about the baby, lady. She's in good hands. Tell us again about these boots and clothes. You peed on them, you said?"

"Yes. I had come home earlier than expected. I had the wrong date for the orientation class. I came home and found him with a girl in my bed. I was so stunned. I can't explain how. In anger, I peed in his boots. All over their clothes on the floor. Then left the apartment. Without him knowing I had been there."

"Peed in his boots?" Detective Logan said, glancing at the detective standing next to him. "You still have those snakeskin boots, McCaffrey? Don't leave them lying around." There was a general snickering. Even in death they found humour.

Detective Logan cleared his throat and became serious. "Now tell us exactly what happened."

"I've told you twice already."

"Tell us again."

The interrogation carried on for so long that she felt dizzy and slightly disorientated. She was getting tired of the questions, the same ones over and over again, with trick questions in between to catch her out. After several hours, they left her alone in the room and a female officer brought her a hamburger and a drink, and asked her what kind of baby formula Bobby Jo was on, and whether she could have any juice. In a daze Joonie told her, and again asked when she could have Bobby Jo back. She felt dirty in the stained clothes. She wanted her child. She didn't know where she would go when she left the precinct, but knew that she would somehow have to return to the apartment because all her and Bobby Jo's things were there.

The hardest part for her was to give the police the name of her parents back home and their telephone number. They were going to contact her father; her family would learn that she had stabbed her boyfriend to death. The news would shock her mother and put her in hospital. Her father would be beside himself. What was wrong with her? Never listening to anyone? He had attacked her, had been entirely at fault, but she had played a part in it. She had come back the second time. If she hadn't come back, he wouldn't be dead. No one would be able to convince her that that wasn't the case.

She was told that she could make a call and was ushered into a different room with a phone. Further down the passage, she saw Aspasia talking to the cops. Her first instinct was to run to her and tell her how sorry she was. But she let go of the idea, fearing his mother's reaction. She didn't feel strong enough to go up to her.

Reggie answered. He immediately grasped what had happened and rushed to the precinct to tell the detectives what they had spoken about in the park. He had a lawyer with him. She could see through the window into the next room where he was being questioned. For more than an hour they made her wait, then a man in a suit and a briefcase, a Mr Larry Garfunkle, arrived to say that he had been appointed as her lawyer. He spoke to the Indian woman and some of the other witnesses, and again the story had to be told.

"Your friend Reggie Philander gave a statement. It seems that your peeing in Mr Dukakis' boots – it's a Piss 'n Boots joke with the cops now," he added with a smile, "– was just too original not to take into account as shedding light on your character. People react differently to news of infidelity. That you stained his boots and the girl's clothing rather than confronting them in bed and going ballistic indicates restraint. It's also obvious from the scene of the crime and your bruises that your action was in self-defence. The witnesses gave exonerating statements. Two of them said that they had heard fighting and shouting on other occasions, but hadn't intervened. One had noticed bruises on your face before. However," he continued more slowly, "you're not out of the woods. The prosecutor's on the case now; he will want to go over everything and also interview you. They will also do a background check on the deceased."

"And my family? They don't have a need to call my family now, right?"

"If they were going to keep you in custody, your parents would've had to be notified because of Bobby Jo. She's an American citizen. She would've had to go into foster care until your parents arrived. But you are being released into the care of Mr Philander who has taken responsibility for you. We have his statement that you spoke to him in the park and that you had articulated your fears to him and were afraid to go home. With all the statements in your favour, and the bruises on your back and face, they can't hold you. But they're still not finished with you. It's all just a process now. I'll speak to the prosecutor again. He's aware that you intended to return to South Africa in a few months' time."

She just stared at the lawyer.

Detective Logan and the two cops came back into the room where she was waiting to be released.

"We're sorry that we have to put you through this," he said, "but a man was killed; we have to investigate everything and everyone. I'm sure you understand."

"I understand, and thank you for believing me."

The detective continued. "You told us earlier that your visa expires by the end of next February. With all that you have told us, and the fact that you can't work in this country without a visa, it might be a good idea for you to be on a plane when this is all over."

They were hard words, but they were words she needed to hear. Never again did she want to go through such trauma.

"One last thing before you go," the detective said. "We have your contact details back home. Don't forget. You can't leave until we've cleared you."

Bobby Jo was brought in to her. She wrapped her arms around her child, tears of relief and gratitude pouring down her face and staining her already sticky dress.

The day before she left New York for good, she took out her writing pad and wrote Aspasia Dukakis a letter.

Dear Aspasia
It is with a sore heart that I am writing this letter to you. I am leaving for South Africa tomorrow and can't leave without telling you how very sorry I am that you have lost your son.

I want you to know that Stavros was good to me and my child and that we had many good times together. However, you were right when you said to Stavros that a fish cannot live with a bird and that our cultural differences and traditions would eventually drive us apart. I now know your words to be true.

I hope you can forgive me and I apologise if I have been rude to you. I will pray every day that your pain goes away. I have pain too, and will have to live forever with what has happened.

Do not think too harshly of me. You were right about many things. A mother does know what is best for her child. Many blessings to you.
Joonie

I often wonder how things might've turned out if I had let the old woman in Retreat flush out my uterus and not had the baby and never left South Africa. Would I have been married now? Would I have had children? I can't say that I would've been content not to learn the true identity of my mother, or that I regret having given birth to Bobby Jo. It was perhaps the only good decision I made, to have her; that, and being there for my mother before she died.

After staying for three weeks at their home, Reggie and Ursula drove me to the airport. I did not say goodbye to Millie and Veronica or any of my card-playing friends. I did not want to talk about what they had read in the papers and discuss any of it with anyone except Reggie, who had come through for me as a real friend. In the end I didn't see the inside of a lecture hall; the course started a week after I moved in with the Philanders. My persistence to do things my own way had cost me. In a telephone call to my parents a few days earlier I had told them the news, to give them time to think about what had happened to me and to prepare them that I was coming home.

Before boarding, while Ursula was at the bookstand buying a magazine for me to read on the plane, I considered having a few words with Reggie. I had got to know Ursula and her British background. She was like any other hopeful who had come to experience the American Dream. I saw how hard it was caring for an autistic child. She was cooped up at home. Most of their arguments were as a result of stress and fatigue. Like me, Ursula was an outsider thrown in amongst a group of squawking pigeons, trying to fit in. The reality is that you never fit in.

"Maybe, Reggie," I said hesitantly, "there's still a chance for you and Ursula to rekindle what you once had. Ursula's tired and she pines for her friends. We come here from tight-knit groups and we're like fish out of water. We flounder. We don't know how to cope. You only succeed if you give in completely to the other side and become one of them."

Reggie nodded. It was true not only of women, it applied to him too.

I did not tell my family the date I was coming back and called my father from a public phone booth at Cape Town airport as soon as Bobby Jo and I had checked through customs. It was early October. "Don't bring anyone with you, Dad. I have a lot of suitcases and I don't want to discuss the case; no family, please, not even Mom. I want to be alone with you and Mom tonight."

It was a different experience from my first visit home. There was no fanfare, no cakes and tarts, just my father and mother and myself in the living room with a cup of tea and a Dean Martin song playing softly on the radio. My mother, slightly bewildered, asked in an almost inaudible voice whether it was true. Yes, I said, I did stab Stavros in self-defence. My father put his arm around me and let me cry into his shirt.

"Is this it now, Joonie?" my mother asked.

"This is it, Mom. I'm back. I'm sorry if what is being whispered behind our backs is going to cause you embarrassment. I'm truly sorry. I didn't mean for any of this to happen; my stubbornness caused this. Stavros would be alive if I hadn't gone back."

"Don't blame yourself," my father said. "But let this be it now, Joonie."

"This is it, Dad. I also want to tell you that I'm not going to stay with you and Mom indefinitely as Blair and I have plans. But I'm back. I have no desire to leave South Africa again."

After a week at home, I felt brave enough to do what I thought was the proper thing to do. It was a huge chance I was taking. The woman had been rude to me the last and only time we had met. But I was a little smarter now than before. I could read between people's sentences and also read into what wasn't said. I had become much more forgiving about other people's behaviour as my own had left so much to be desired, so many times.

I dressed Bobby Jo in a pretty pink frilly frock with shoulder straps and wheeled her down the street in the stroller. I turned right at the second street and saw two cars in front of the house, one, a Toyota Corolla and the other, an army vehicle. For a moment I thought that Blair had come back early and was in the house.

I took a deep breath and rang the bell. A man my father's age, in a blue suit, opened the door. "Can I help you?"

"Yes, please. My name's Joonie. I'm Blair's friend. He told me that his mother is ill. I've come to see how she is."

"She doesn't want visitors. But do come in." I followed him to the bedroom where Blair's mother sat propped up with pillows. She had always been thin, but looked even thinner now than before, with deep hollows under her eyes. Two men in brown uniforms stood respectfully at the side of the bed, their army caps in their hands. I didn't think anything of it. They were probably Blair's friends who were on leave in Cape Town and had come to visit.

"Ronelle, hier is iemand vir jou."

Blair's mother turned her head. For a moment I thought she didn't recognise me, but her eyes widened in surprise.

"I hope I'm not intruding. Blair told me that you were not feeling well. I thought I would come in for a few minutes and see how you are – if I could get you anything from the shop, or do something for you."

"I don't need anything, thank you – but thank you for coming."

Her eyes drifted down to Bobby Jo in the stroller. She looked back up at me.

"That's your baby?"

"Yes."

"She's a pretty little thing."

"Thank you."

She turned to the man in the blue suit. "This is my brother, Jack. Give her that photograph on the dresser, Jack."

He handed it to me. It was a photograph of a baby about a year old sitting in a pram. There was no mistaking the similarities between Blair as a toddler and Bobby Jo.

I knew then that she knew. And that she knew I knew. Nothing more had to be said. She had accepted that I would be in her son's life.

"These boys are here with some bad news," she said, starting to sob. "Blair was killed on the Angolan border last night."

Dear Joonie
I'm hurrying to write this letter before we take off on a mission up north. I don't know when you'll get it, but this will be my last communication from here. I love you, my angel, and can't wait to see you. I've received the photos. The one with you and BJ in the park with the sprinklers is my favourite.

I called my father last night and told him about you and our plans to marry next Easter. He didn't say much, but he is happy at least that I will have done my duty for my country, and understands that I want to leave. The army's been good for me. It's given me direction and made me think hard about what I want to do with my life. I know for certain now that I want to be out in the bush. But not as a soldier. I want to work with animals. I want you and Bobby Jo to be with me. I never knew that I could feel this way about someone and that I would want to be with you all the time. Hope you like this photo I sent you.

About my mother, her condition is getting worse. The doctor said that pancreatic cancer is one of the worst cancers and that she does not have long to live. I hope that I'll get back in time. I so much want her to see her grandchild before she leaves this world, but I'm not sure that she will still be around when you return next April.

I'll phone you as soon as I'm back in civvie street! Probably from Windhoek. Can't wait to hear your voice.
Love you, Joons
Blair

I never wrote another letter again, to any man. It took me years to overcome what had happened and it left me deeply depressed. My thinking was impaired, my anger clouded my reasoning and I wasted years blaming God. I didn't understand how I could have had so many things go wrong in my life, and just when I seemed in reach of happiness with the father of my child, that I should lose him to a landmine. When Mandela was released from prison in the early nineties and became president, the country underwent a change and all those Draconian laws that had caused so much terror in people's lives were scrapped and interracial marriage was allowed – an irony after all I'd gone through. After a tiring and fruitless battle with God, I accepted my part in the tragedy and tried to get on with my life. My father had been right, I thought. There was your plan for yourself, and then there was providence.

I quietened down as the years passed. I saw my little girl grow up and get married and have two little girls of her own. I had offers of marriage, but found that I had lost interest in wanting to be close to a man. I just did not have those feelings anymore, and I didn't want them aroused. I wanted no one sharing my bed and didn't want to commit to a partnership with anyone. I was too set in my ways to make space for someone whose baggage I would have to take on. I know now that marriage is one of God's brilliant devices to keep people together so that they can wade together through the heavy waters of life. Sex was the key in keeping the man around. When the sex waned, you stayed together out of good conscience and respect for God's Word. I would be alone on my own terms, and understand now how polygamy can save a marriage that is in decline. It's impossible to feel the same way about someone at fifty as you felt at sixteen. I had discovered long ago that you can be attracted to more than one person at the same time. I am too old now for games and the rigours of pleasing a man and certainly don't want to be part of that lonely brigade of women who look constantly for love and feel unfulfilled without a man around. The love I had searched for my whole life had eluded me, and I am accepting of it.

I once heard an actor say in a movie that God is either dead or He despises us. I thought about that for a long time, and in the end decided it not to be true. God doesn't hate us. If God was guilty of anything, it was that He was scared for the choices we made. God wouldn't have sent so many great men to deliver His Word and provide us with a life compass if He didn't care.

I saw quite a bit of Hilary after I returned from New York with Bobby Jo. She was involved with an actress and I learned for the first time that she was gay. I told her everything about that fateful day when I had discovered Stavros in bed with Maria and the fight that ensued resulting in his death. She said the right words, she comforted me, and it was with sadness when less than a year later I learned that she was found dead in her flat from an overdose of pills.

When my parents passed on and it seemed that the world had forgotten me, I had a most surprising visitor show up at my house. Reggie. He was back in South Africa. His son had died after an accident in the park, and Ursula finally left him and returned to London where she married an Englishman. I was surprised to see him. He was in his late fifties now, but still a good-looking man who could still make me laugh.

Reggie was God's gift to me. He arrived at a time when I needed a little tenderness, and he needed a little caring himself. He came every day after having done a little plumbing or renovation work in the morning. At six o'clock he would go to his sister's house, and the next day be back at noon. We would work in my garden together, read the newspaper in the front room where there was sun in the late afternoons and have cake and tea. We were much more than friends. Reggie understood my moods and loved me with all his heart. In return, I allowed myself to be cuddled and hugged and sometimes indulge in an open-mouth kiss. It was sad that I had to receive this love and affection at a time when my heart had almost turned to stone, but I was happy with the small pleasures we shared. Reggie and I had a strong emotional tie and a physical relationship would've enhanced and escalated our friendship and bound us together even more, but I decided not to risk the one true friendship I had.

When Bobby Jo left for America with my two grandchildren, to show them the country of her birth, I only cried after she had left. She would never know how much I could've told her, but she is exactly like me – stubborn and with all the answers – and I had to let her make her own mistakes.

For nine years Reggie came every day to my house. One day he never showed up, and I called his sister who told me Reggie had died in his sleep. I didn't cry at the funeral. I now only cry when I am happy. I was fortunate to have had Reggie. God had put him in my path all those years ago so that one day he could give me comfort when I was all by myself. I had loved Blair with the impatience of a little puppy and the greediness of young love. I had loved

Reggie for loving me with all my faults.

"You are selfish, Joonie, you know that?" he said to me once.

"Yes," I laughed, "but I'm not selfish with you."

"Knock, knock."

"Who's there?"

"Cyril."

"Cyril who?"

"Cyriliddle closer."

I think God sees what we cannot with our veiled vision, and opens our hearts when we are ready to receive Him.

Other titles by Rayda Jacobs

The Middle Children
Eyes of the Sky
The Slave Book
Sachs Street
Confessions of a Gambler
Postcards from South Africa
The Mecca Diaries
My Father's Orchid
Masquerade